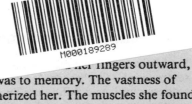

Tonight th...

Fantasy took h... ...her fingers outward, committing all he was to memory. The vastness of his shoulders mesmerized her. The muscles she found said a great deal about commitment and personal pride. By the time she'd explored his limits, her arms and hands were widespread. She rocked forward, bringing her body against his, and reveled in her power when his groan reached her.

Joe's hands had remained still while Tina made her exploration. Tonight could be right; he believed that. And yet because the past still had its claim on him, he willed himself to take it slow. Only when he was sure it was what she wanted would he lift his hands and find a home for them in the softness of her hair. "I was just wondering if they'll lock this park up soon," he said raggedly.

"Then we'll stay the night."

The night. She was willing to give him that much. Although he shuddered, Joe felt a strength that had never been his before . . . .

Dear Reader,

Sophisticated but sensitive, savvy yet unabashedly sentimental—that's today's woman, today's romance reader—you! And Silhouette Special Editions are written expressly to reward your quest for substantial, emotionally involving love stories.

So take a leisurely stroll under the cover's lavender arch into a garden of romantic delights. Pick and choose among titles if you must—we hope you'll soon equate all six Special Editions each month with consistently gratifying romantic reading.

Watch for sparkling new stories from your Silhouette favorites—Nora Roberts, Tracy Sinclair, Ginna Gray, Lindsay McKenna, Curtiss Ann Matlock, among others—along with some exciting newcomers to Silhouette, such as Karen Keast and Patricia Coughlin. Be on the lookout, too, for the new Silhouette Classics, a distinctive collection of bestselling Special Editions and Silhouette Intimate Moments now brought back to the stands—two each month—by popular demand.

On behalf of all the authors and editors of Special Editions,
Warmest wishes,

Leslie Kazanjian
Senior Editor

DAWN FLINDT
The Power Within

Silhouette Special Edition

Published by Silhouette Books New York

America's Publisher of Contemporary Romance

SILHOUETTE BOOKS
300 East 42nd St., New York, N.Y. 10017

ISBN: 0-373-09448-5

First Silhouette Books printing April 1988

America's Publisher of Contemporary Romance

Printed in the U.S.A.

DAWN FLINDT

Having a mother and a grandmother who were teachers and growing up in rural areas without television reception paved the way to a love of reading for this Oregon writer. Her first writing attempts were comic books—with horses as the main characters! These "literary masterpieces" failed to bring her international acclaim, but the author says her sister loyally appreciated her efforts. Although Dawn has done everything from newspaper work to magazine articles, fiction remains her first love. Married to a social worker and the mother of two teenage sons, Dawn Flindt also writes as Vella Munn.

THE WESTERN UNITED STATES

Chapter One

Tina Morton, once voted most delectable coed at her high school, never heard the boat that sliced across the towline she was holding. It was one of those perfect spring days in eastern Texas meant for water-skiing and sun tanning. In the boat pulling her was her fiancé. Next to him was her best friend and that best friend's latest beau. Ordinary people doing ordinary things.

When she first saw the swift-moving shadow to her left, Tina's head was thrown back to catch the wind and spray. She was laughing with the pure joy of being alive. For almost two seconds she didn't react. She'd been water-skiing at Lake O'the Pines all her life. Despite the congestion caused by the powerful boats on the dam-created lake, most operators respected each other's right-of-way. Accidents didn't happen.

Until today.

The gleaming red boat was bearing straight for her. Even as she violently twisted her body and leaned low to change direction, Tina knew the speedboat was going to hit her. Tina screamed, her voice a hard, angry cry laden with fear. She was twenty-five years old and she was about to die in a Texas lake on a Sunday afternoon.

No one heard Tina's scream over the roar of the motors, but one man turned toward the lake at the moment the red racer made a desperate last attempt to change course. Joe Rustin had been sunbathing. He never knew what force stripped lethargy from his muscles and pulled him into a sitting position. Someone needed him. That was the only thing he knew.

He was still trying to focus through the harsh glare of the sun when the line connecting Tina to the boat towing her was severed and she was sucked under toward the racer's churning propeller.

Joe was on his feet with a speed and grace that belied his 237 pounds. He didn't wait to see if the small dark head sinking from view in the seething water was going to resurface. His upper body knotted with tension as he plunged into the lake. Swimming had never been Joe's forte, since his muscularity made floating all but impossible, but his powerful arms cut relentlessly through the water to where the two craft were already milling in confusion.

"Damn! Where is she?" he heard someone yell. "I can't see her!" The words spurred Joe on until he was less than ten feet from where the boat that had been towing the water-skier now bounced in its own wake. A woman. An injured woman was somewhere beneath them.

The two men and one woman in the tow boat were hanging over the side while the three men in the red racer seemed more concerned with something in it than the plight of whoever they'd come within inches of cutting in two.

With a curse, Joe lowered his head and dived under the racer. There might be others more capable, but the thought didn't enter Joe's head. He had to find her before it was too late.

He swam directly under the speedboat and came up at the opposite side. His right hand touched something hard and smooth—one of the water skis the woman had been using. He didn't want to think about what might have happened to the other one. He yelled at the driver of the red boat not to start his engine again, but the three men were so intent on arguing with each other that he wasn't sure they'd heard. Despite the forces holding him low in the water, Joe was able to look around enough to realize that the woman still wasn't on the surface. By now several other people were swimming out toward the two boats. Joe didn't intend to wait for them.

When he went under this time his goal was to search the underside of the tow boat. At least that driver had had the sense to kill his motor.

The silent, watery world was dark but not so dark as to totally envelop the form floating facedown with her back jammed against the underside of the boat. Joe didn't have time to think about the possibility of injuring the woman further by grabbing her. He didn't think about anything except getting her to the surface and lifesaving oxygen.

He was holding her by the shoulder, pushing her head upward when they broke the surface. Her head fell forward instead of reaching up for air. He pleaded with whatever gods were listening not to let her die before he yelled for assistance. A moment later, hands were reaching for the woman's body. Before they could haul her out of the water Joe yelled a warning. "Easy! You don't know what's broken! Wait!" Quickly he dived under the water so he could grab her ankles and push upward as her limp form was gently lifted into the boat.

By the time Joe hooked his arms over the side of the boat, someone was breathing into the young woman's mouth. Because he was afraid that hauling himself into the boat might tip it over, Joe was helpless to do anything except watch. The skier's lips were blue but not so discolored that he wasn't aware of their soft perfection, and her black hair was plastered to her forehead, drawing his eyes to her thick dark brows and long wet lashes. She was tiny, so slender inside the revealing white bathing suit that she seemed like a doll. She would have looked even more flawless if it hadn't been for the deep wound on her thigh.

"Is she breathing?" Joe asked. He was stopped by the lack of emotion in his voice that had nothing to do with what he was feeling.

One of the men in the boat turned toward him, opened his mouth and stared. Joe had seen that look on men's faces before, a look that acknowledged Joe Rustin's physical superiority. For a moment two sets of eyes met and held. "I don't know," the man managed before going back to kneeling over the limp form.

"Start the boat," Joe ordered. "We've got to get her to shore." He struck out in an even crawl toward the knot of people on the bank as soon as the other woman in the boat moved to obey him. He didn't give a damn what the men in the red racer did as long as they stayed away from him. He wasn't sure what he would do if they'd killed her.

Because the boat carrying the woman was moving at a snail's pace, Joe reached shore before it did. He stood in waist-deep water with moisture sheeting off his massive chest, guiding the boat the last few feet to the ramp.

"Has anyone called an ambulance?" he asked in a tone that was more order than question. Helping hands were everywhere, but he didn't want any untrained volunteer hauling the woman out of the boat when none of them knew what was wrong. The man who'd been giving her mouth-to-mouth was still at work, his flushed face a vivid contrast to the sickening white under the unconscious woman's tan.

"There's an ambulance on the way but it's going to be a while," someone supplied. Joe nodded and held the boat up to the dock until a couple of teenagers secured it. Only then was Joe able to concentrate on more than the young woman's leg wound. Joe wasn't trained in first aid, but he'd worked with enough bodies to know when something was wrong with one. He didn't have to touch the swelling on the lower part of her left leg to know that the tibia was broken. But it was her silent chest that frightened him.

The woman who'd brought the boat to shore was scrambling toward Joe. "Those stupid fools! Who let them in a boat? My God, what could they have been thinking about?"

Joe didn't have any answers. He'd built his life around control and power—but today he felt as helpless as he had the day two years ago when Shannon had walked out on him and turned his world inside out.

A moment later the crowd started muttering and pointing. Without catching the words themselves, Joe saw that something by the parking lot was drawing their attention. He stood and turned around as the three men who'd been in the red boat reached their car. "They're trying to leave!" someone yelled.

Although several others started toward the men, Joe ran with them. Rage and frustration and fear had built to a level that could be controlled only with action. This was something he could do—maybe it was the *only* thing he could do for the injured young woman. At least five men got to the car at the same time, but it was Joe who took that final step, placing himself between the vehicle and the way out.

Maybe they'd killed the beautiful skier. If they had, somehow, they were going to pay.

"You're not going anywhere," he said in a voice that carried despite the rolled-up windows. He placed his hands on the hood of the car and expanded his naked chest. His nails bit into metal as he took a deep breath of hot humid air. The scent of pitch and new-mowed grass reached his brain, bringing him back to the moment. Most of the time Joe didn't believe in calling attention to his size and strength, but today that had been enough to defuse the three men.

The car's engine died, and the driver dropped his head forward onto the steering wheel. The blank, befuddled look from the other men told Joe everything he needed to know: liquor had piloted the boat that maybe had cost a woman her life.

Anger was an emotion Joe seldom allowed himself to acknowledge. That, coupled with his physical strength, could mean an explosion only he could bring under control. But controlling himself didn't come easily. Anger was the only emotion that made sense now. Joe Rustin had come to the lake because he'd been training intensely for the past two months and needed a day off. None of this was his idea of a relaxing afternoon, but he was grateful he'd been there to help.

"Get the hell out of there!" he ordered as he violently pulled the car door open. "You're not going anywhere!" He didn't let go of the door until the men were out of the car and turned over to someone who identified himself as responsible for security at the lake. Joe was aware of more looks as he slammed the door, but he didn't give a damn what they were thinking. He couldn't remember how long he'd been away from the unconscious woman. All he was aware of was the need to get back there. He wouldn't be able to leave until her chest rose and fell on its own.

The woman who'd driven the boat was blinking back tears, but Joe didn't allow himself to think about why. Onlookers parted as he pushed his way forward and again dropped to his knees on the dock. The two men from the boat were still huddled around the slim form, but no one touched her.

A wave of nausea washed over Joe. People didn't die on cloudless days like this at a lake where families brought their children and lovers looked for secluded corners. He'd pulled her out of the watery darkness and into the sunlight; she had no right dying on him!

"Is she—" he started. A whimpering cry answered his question.

Joe wasn't aware of the long sigh that escaped his own lungs. He wasn't aware of anything except a bone-deep sense of relief. The woman was alive!

And badly injured.

Her hands were clenching and unclenching, and the fine bones beneath her tanned skin fascinated Joe. He desperately wanted to see those hands holding on to a towline and not blindly searching for anything that would turn her nightmare into something that made sense. He didn't think about what he was doing when he gently covered her hands with his. Their restless movement stilled, and he thought she was breathing less spasmodically.

"Hang in there, sunshine. You aren't alone. Can you hear me? You aren't alone." He wasn't going to tell her everything was going to be all right. "What's her name?" Knowing that had become essential.

"Tina. Tina Morton."

Tina. A musical name. Joe glanced at the man who'd spoken, taking in how he was staring at the joined hands. Joe wondered if the other man should be doing that. His face was ashen and his pupils were too large. Maybe this was Tina's husband or lover. If he was, Joe could only hope Tina wouldn't depend on him too much.

There wasn't much anyone could do while they waited for the ambulance to arrive. Someone supplied a blanket to cover Tina's upper body and someone else applied pressure to the wound on her thigh to stem the bleeding. Joe felt the sun drying his broad, bare back but time had no meaning. He was aware of very little except that when he tried to let go of Tina's hands, she grabbed him with a strength he didn't think her body possessed. He wanted, desperately, for her to open her eyes, to show him what he already knew: with brows, hair and lashes that dark, her eyes would be dusky pools.

Joe's legs had gone to sleep and the sun was sending prickles across his shoulder blades by the time he heard the eerie whine of an ambulance. He bent close to Tina's ears, smelling lake water and something undeniably feminine. "Help's here, sunshine. They'll get you to a hospital now."

Her lids fluttered, fought a great weight and then opened. He was right. Her eyes were bottomless. She opened her mouth and swallowed but nothing came out.

"Don't worry," Joe repeated in response to the nails digging into his hands. "They aren't going to hurt you."

Thank you. She hadn't spoken; Joe was sure of that. And yet he sensed the two words as clearly as if they'd been whispered for his ears alone.

"You're welcome, sunshine." This was crazy. It couldn't be happening and yet it was. Joe was sharing one mind with Tina Morton. For the first time in two years he wasn't putting emotional distance between himself and a woman.

Maybe the bonding started the moment of the accident when a force he didn't understand catapulted him into action. All he wanted to do was hold her in his arms for hours on end.

Joe tried to step back so the two paramedics could place a stretcher beside Tina, but she held fast, her desperation making her incredibly strong.

Don't go. Please.

Never. Joe shook off the thought but didn't try to break her hold on him. He managed to shift his body so the attendants could do their work, but when she was on the stretcher and being carried toward the ambulance, Joe was still with her.

He turned questioning eyes on the attendants. "She wants me to go with her." He held up his captured hands as proof.

"I guess it's all right," one of the attendants replied. "But it's going to be awfully crowded with you in there."

Joe wanted to blend into the background, to simply be there when Tina needed him. But that wasn't possible. Joe

Rustin hadn't blended into the background for years. He hoisted himself into the back of the ambulance and then looked around for the teenagers who'd helped secure the boat. He asked one of them to get his keys and drive his car back to Longview for him. "Just leave it in the hospital parking lot," he finished. "I'll find it."

As the ambulance door was closing, Joe caught a glimpse of the man who'd told him Tina's name. His lips were as white as they'd been before. He was staring at Tina with a kind of horror in his eyes.

Joe's anger rose like bile in his throat before he looked down at the woman by his side.

The attendant didn't do much more than monitor Tina's pulse and breathing during the ride to Longview. He applied a fresh pressure bandage to the leg wound, but the bleeding had slowed to the point that Joe wasn't worried she would lose too much more blood.

If he hadn't known what she'd gone through, Joe would have thought Tina was sleeping. Her fingers slowly gave up their relentless strength and her eyes lay quietly closed. She wasn't interested in him or her surroundings. To Joe that meant one thing: concussion. He wanted to ask the attendant about that but remained silent. Just because Tina was quiet didn't mean she wasn't conscious enough to pick up on anything that was said. She had to be terrified and in pain, and he didn't want to frighten her any more than she already was.

When they arrived at the hospital, Joe managed to free his hands and hoist himself out of the ambulance to give the attendants room to maneuver, but he was beside the stretcher when the group entered the hospital. Joe had been thinking about the long wait he'd had the time he'd injured his back during a power-lifting meet. Although he'd been unable to stand straight in the hospital emergency room, he'd had to wait at least fifteen minutes before his turn came.

This time there was no waiting. The attendants headed for one of the examination rooms with Joe staying too close to be left behind. He had no business among the white-clad professionals and felt foolish wearing only swimming trunks. He also knew that not many people tried to tell Joe Rustin that he couldn't go wherever he wanted.

"Where's the doctor?" Joe asked as a couple of nurses joined the attendants. "There's got to be one on duty."

"Several," a middle-aged nurse said shortly. "We'll call one in a moment."

"In a moment nothing." As Tina's hands started searching the air, Joe again took her strangely cold fingers. For a moment the contact left no room for words. "Look, you've got an Albert Reynolds here. He's some kind of bone specialist. You tell that underdeveloped quack to get his tail in here, now."

"Who are you?" the nurse challenged. "You can't talk about the doctors like that."

Despite the threads of communication forged by locked fingers, Joe found the necessary words. "I can say anything I like about Al. You tell him that Joe's going to tie him in a knot if he doesn't get here on the double."

The nurse snorted her disapproval but hurried out of the room just the same. Joe could almost taste the silence that followed his outburst. He hadn't meant to throw his weight around, but damn it, Tina was slowly rolling her head back and forth on the table and moaning every time she did—and it terrified him.

"I've seen her somewhere," the younger nurse said as she checked Tina's pulse. "I just can't think where."

One of the attendants agreed that Tina's face looked familiar but Joe didn't have anything to add. He'd been looking at the waist he knew he could circle with his hands. He hadn't taken time to step back and study all of her.

"On TV." The nurse grinned as if that was the most important thing she'd said all day. "Doesn't she do those ads for that boat place? Boat World. You know, they have those speedboats that cost more than my house did.''

"Maybe," Joe mused. He could care less about that. He was about to ask why they couldn't get a doctor when they needed one, when Dr. Albert Reynolds walked in the door.

"I figured it was you." The tall, well-built doctor laughed. "You're the only man I know who could make good on a threat to tie me in a knot. What have we got here?"

Quickly Joe told the doctor about the accident. It was strange. He'd never thought much about Al being a doctor when they were working out together, but now he was glad to be able to count a bone specialist among his friends.

"And you decided to come along for the ride," Al said as he turned toward his patient. "What's the matter? Can't you find any clothes that fit?"

Joe would have thrown Al into a headlock except that would have meant letting go of Tina's hands and she was back to gripping him tightly. "Why don't you earn your keep and stop worrying about what I'm wearing. Do you think she's got a concussion?"

It seemed to Joe as if the wheels of the hospital moved exceedingly slowly, and yet he understood the necessity of a thorough examination. While Al was arranging for X rays, one of the teenagers from the lake poked his head in the door. He held out the car keys plus the clothes Joe had left where he'd been napping. "I thought you might need these," the young man said before starting to slide back out again.

Joe stopped him with a look. He let go of Tina's hands and stepped outside with the youth. "What about the people who were with her?" he asked. "A woman and a couple of men."

"I don't know." The teenager shrugged. "They left before I did. I thought they'd be here by now." He watched while Joe pulled a sleeveless sweatshirt over his head and shrugged it past his massive chest. "The men were really shook-up. I think the woman was driving."

Joe thanked the teenager and then shook his hand when the young man turned down Joe's offer to pay him for driving his car. He'd turned back toward Tina when he glanced in the direction of the waiting room he'd hurried past earlier. The area contained a nurses' station plus several groupings of chairs. The two men and woman he'd seen before were in a far corner of the room, fully dressed now. Although the woman had gotten to her feet and was starting toward Joe, neither of the men had moved.

"Do you know anything?" she asked. She rolled her eyes skyward as if dismissing the men. "Is she going to be all right?"

"She isn't going to die. But she's pretty out of it and there's at least one broken bone."

"Maybe more?"

"They won't know for certain until they see the X rays," Joe said simply. He didn't know the woman's name, but he liked her. She was taller than Tina, with long slender arms and legs that probably stayed that way through hard work.

"What about the leg with the cut?"

The woman didn't sidestep painful questions. Joe gave her credit for that. "The doctor's a friend of mine. He says there's some muscle damage."

"Damn. What about a scar?"

Joe hadn't given that much thought. In his world, muscles were more important than skin. "They're calling in a plastic surgeon so I guess it'll be all right."

"You don't know Tina," the woman said softly. "If there's a lot of scarring—"

"As long as she can walk. That's the main thing." Joe started to turn away. He'd been away from the semiconscious woman too long. He stopped. "Is she married?"

"Not yet. It's on the agenda, or at least it was before this came up." The woman snorted. "It's funny how an emergency brings out the true nature of people. Paul's always so in control at work that I never guessed he'd cave in like this. I wish, for Tina's sake, that he was more like you.''

Joe wasn't sure he was being like anything. All he knew was that there wasn't another place in the world he would rather be than at the side of the young woman with the thick black hair. But she was engaged. In love. He should have known.

As he went back into the examination room, Joe remembered what the other woman had said about Tina's reaction to a scar. It made sense. As far as he could see, there wasn't a mark on Tina's body. A beautiful young woman would think about something like that.

But that's not the important thing, Joe thought as he once again took up his position near Tina's head. There was some muscle damage. It'll come out all right, he told her through the wordless communication that had worked before. I can help.

Joe wished he could.

Al held up the developed X ray of Tina's leg and pointed to a spot. ''You were right, of course,'' he told Joe. ''She's broken her tibia, but it looks clean.''

''What about her head? She was unconscious a long time.'' Joe noted that Tina was looking more alert and wondered how much she understood.

''We'll keep an eye on that, but I don't think that's going to be a problem. Poor kid. The cast on her leg'll really knock her out of circulation.''

''Doctor?''

It was the first time Joe had heard Tina Morton speak. Her voice was little more than a fluttering whisper and yet Joe felt the sound deep inside him. He was drawn to it as surely as if she'd uttered a command. He leaned over, not caring that other people needed access to her. And yet it was Al she had spoken to.

''What is it, Tina?'' Al asked softly.

"What . . . I don't know where I am."

"I don't expect you to." The doctor laughed softly. "Don't worry about it, young lady. You're in a hospital. We're going to take care of you."

"It hurts."

"What does?" Al asked, while Joe would have done everything in his power to take over those simple words for her.

It took Tina a moment to respond. "Everywhere."

"Well, that narrows it down." Al chuckled again. "Didn't anyone ever tell you not to pick a fight with a boat? You have a bit of a concussion on top of everything else, which means you're going to have quite a headache for a while."

"My legs?"

The question tore through Joe. He was glad she wasn't able to see the thigh wound or the unnatural bump from the broken bone. He leaned ever closer, desperate for a way to give her something else to think about. "Do you remember the accident?" he asked, although he wasn't sure that was the right way to distract her.

"Accident?" She licked her lips. Her eyes were on his and yet they had a faraway quality. "I remember . . . you."

She remembered him. Joe had been paid his share of compliments in his thirty years but none of them touched him the way those simple words did. He wanted to tell her about the accident and his role in it and yet he didn't. He wished— He wished there was nothing more to the day than what they'd each separately been experiencing before a red boat driven by a drunk had changed everything. He would have traded getting to look into those incredibly dark eyes for that.

"That's a start," Al was saying. "Most accident victims can't remember anything. There isn't any identification tucked away in that bathing suit. Who should we be notifying?"

Tina tore her eyes away from Joe, but the look she gave the doctor was without comprehension. "Notify?"

"A husband, parents," Al supplied. "Does your family live nearby?"

"Don't call them. Don't tell my mother." Tina reached out. Her hand circled what it could of Joe's wrist as pain contorted her face. "She can't see me like this."

Al exchanged looks with Joe. "You need to give your mother more credit, Tina. I'm sure she saw her share of bumps and bruises while you were growing up. You'd be surprised what mothers can handle."

"No." Tina tried to shake her head but her eyes told Joe that she was in pain. "She won't—" Tina closed her eyes.

"All right," Al said as the two men exchanged another look. "What about someone else? Joe said you were with three others when the accident happened."

Tina licked her lips but didn't open her eyes. "Paul."

"Paul who?" Al asked while Joe fought off the impact of hearing that name coming from Tina's lips. Despite the fact that he'd only just met her, it hurt Joe that there was another man for Tina to turn to.

"Kenney. What's wrong with me?"

"Everything you're feeling is to be expected, Tina. Actually, from what Joe's told me, it could be a lot worse. You're lucky he got you out of the water before you'd been cut off from oxygen too long."

Tina's eyes opened. Joe read fear and shock and confusion in her blue-black eyes. He tried to concentrate on what Al was telling her about her injuries, but as long as she continued to look at him, nothing registered except her incredible eyes searching his face. He wasn't sure how aware she was of what she was doing and what was happening to her, but he was sure of one thing: they were communicating in a way that went far beyond words. It was the same communication that had pulled him into the water earlier.

It wasn't until Al cleared his throat that Joe tore himself away. There was no mistaking the teasing look in the doctor's eyes. "If I can get your attention, Joe—" Al stressed every word "—we're going to get started on repairing the damage. You are definitely going to be in the way of the plastic surgeon."

"Oh." Joe felt cast adrift. Everything he was and felt and experienced was tied up in Tina Morton. He didn't know what he was going to do with himself.

"Are you listening?" Al stressed. "Why don't you go find some clothes?"

Joe ran his hands down his chest, over the rocklike muscles under the worn shirt. He was feeling helpless and useless, two emotions that seldom entered his life. "How long will it take?"

"Long enough for you to find your shoes, Joe."

Joe backed away from the table supporting Tina. He'd done everything he could; there was no reason for him to stay here. Her fiancé, or whoever this Paul person was, should be taking over now. "Thanks, Al," he said automatically. "You'll keep me posted, won't you?"

Al's "Of course" was followed by a simple, whispered sentence.

"Please don't leave me, Joe."

Chapter Two

The world was floating somewhere just beyond Tina's grasp. Part of her knew she had a responsibility to enter the world, but there was still much of her that was content to remain in the quiet cocoon she'd found. She was vaguely aware of physical discomfort, but as long as she didn't move she didn't have to think about that.

She was mildly curious as to why she was where she was—something to do with water and a big man. How or why the two were connected was beyond her.

"Tina. Tina. You have company. Wake up."

I'm not interested. It should be easy enough to tell whoever was speaking to go away, but she'd lost the ability to speak. With an effort, Tina opened her eyes and focused on the white figure bending over her. She was relieved to find a nurse with her. "What?" The question sounded both stupid and terribly profound.

"I said you have company, Tina. You've been asleep a long time."

Tina wasn't sure that was right, but then nothing about what was happening to her had ever happened before. She blinked several times in an effort to make the white figure come into focus. Tina didn't recognize the nurse, but she did recognize the woman standing near her. "Ginger. What are you doing here?"

"Just offhand, I'd say I've come to see how you are. Do you have any idea what you put us through yesterday?"

"No. What am I doing here, Ginger?" Reality was rapidly taking over. Tina could no longer avoid it, but she just wasn't sure she was ready for what was waiting.

The nurse and Ginger exchanged looks and then the nurse slowly walked out of the room. Ginger waited until they were alone. "Are you sure you really want to hear this?" her friend asked. "The doctor said you probably wouldn't remember anything of the accident."

"What accident?" Tina started to ask. She tried to shift her weight in the bed, but something was holding her in one position. That wasn't right. "Ginger, what's wrong?"

Ginger touched her cheek, a gesture that took away some of the fear Tina was feeling. "You're trussed up like a Christmas turkey, that's what. I hope you're ready for this because it's quite a list. Your left leg is broken and in traction—but the doctor said it's a clean break, which is good—and there are God knows how many stitches in your right leg. Aside from a slight concussion, you're in tip-top shape."

"I don't understand." Tina wanted to take Ginger's hand but was afraid to move. Yesterday was still a blank, but she did remember something about grabbing on to a big hand and wanting to hold it forever. It might have been Paul, but she didn't think so. Paul's hand wasn't that large. "What happened?"

Ginger took a minute to pull a chair up next to the bed and then described the accident as briefly as possible.

"There are more details," she wound up. "But the doctor said to spring them on you slowly."

"Yesterday? It happened yesterday?"

"I'm afraid so, kid. You've already blown the weekend. I wanted to let you sleep some more, but the hospital staff said it was time for you to wake up." Ginger was holding Tina's hand now. It was a simple gesture, but Tina was grateful for it.

"Where's Paul?" she asked.

Disgust ruined Ginger's usually attractive features. "Waiting for you to heal before he ventures in here, I guess. I'm sorry," Ginger relented. "I probably shouldn't be so hard on him, but he was as much help yesterday as a saddle on a sow. Some people come through in an emergency— then there's dear old Paul."

Paul. No image came to mind. "You said some man pulled me out of the water? I'd like to thank him."

"Me, too." Ginger's eyes widened. "That has to be the biggest person I've ever seen. I think maybe that's what intimidated Paul. I might as well give Paul the benefit of the doubt."

Tina wanted to know more about the man who'd saved her life, but the feathers of pain she'd been able to keep at bay earlier were gaining in strength. She closed her eyes against the feeling. "Do you think you could ask someone for an aspirin?"

"I think you're going to need more than an aspirin for a few days. Hold on. I'll see what I can come up with." Ginger gently patted Tina on the shoulder before leaving the room. Even flat on her back, Tina could see her left leg suspended from some kind of apparatus. She couldn't see her right leg but could feel the bandage wrapped around her thigh.

The thought of any kind of injury sent shock waves through her. It hadn't seemed so bad when Ginger was talking about it, but now she could see and feel the damage. Tina took several deep breaths of air in an attempt to keep the fear from rising up her throat. She was desperately grateful when Ginger and a nurse entered her room. She wanted to think about a painkiller, not broken bones and stitches.

"Do you want me to leave now?" Ginger asked after the nurse had given her a shot. "Maybe you want to sleep some more."

"In a minute. Ginger, what—" She couldn't finish. She didn't want to know about the possibility of scars, disfigurement, maybe even being crippled. "What about my folks?"

Ginger ran her hand over her face. "They don't know yet."

"They— I don't understand."

"It was Joe Rustin, the guy who pulled you out of the water. Tina, you were really out of it in the emergency room, but you begged him not to tell your parents. He made us promise to wait until you were awake."

Thank God. Tina remembered nothing of being in the emergency room, but she wasn't surprised that she'd begged everyone not to tell her family, especially her mother. This had to be done carefully. "They have to know." She didn't try to keep the resignation out of her voice.

"I know. Do you want me to do it?"

Tina didn't have a ready answer. Her mother would panic. Her father's energies would go into trying to calm his wife. They would be locked up in each other with her feeling like a spectator instead of the injured party. Tina wasn't ready for that and yet she knew she had no choice. "You know Mom. She's going to fall apart. What are they going to think when they find out it was yesterday?"

Ginger grimaced. "Let me worry about that, Tina. I'll make sure they understand you aren't dying. Broken bones heal. You aren't the first person in the world who's had an accident. Look, one more thing before I take off. That Rustin guy wants to see you.''

"Now?'' It was probably the painkiller, but Tina's eyelids were gaining weight with every second.

"I don't think he's pushing that hard," Ginger said warmly. "I'll tell him to wait until you've had some rest. But you don't mind seeing him?''

"No. Ginger, I owe him so much.''

"I know. It's just that, well, Paul's been hanging around, too. It could get awkward.''

"Oh,'' Tina mouthed as she drifted off. Her last thought was to wonder why Paul hadn't been the first person to see her.

It was early evening when Tina woke up again. She supposed it was the sound of meals being delivered that roused her, but because there was less pain this time, she didn't mind. She was starting to rebel against the feeling that she was tied to the bed, totally dependent on others. Tina Morton loved life. She had an exciting job with the largest boat business in this part of the state. Trying out Paul's new water skis had been her idea. Being hospitalized was not.

By inching her body around, Tina was able to get her fingers on the call button. To her relief, the nurse informed her that she could indeed have something to eat. Tina wasn't hungry so much as thirsty, but when the nurse brought in a fruit salad and helped her with it, Tina ate with an abandon she hadn't allowed herself for a long time. Staying a size eight took constant calorie counting. "Are you ready for some company?'' the nurse asked after she'd finished.

"My parents?''

"No. I'm sorry. Your friend said to tell you that she hasn't been able to get in touch with them yet. But there's this guy who looks like Tarzan sitting out there who's going to break a chair if he sits in it much longer. Then someone phoned who says he's your fiancé. He asked us to call him when you wake up.''

Paul wasn't here and yet a stranger was. "I'd like to see—" She paused, thinking. "Joe something."

"Good choice." The nurse smiled. "Find out if he's married, will you? I'd probably have to make all his clothes, but I have a feeling he'd be worth it."

Tina allowed herself a small smile, the first since she'd been injured. The nurse was probably in her fifties, and Tina enjoyed her outlook. But Tina had a different interest in this Joe person. She had things she wanted to say to the man who'd saved her life.

He was big.

He was more than that. He first filled the doorway and then made it impossible for Tina to think about anything except his presence. There wasn't an ounce of extra flesh on him. He was wearing a polo shirt that pulled tightly across his upper arms and jeans that stretched over the most muscular thighs she'd ever seen. He looked as if he could make a pack of Dobermans back down. She wondered if he ever had to prove himself to others or if his size alone was enough intimidation. She understood what the nurse meant about needing someone to make his clothes. There probably wasn't a manufactured suit in the world that would accommodate those shoulders.

"Hi," he said, with a softness that belied his size.

"Hi, yourself." Sunshine. That's what he'd called her. Tina had no idea how she knew that, only that she'd heard the word rolling softly off the man's tongue when nothing in her life was going right. She looked into his dark ash eyes, saw intelligence, caring and tenderness, and forgot everything she'd ever heard about muscle-bound apes.

"You look—" He stopped.

"I look like I lost a fight with a professional wrestler." Tina's eyes were drawn to his hands. There were several crescent-shaped nail marks in the back of the right one. "Did I do that?"

"You were holding on pretty tight." He glanced at the molded plastic chair Ginger had used but didn't sit down. "You're going to be all right. Did they tell you that?"

"I haven't seen my doctor or maybe he came while I was sleeping." This wasn't what she wanted to be talking to Joe about. She wanted to— Good God, she wanted him to lift her into his powerful arms and take her home!

"The doctor's a member of my gym," Joe explained. "I'm glad Al was on duty. He's a good man."

"He's the one responsible for all this hardware?" Tina nodded her head in the direction of her legs.

"I'm afraid so." Again Joe glanced at the flimsy chair near her bed. He folded his arms across his chest, and Tina's thoughts went with the movement.

He's Gulliver in Lilliput. "I want— Thank you." The words weren't enough. She wouldn't be alive if it weren't for him.

"I didn't do it all," Joe was saying. "One of the men in your boat got you breathing again."

She hadn't known it was that bad. Tina started to shudder, but the fear and panic she expected didn't come. Joe had been there; she wouldn't have died with him there.

Tina tore herself away from the thought. Joe was a man, not a miracle worker. It wasn't fair to give him that awesome responsibility. "I still owe you so much," she said simply.

Joe nodded. It wasn't a boastful gesture but neither did he try to make light of what he'd done. Tina respected him for that. "I don't know what's going to happen to the men who hit you. They'd been drinking."

"I don't remember any of that," Tina admitted. Again she glanced at the marks on the back of Joe's hand. "I remember holding on to you."

Gently Joe took one of her hands in his. He turned it around, studying the manicured nails. "You're stronger than you look."

"Fear has a way of doing that, I guess. I wish I could remember," she groaned. Having him hold her hand took away the last of her hatred of being trapped here. She was alive. She'd get back on her feet—with his help.

She was doing it again. She had no business, no right, trying to make Joe into more than what he was. And yet— she felt safe and right and at home with her hand in his.

"My friend said you've been here a lot of the time," she said after a minute of silence. "You didn't have to do that."

"I know." Joe smiled faintly, a nice gesture that showed a little of the boy still living in his deep-set gray eyes. "I tried to work today but I couldn't get you off my mind. I wanted to see you awake." He released her hand but stayed close enough to the bed that she could feel his body heat. "I told myself I didn't have to come again, but—I'm here."

Something was wrong and he wasn't going to tell her what that was—she could sense that much. "I'm awake, all right. Although I'm not sure that's what I want at the moment." She indicated her legs to make her point. "Where do you work?"

"I own a gym."

"It sounds interesting. I've always wondered what it would be like to have my own business." Tina knew she was rattling on, but talking about what Joe did for a living was better than talking about her accident. "I belong to a fitness gym. The owners are into aerobics. They put me through my paces three mornings a week."

"The Muscle Mill isn't like that. It's mostly deadweights for power lifting. I have some members who are body-builders."

"Oh." Tina knew almost nothing about what Joe was saying. Her job and a lot more depended on her maintaining her figure. She understood dieting and exercise, but not anything to do with weights. "Is that what you are, a body-builder?"

Joe laughed but the sound was a little forced. "Not likely. I'm after strength, not looks. Dead lifts, squats, bench presses. I compete in those categories."

"I hope you'll tell me about it," Tina started, but before she could finish, the phone in the room rang. Tina looked helplessly at it. There was no way she could reach it. "Please," she asked.

Joe picked up the receiver and started answering questions, but from his short replies, Tina had no clue as to whom he was talking to. Finally he told the caller that she was ready for visitors and then hung up. "That was Paul."

Tina closed her eyes. Paul. She wanted to feel something—anything. There had to have been a reason for their having gotten engaged, but whatever it had been now escaped her. "What did he have to say?"

"He's bringing your parents with him."

Tina's eyes flew open. "Oh, no! I'm sorry," she relented. "I have to face them sometime, don't I?"

Joe smiled. Really smiled. The gesture told her that he understood that relationships between parents and children could be complicated. "You were adamant about them not being told yesterday."

"I don't remember." It frightened her that there were so many blank places.

As if he understood what she was thinking, Joe smiled and touched her on the cheek. His touch was a hundred times more comforting that Ginger's had been. "Al says some of your memory will come back, but for you not to be surprised if your mind continues to reject certain things."

He'd talked to the doctor about what was ahead of her. "I guess that's to be expected," she said. "I mean, there's probably things I don't want to remember."

"Why didn't you want your folks to know?"

He had no right asking that. Just because he'd saved her life didn't give him access to it. And yet, maybe he did have that right. "My parents, my mother especially, think I'm a porcelain doll. She had a terrible time carrying me. I was premature and the doctors hadn't been certain that I'd make it. They're going to fall apart when they see me like this." It went further, deeper than that, but Tina wasn't ready to tell Joe that, or herself.

"You don't look that bad."

He was lying. She didn't like being lied to. "I look like hell." Neither Paul nor her parents had ever heard her swear.

"It's not so bad," Joe continued in a tone so mild that she realized he hadn't taken offense. "There's some bruising around your neck and you have a bump on your right jaw, but they're going to heal soon."

Bruises. Bumps. Tina tried to swallow. She had a commercial scheduled for later in the week. They'd have to postpone it. "Ginger didn't tell me about that."

"She probably didn't want to upset you."

"It doesn't bother you? My bruises, I mean." She wanted to touch her jaw but it hurt too much to try to move her hand that far. She hated the little-girl quality that had slid into her voice, but she couldn't help it. Looking right physically was what her job hinged on. The outer package mattered.

"They'll go away. It's—" He paused. "It's your bones and muscles that count."

Tina had no defense against the desperation that clawed its way through her. She hadn't allowed herself to think about being crippled before. "What did your doctor friend say about that?" she demanded. "What's wrong with me?"

Joe was leaning over her, his face inches from hers. She wasn't aware of his having moved, only that suddenly, when she needed him most, he was there. She hadn't had to give voice to her fears. Somehow he'd known what she was thinking. "You're going to be able to walk. Believe me, you aren't going to spend your life in a wheelchair."

"But I'm not going to jump out of bed tomorrow either, am I?" She spoke the words with finality. Her legs weren't right, at least her right one wasn't. It felt numb.

"There's been some muscle damage." Joe hadn't moved. He was still giving her himself.

"Tell me." She wanted to close her eyes, to block out his words and yet she needed to go on looking at him. In the space of a day, he'd become the most important and most honest person in her life.

"They don't know everything yet, Tina. Al said we'll have to wait and see how much healing your body is capable of. But you will need physical therapy for the right leg."

"What's it going to look like?" She would have given anything not to have to ask that question, but she had to have certain answers. She trusted Joe to tell her the truth.

Joe shrugged, the muscles under the molded shirt moving with a power that pulled Tina's thoughts out of the depths they'd plunged into. "Don't worry about a scar, Tina. You're a beautiful woman. That hasn't changed."

Don't worry about a scar. "What is it going to look like?" she repeated.

"I don't know." He was still inches away, his breath warming her face. "A plastic surgeon did the work. Al says he's good."

"Al says." Tina hated the cynicism she heard in her voice, but she couldn't help it. For twenty-five years she'd heard that her looks were what unlocked and would continue to unlock the doors in her life. Joe couldn't possibly understand that. "It doesn't matter if a man has scars. It's different for a—for me."

"Why?"

"Because I'm out of a job if I don't measure up," Tina said in exasperation, knowing that that really didn't explain anything.

"I find that hard to believe. Tina." Joe's voice dropped to a husky whisper. "Let's get you out of this damn bed first. Then we'll take the next step."

We? Tina wanted to ask him what he meant, but he didn't give her the chance. She didn't know that he was going to kiss her until she felt his lips on hers. They were soft, maybe the only soft thing about him. She closed her eyes and shut out the world, allowed Joe Rustin's presence to take over everything. Despite the painkiller invading her body and the cast insulating her from him, Tina felt the first stirring of something precious. It wasn't a kiss between rescuer and victim; it wasn't a kiss between friends. It was, undeniably, a kiss like no other she'd ever experienced.

"It's going to be all right, Tina."

When Tina opened her eyes, Joe was back to standing over her, his body a tower capable of warding off the world. He couldn't lie; he'd make everything all right—or at least as right as things could be.

"I hope you mean it," she admitted.

Joe tapped his head. "If you think it is, it will be."

"Is that your philosophy in life?" Part of her was still tied up in their kiss, but she needed to talk to him. "Mind over matter."

"The power of positive thinking." Joe nodded. "Set your mind on getting out of here. That's your first goal."

Tina tilted her head slightly and stared up at him. "Is that an order?"

"Yes, that's an order. Give yourself a goal each day. Your leg isn't going to be hooked up to that contraption very long. Then you can get into a wheelchair."

He was right. That was a goal to shoot for. Just thinking about getting out of bed set Tina's pulse to racing. There were so many things she wanted to do—get back to work, water the plants in her apartment, find out if there was anything left of the water skis. Have Joe take her to the Muscle Mill. And Paul. He should be part of her plans. "I thought I'd never be excited about a wheelchair," she admitted. "But I'm going to have to do this one step at a time, aren't I?"

"We. We'll do it one step at a time." The smile left Joe's face. "You'll do it, Tina. You have your family to help, and Paul. Look, they're going to be here soon. I have to leave."

Please don't. Not ever. "Why?"

"Paul's with your parents."

"I don't care." Tina closed her eyes against what she was saying. "What I mean is, my folks are going to want to thank you."

"They don't have to do that. Look, Tina, it's going to be uncomfortable if I'm here when you see Paul. You need some time alone with him."

"My folks are going to be here. Besides, I'm not so sure I want time alone with Paul." She opened her eyes to find Joe watching her. "I've never been nervous around Paul before, but I'm nervous now. Maybe *nervous* isn't the right word. I don't think I want to hear what he's going to say."

"About what?" Joe's hands were hanging at his sides but at an angle created by his massive chest. "If he loves you, what you look like today isn't going to change that."

If he loves me. "Please don't leave, Joe."

"You said that yesterday."

"I did? What did you do?"

"I stayed."

"Then stay today." Stay and give me some of your strength.

The door opened, shattering the electricity created by their words. Tina shot Joe a private look before pasting on the smile her parents and Paul would be expecting. Her face felt as if it was breaking, but she didn't dare let go. It could be harder. Joe might have left.

"Tina! My darling! What have they done to you?" Tina's mother hurried to Tina's side but stopped just short of touching her. "Your face."

"What about my face?" Tina fought off the panic that radiated out from her mother and threatened to engulf her as well. She didn't remember her first weeks of life, but the pattern had been set during that time. Tina was a fragile gift given to frightened parents. Although the twenty-five-year-old woman knew she was going to live, remnants of that premature baby remained.

"There's the most horrible lump on your cheek. And your whole neck is purple. Oh, Tina, you haven't broken your neck, have you?" Tina's mother was actually shaking.

"No. She hasn't broken her neck. And it's just part of her neck that's bruised," Joe said, his voice low and yet commanding. "Tina, I'm going to be leaving now."

Don't! Don't leave me. "Do you have to?" she asked, unmindful of the looks flashing between her parents and Paul.

"Yes." He said the word slowly. "Some things you have to do on your own, sunshine. I'll be back in the morning."

Joe was gone, taking with him some of the strength she needed. And yet he was right. He couldn't face her parents for her. He wasn't part of her life—at least not yet.

Tina didn't try to speak until she could no longer hear Joe's solid footsteps going down the hall. She concentrated on her parents, trying to put herself in their place. They were loving and concerned—and exhausting. "That's the man who rescued me," she said, wondering if her parents were aware of how much they all owed Joe Rustin.

Paul had been standing near the door but now he came forward and thrust out a perfect flower-shop bouquet. "For you," he said before placing it on her bedside table. "You're looking better."

Better than what? Tina wondered, but she didn't ask. It wasn't fair to compare Paul to Joe, but she couldn't help it. Joe had taken up the room; Paul occupied a corner of it. Something of Joe had spilled over for her to absorb; Paul stood in a hard line, letting her know nothing of his thoughts. Paul was a handsome man, perhaps the best-looking man she'd ever dated, but his mind was occupied with the golf course he was developing. Before Sunday Tina had admired Paul for his intelligence and his commitment to his career. Now, somehow, that just wasn't enough.

He hadn't touched her since coming into the room. She didn't think he had touched her yesterday.

"What do you think?" Tina baited him. "Do I look like something out of a horror movie?" She didn't want to hurt Paul and yet maybe she did. She'd always been tuned in to other people's feelings. As a consequence, she put their wants and needs before hers. This time, however, her world had been turned on edge. Paul should know she needed him without her having to ask.

"Don't say things like that, Tina," her mother begged before Paul could open his mouth. Tina didn't need to hear him respond. He was looking at her and yet he wasn't, reminding her of the way people look at someone in a wheelchair.

Tina gave up. Paul wasn't ready to give her anything, and certainly she wasn't going to beg. "It's true, Mom," she said, knowing there was no sidestepping what was on her mother's mind. "I'm a mess."

Her mother leaned over and brushed a limp curl away from Tina's forehead. "My poor baby. When Paul told us— I've always thought that if we could just get you out of your teens, we wouldn't have to worry about you getting hurt anymore." Tears glistened in the woman's eyes.

"I could have been killed, Mother—but I wasn't, and I'm going to be back on my two feet again." Tina loved her parents. She just wished they'd realize that she'd cut her half of the apron strings a long time ago. Tina hadn't seen her face since the accident, but she had a pretty good idea what she looked like—and it wasn't the image of Tina Morton people were used to. Well, she couldn't help that. Once, just once in her life, Tina needed to hear her mother talk of something other than appearances.

"That's the spirit," her father said, but his smile was forced. "I've asked to talk to your doctor. As soon as we know everything we can start making plans."

"For what?" Tina asked.

"For..." Her father's voice trailed off. "Have you talked to Mr. Pardee yet? Has he said anything about your job?"

Tina closed her eyes. Her job was the least of her concerns, but her father had been the one to promote her to Larry Pardee in the first place. Her parents sounded as if they were planning her funeral; and yet she really didn't expect anything different. She'd always been their perfect little girl. They didn't quite know how to react now that reality had set in. "I've been a little tied up," she said lightly. "Paul? Could you do that?" She watched his response.

"Of course, Tina. I wonder what he's going to do, now that you can't be part of the advertising campaign. It's going to call for some radical changes in Boat World's public image."

Tina had expected Paul to say that. It was his practical, businesslike mind talking. Although Tina preferred her role as saleswoman to the advertising she did, realistically, Larry wouldn't like it if she wasn't able to perform both roles. "I can't worry about that now," she said tiredly. "I guess that's Larry's problem."

"Mr. Pardee can't see you looking like this," Tina's mother was saying. "We have to get you fixed up first. Where's your makeup case?"

"Slow down, Mom," Tina tried. She understood that her mother's nerves were doing the talking. Still: "He isn't going to be here within the next five minutes. Besides, don't you think he'll understand if I don't have my false eyelashes on?" She was laying it on a little thick, but Tina couldn't think of any other way to get her mother to realize what she was saying.

"I don't know if we can cover up the bruising," her mother continued, obviously not listening to her daughter. She was doing her best not to look at Tina, but her eyes revealed her panic. "I'll try my best. But that bump. Maybe if you turn your head to one side no one will see it."

"Mom. Please." The words were hollow and spoken without conviction. Tina needed to hear her mother concern herself with what was going on inside her daughter and not just the surface picture. But maybe it was too late for that. "I really don't care. I was almost killed yesterday. I'm not going to look like a beauty contestant."

"Maybe not." Her mother was trying to fluff up Tina's hair. "But you'll feel better if you look your best. I'll bring my hair curler in the morning and I'm sure I can find your makeup."

"Whatever you want." Tina was too exhausted to argue.

At least her father seemed to understand a little of what Tina was going through. He planted a light kiss on her forehead and then drew his wife away. "Our girl needs her rest. We can see her later, dear," he said firmly.

"I'll have to come early," her mother was saying as they left the room. "I want to get her fixed up before Mr. Pardee or anyone shows up."

Again Tina closed her eyes, but there was no hiding the fact that neither of her parents had really looked at her. She could understand that they hated to see their only child injured, but she couldn't imagine not wanting to know everything if she was in their place. "Poor Mom and Dad. They still think of me as that tiny, premature baby, don't they?"

"Tina, do you want me to leave, too?"

Tina focused on Paul. A few days ago they'd gone to a community theater production together. She'd enjoyed being on his arm, dressed to the nines, but now that night seemed a lifetime away. "What do you feel like doing?" she asked. In a perverse way, Tina wanted to test Paul, and see what he really felt for her. The established order no longer existed. She didn't have to try to fit herself into the molds others had created for her.

"You really don't remember anything of the accident?" Paul asked as he came closer. Paul continued to stand, as Joe had done earlier.

"Nothing," Tina lied. She remembered one thing. A powerful hand offered as a lifeline.

"Do you want to hear about it?"

"Why not?" Tina laughed. "After all, there's no way I'm going to be able to pretend it didn't happen."

Paul sighed before launching into his explanation. He reminded Tina that she was the one who wanted to try out the new skis, before telling her about the crazily driven boat that put a sudden end to a quiet day. "We couldn't see you from the boat, and I didn't want to get in the water because I was sure you'd surface any moment. When that man found you, Ron and I lifted you into the boat and started artificial respiration."

"You did that?" It would have meant so much to Tina to hear that Paul had done that for her.

Paul glanced away. "Actually, Ron gave you mouth-to-mouth. Someone had to handle the boat, Tina," he continued. "Other boats were coming up and causing wakes. Someone had to keep things as calm as possible for you."

Tina didn't say anything. Ginger had said she'd been manning the boat; Joe had said it was a woman at the controls. "How long was it before I started breathing on my own?" she asked. She wasn't ready to think about what she was learning about Paul.

"I'm not sure," Paul went on. "The men who struck you tried to leave. We had to stop them. I don't know how much time elapsed."

Ginger hadn't said anything about Paul being involved in that, either. Maybe he was lying to himself as well as to her. She asked a few more questions about the day, but because she had no memory of the accident, it was as if it had happened to someone else. "I'm going to be here awhile," she said at length. "What are you going to do with yourself?"

Obviously Paul hadn't expected that question. "Work, I guess. And come to see you. Tina, I might have to go to Dallas later in the week. I'm sorry."

Tina wondered if he really was, or if Dallas was an excuse for not having to see her. She couldn't imagine herself deserting Paul if the tables were turned.

She knew that wasn't fair. He was here now. Maybe she was expecting him to be Superman when all he could be was a human being.

"Oh," Tina said around an emotion that felt too much like something dying. "Thanks for the flowers." She didn't know why she was still trying. Paul was shifting from one foot to the other, obviously uncomfortable. He hadn't kissed her.

Joe had, but Paul hadn't.

"You're welcome," Paul said after a long stretch of silence. "Look, Tina, I have to get up early tomorrow."

"Of course. When will I see you?"

Paul stirred and jammed his hands into his pockets. "I'm not sure. I'm going to be out at the site much of the day. Look, I'll call you." He leaned over and brushed his lips against her forehead. "Get some sleep."

Tina watched Paul leave. He said he'd call, but it didn't matter. He'd told her to get some sleep. That was the kind of thing people said when they couldn't think of anything else. She wondered why he hadn't kissed her on the lips—did she scare him that much?

Chapter Three

Tina was kept flat on her back for four days. Paul visited only once during that time, but then he was in Dallas three of those days. The one short visit was painful for Tina and, she suspected, for Paul as well. Conversation that before had always come easily died after a few awkward sentences.

Her mother came by twice a day, armed with makeup. Every day Alice Morton had different plans for Tina's future. Because she was unable to accept the doctor's reassurance that Tina's bumps and bruises would heal, given time, she called in another plastic surgeon for reassurance that the right side of Tina's face wouldn't remain disfigured. The older woman had even contacted a beautician to come in and do Tina's hair, although orders were for Tina not to attempt sitting up. Then came talk of sending Tina to a spa after her release. "What you need is a make-over," Alice informed her. "You'd feel much better if you had your hair lightened."

Tina loved her dark coloring, but didn't feel up to getting into a discussion about that. She understood that her mother needed time to put the accident into perspective and reassure herself that Tina was going to live. She silently accepted her mother's nervous hovering while trying not to notice that her mother still wasn't talking about anything more important than the color of her hair.

She told Joe that. She talked Ginger into dialing the number for the Muscle Mill when Monday passed without seeing him. "Don't desert me just because my black-and-blue face is turning orange," she told him with a lightness she didn't feel. In the background she could hear weights thudding to the floor, and pain-racked yells. What was this Muscle Mill, anyway? "I need a friend who doesn't look at me like I'm a sideshow freak."

"You're hardly that, Tina." Joe's voice was low as if to ward against the possibility of being overheard. "I figured—well, I figured you'd have friends around. You don't need me."

"But I *do* need you, Joe." Tina ignored Ginger's startled look but lightened her tone. "I'm rewriting my will to make you heir to all my millions. You wouldn't want to jeopardize your status, would you?"

"Are you sure it's all right? What about Paul?"

"What *about* Paul? Don't let him chase you away. You—you're not telling me you don't want to see me anymore, are you?"

"I'm not telling you that, Tina." Joe was silent a moment. "If I had the brains I was born with I would, but I'm not going to."

"Good. I need your opinion on what I'd look like as a blonde."

"I like you the way you are," Joe said, as Tina knew he would. "But yes, I'll come."

After Joe showed up Tuesday morning in time to help with her breakfast, Tina stopped wondering why this man was rearranging his life to accommodate her. She needed him to help her sort through the things the accident had changed and was continuing to change about her. She would take anything he gave her.

He was the only one she told about what took place when her boss dropped by to visit. "I should have known it was coming," she admitted after Joe took up his station by the bed that evening. Somehow he'd found a chair capable of accommodating him and had moved it into her room. Now he sat with his arms folded across his chest, moisture holding his sleeveless shirt against his body. "I'm the best salesperson Boat World has, but that certainly isn't the way Larry sees it."

"How does he see it?" Joe tossed his head to one side in an attempt to lift his hair off his forehead. He didn't have to tell her that he'd just finished working out and his shower had been a quick one.

"I'm a come-on." Tina gritted her teeth against the reality she was revealing. She'd never spelled it out like that with Paul. Or maybe with herself, either. "I don't know if you've seen the TV ads Boat World uses, but I'm in all of them." She pasted a doll-like smile on her face. "One of the local dress stores loans us the outfits I wear. And we have a hairdresser and makeup person come in to 'prepare' me for the camera. Then—" Tina paused. "Then I come on to whatever boat Larry's featuring—the message being, buy our boats and get the girls as well."

"I've seen the ads," Joe said tersely.

"Then you know." Tina wasn't sure why she was continuing on this self-demeaning course but once she started she couldn't stop. "Basically I go in front of the camera and make a fool of myself."

"Then why do you do it?"

That wasn't fair. It wasn't the response she was looking for. "Why do you spend hours every day developing your muscles?"

"Because I'm proud of what I am—and it pays the bills."

Tina started to close her eyes against the reality of what Joe was making her face, but stopped herself. "You're lucky. I'm proud of what I know about boats and the fact that I can sell the right boat at the right price to the right person. That's the main reason I work for Larry, not because I'm that crazy about seeing myself on TV. But Joe—" She stopped long enough to gather strength for the rest. "I'm the teaser. I'm not naive. I know that. Larry parades me in front of the public—I let myself be paraded. Men come in because they want to see the girl who falls all over the boats on TV."

Joe stopped her. "It isn't that bad. Don't put yourself down."

"Why shouldn't I?" Tina asked almost desperately. "It can't be nearly as bad as what Larry said to me today."

"What did he say?"

Tina stared at the ceiling because she couldn't concentrate when she was staring into Joe's eyes. His eyes had a way of making her forget a lot of things. "He told me that my primary value to the business is as a spokesperson—the public image. He—said he'd hired me because I have great legs and a sexy, outdoor look. *Sexy!* I hate that word when it's used that way. The fact that I know the business and can sell doesn't seem to matter much to him. He doesn't want a spokesperson who has to wear slacks to cover up her scars."

"Forget the damn scar!"

"I'd like to," Tina moaned. "Just like I wish none of this had ever happened. But Joe, my legs have always been on the commercials. If you've seen them, you know I wear bathing suits."

"So let someone else do the damn commercials. You're still a saleswoman."

"I'm not so sure." This was what she had to tell her parents, what she was first telling Joe. "I don't know where I stand."

"He fired you?" Joe took her hand, but Tina lacked the strength to respond. She continued to stare at the ceiling.

"Those weren't the words he used. Larry Pardee has too much savvy for that. I might have grounds for a suit if he does that. He— I believe his argument was that it'll be a long time before I can go back to work, and in the meantime, his advertising campaign has to continue. Advertising! We film the commercials right in the showroom. They can be filmed and run the same day if need be. They might not be slick, but they're cheap." Tina blinked, turned her head and found Joe's eyes. "I'm being replaced by an eighteen-year-old just out of high school. She won some kind of local beauty contest. She doesn't know finance charges from an outboard motor, but her braces are off."

"You're bitter."

Tina thought about that. She should be but she wasn't. "I don't know what I feel right now," she admitted. "I think I'm in shock. I really hadn't expected him to kick me while I was down."

"You'll land on your feet, Tina. You still have a job. Besides, that kid might fall on her face."

Tina absorbed the conviction she heard in his voice. "Tell that to my mother, will you? She told me not to let Larry see me until the bruising faded."

"Do you think that would have made a difference?"

Tina shook her head. The gesture still hurt but at least she no longer felt as if the top of her head was going to come off every time she moved. "Probably not. I don't care."

"I don't believe that." Joe brought his face closer to hers. "You're a fighter."

"Not right now." Tina hated the depression settling around her, but she had no defense against it. Her boss's words hadn't truly sunk in until now. "I don't know if I'm going to get up off the canvas this time," she admitted.

Joe didn't try to argue Tina out of her depression but neither did he walk out of the room. For a minute he watched her, his eyes easy on her body. Tina didn't know whether he was aware of her or lost somewhere within himself. When he spoke it was of everyday things. He'd just signed up a couple of new members. One was a teenager with the goal of making the high-school football team. The other was a man in his late fifties who'd just moved here and wanted to continue a lifetime commitment to fitness. "I hope you can meet him someday," Joe said. "He can out-lift a lot of men thirty years younger than he is. I'm sponsoring a power-lifting contest later this year. He wants me to add a special event for older lifters."

"Are you going to do it?" Tina asked. She was grateful to Joe for giving her something else to think about.

"Yes. I think so. The contest is already set up so teens and women can compete with each other. I think you'd enjoy watching."

"If I'm out of here."

"You'll be out of here long before that," he reassured her.

"Can you be sure, Joe? Can you promise me that?"

"I can't promise you anything, Tina. You're the only one who can make your life work."

"I'm frightened."

"We're all frightened sometimes, Tina."

"Even you, Joe?"

For answer, Joe placed her hand against his chest and brought his lips inches from hers. He'd kissed her that way once before. Tina licked her dry lips and waited, wanting nothing else in life.

This time she could feel the beating of his heart through her hand. His lips made a slow, gentle invasion. It wasn't the passionate kiss of lovers; neither was it the chaste kiss reserved for acquaintances. What they shared was an admission that they'd gone beyond the first stages. Tina had remained passive the first time he kissed her, but now she had something to give. That something was gratitude, a request for friendship—and maybe more.

Tina couldn't remember much of what happened after that. She knew that Joe stayed for maybe another half hour and they talked the whole time. But when she was trying to fall asleep, what stood out was when he bent over her and showed her the world in a kiss.

He came by again the next morning just after her mother left and then returned that evening to read the paper to her. On Thursday he brought pictures of the contest he'd sponsored the year before and talked about traveling to Europe to compete with other world-class lifters. When she asked questions about what drove him to demand that much of his body, he gave her incomplete answers and turned the conversation around to other things. His explanation of what it took to be considered world-class was equally sketchy. Later, after another kiss that would stay with her for hours, he left without saying anything about seeing her again. But Joe was there before breakfast the next morning with a chocolate milk shake tucked under the shirt he carried over his arm. In the evening he brought strawberries and fed them to her one by one. They talked about Tina's feelings toward her boss, her parents, even Paul. At the end of each visit Joe left without telling her when, or if, she'd see him again, but he always returned.

By the end of the week, Tina's life revolved around Joe's visits.

"Don't you have a business to run?" she asked when he presented her with a women's magazine and then settled back to read an article to her. "I can't believe you don't have anything better to do than entertain me."

Joe's smile, as it always did, made Tina forget what they'd been talking about. "I could tune up my car, go over the books at the Muscle Mill, agree to be interviewed for a magazine article.''

Tina picked up on that. "What kind of article?"

Joe shrugged his massive shoulders. "On power lifting. Some reporter heard about me and now he wants to do some local-boy-makes-good article."

That was the first time Tina had heard Joe refer to himself as a local product. The truth was she knew almost nothing about his background. "And you don't want to talk to this reporter, do you?"

"No."

"Why? Dr. Reynolds said you dead-lift over eight hundred pounds. That's incredible!"

"Yeah? Maybe so." Joe was obviously uncomfortable.

"Why don't you like talking about it?" she pressed. He wasn't going to get away that easily. He knew so much about her; it was time for an exchange. "Dr. Reynolds says you have all kinds of trophies at your place, and that you even went to the Olympics. If it was me, I'd be asking for a front-page spread." She sobered. "What you do is so different from what I do—what I did. You've had to work for years to get where you are. All I had to do was be born with good legs."

Joe rose to his feet and walked to the window at the far end of the room. By turning her head Tina could just barely see him.

He started slowly. "I'm a private person, Tina. At least I try to be. It's one thing to compete on a world-class level. It's another to talk to a reporter about it."

"Why?"

"It's a complicated story." A few minutes later he returned and sat down to finish the article, but Tina listened only halfheartedly. She could feel the barrier Joe had erected between himself and the world—herself included.

But maybe being that strong carried with it a set of problems not many people understood. Joe was, quite frankly, physically intimidating. If she hadn't been privileged to see that quiet, gentle side of him, she might have gone around the corner to avoid him. She'd certainly think twice about dating a man who could easily have his way with any woman he wanted.

She couldn't be the only woman who felt that way.

Her mother showed up before Joe left, which meant there was no special kiss to keep Tina awake that night, and yet sleep didn't come easily. Joe was all male—his kisses told her that. He'd never been married, and judging from the amount of time he spent with her, she doubted there was anyone special in his life.

That didn't add up. A man with as much to give as Joe was giving her shouldn't be alone.

Shortly before noon on Friday, Joe and the doctor showed up at the same time. Tina was surprised to see Joe in the middle of the day, but she didn't have to wait long to find out why he was there.

"How would you like to get out of this torture chamber?" Al asked.

"I can go home?" Tina gasped. She thought about her second-story apartment, unable to picture herself clomping up the stairs.

"Not so fast." Al stopped her. "One step at a time. But it is time you started moving around. First this." To emphasize his point, he reached for the contraption holding her left leg in place and released it carefully while Joe stood beside her looking as if he'd been given the only thing he'd asked for for Christmas.

Tina groaned in relief when she felt the blood return to her leg. She moved her hips on the bed, loving the sense of freedom. "Can I sit up?" she asked.

"You can do more than that. You can get out of bed if you want. If you could do anything you wanted within the confines of this establishment, what would it be?"

Tina didn't have to think. "Wash my hair. Take a shower." She grinned in anticipation.

Al agreed to see what he could do and left to find a nurse. Tina wasn't sure how she was going to manage sitting up on her own, but Joe solved that. He carefully ran his hands behind her back and lifted upward. To her relief she felt no pain. She tried to hold on to Joe's arms but the strength that made it possible for her to water-ski a week ago had deserted her. "I feel so damn weak," she groaned as Joe mechanically raised her bed and placed pillows behind her back. "I hate feeling this way."

"Maybe you can start some exercises." He didn't have to be touching her any longer, but he continued to rest his hands on her shoulders.

"I'm the worst person in the world to talk to about exercising," Tina admitted. "I dropped out of two exercise classes this past year."

"Your motive will be different this time," he pointed out. "Getting yourself on your feet again is a lot more important than trying to keep your stomach flat."

Tina knew what Joe was getting at and yet she resented his attitude that her previous exercising had been for vanity's sake. "Just as long as I don't wind up muscle-bound," she said rather sharply.

"Like me?"

"I was talking about me, not you."

"I'm asking what you were thinking about."

It was an honest question. True, he was bigger, stronger, harder than any other man she'd ever known, but because she couldn't imagine him being any other way, his size didn't intimidate her. At least it didn't now. "No," she answered. "I wasn't thinking about you. Joe, I can't believe you're self-conscious about your size."

"Not when I'm in the gym."

He'd been her lifeline to sanity for a week. She felt she could ask him anything. "What about the rest of the time,

Joe?'' she asked softly. Her searching hand found his forearm. ''Do you ever feel out of place?''

''We all feel out of place sometimes, Tina. It doesn't bother me when people stare at me; I'm used to that. I'm used to being the one people call on when they're moving furniture or lifting an engine out of a car.'' Joe brought his eyes to rest on Tina's small hand trying to span his forearm. ''What I don't like is having people afraid of me.''

Oh, God, Tina thought as a wave of emotion swept over her. Joe had said so little and yet he'd exposed so much of himself with those few words. People who didn't take time to get to know the gentle side of his nature might not understand. ''Has that happened?''

''More than I want it to. I'm not a gorilla.''

''I know that.'' Tina found his hand and laced her fingers through his. She wanted to pull him close, but he needed time to work through his emotions.

''Some people don't.'' His eyes fastened on hers. ''Some women don't.''

Is that what it all boils down to? Tina wondered as a nurse entered the room and put an end to a rare, fragile closeness. The wall around Joe Rustin had been forged by women. Or maybe by one woman.

Although Tina had been staying awake nights dreaming of the luxury of a shower, she now wanted to put it off. She and Joe hadn't said enough to each other. She sensed a door opening between them; it might close again if she didn't try to step through now.

But there was nothing she could do. The nursing staff was shorthanded and the nurse who'd come to assist Tina with her first shower in the better part of a week looked a little frayed around the edges. She removed the IV that had been taped to the back of Tina's left hand and started to fuss with Tina's gown. It wasn't until she'd glanced at Joe twice that Tina understood.

"I think you're being kicked out," Tina explained. "I'm about to be indecently exposed."

Joe nodded and left without a word, much to Tina's disappointment. A few minutes later the nurse spoke. "Is he your husband?"

"Hardly." Tina laughed although the word *husband* had a nice sound. "Why?"

"He's so imposing. I didn't know what I was going to do if he refused to leave."

"Why would he do that?"

"I don't know." The nurse shrugged. "I guess, well, he looks like a brick wall, and I'd hate to get on his bad side— if you know what I mean."

"He's a human being, just like everyone else," Tina said quietly—but she didn't elaborate. What she was learning about Joe Rustin was too precious to share with the woman wheeling her down the hall.

Because of the cast and the stitches, Tina was unable to take a true shower, but with the nurse's help she was able to shampoo her hair and rid her body of the feel of a hospital bed. She hated getting back into an ugly hospital gown, but at least it was a fresh one. Her bed had even been changed in her absence. After the nurse left, Tina entertained herself by learning what her bed was capable of doing and going to the bathroom by herself. That expedition exhausted her.

Her parents weren't due to visit for several hours and Joe had apparently gone back to work. Maybe it was just as well. Closeness couldn't be pushed. It had to grow at its own pace. After resting a few minutes, Tina turned on the overhead TV, but the daytime programs failed to interest her. She was feeling like an ill child confined to her room while everyone else was outside playing, when her phone rang. It took a superhuman effort to reach the instrument.

It was Paul. "I got back this morning. For once my flight was on time. I didn't know if you were there," he said. "It took you so long to answer."

"I'm a little tied up," she explained. A few weeks ago the sound of Paul's voice over the phone gave her day a lift. Now she felt nothing. "I got out of traction today," she explained. "If I ever have a dog, I'm never going to tie it up. There isn't a creature alive who deserves that."

"You're sounding pretty chipper," Paul observed.

"Actually, I'm bored. And weak. I feel like a bowl of Jell-O. What are you up to?"

Paul said something about meeting with some of the investors for the golf course, and Tina patiently waited for him to finish. Paul was so absorbed in what he did that he expected everyone else to be just as interested. Today Tina found his devotion to the golf course exhausting. "Are you going to drop by the hospital after work?" she asked, wondering if he was capable of talking about anything except sand traps and bunkers.

Paul was quiet for a minute. "I don't think I can, Tina. I'm supposed to have dinner with one of the investors. He's thinking of backing another project and wants my input."

Of course. That was more important than hearing that Tina had finally been able to wash her hair. "That's all right."

"No, it isn't," Paul said almost before she could get the words out of her mouth. "Tina, I'm not very proud of myself."

"Oh?" Tina said quietly.

"I didn't do anything the day of the accident." Paul sighed. "I sat there frozen while that big guy dived in after you. I guess what I'm saying is that I've found I don't handle a human crisis very well. Give me a business venture and I feel in charge, but show me a little blood and—"

"That's all right," Tina repeated. Her voice gave away nothing of what she was feeling—or not feeling. "I appreciate your honesty. I'm sure it wasn't easy."

"We need to talk, Tina."

"I know." Tina was gnawing at her lower lip. Paul was a familiar element. He had been part of her world—her future. The fact that that was going to change was frightening—because then nothing of the old status quo would remain. "When?"

"I'm not sure. I think we need to be alone—we'll talk soon, Tina. Call me when it feels right."

"I will," Tina said before hanging up, although she didn't know when that would be.

Her parents came by as Tina was trying to cut into her slice of roast beef. Her father took over that chore but Tina insisted on manning the fork herself. Regaining independence was something she could focus on. It kept her from thinking about what she and Paul would have to say to each other. "I can do it myself, Mom," she stressed when her mother tried to take the fork from her. "I'm a big girl now."

Her mother looked skeptical, which prompted Tina to finish everything on her plate, even the tasteless carrots. Tina sensed that her mother wanted to say something but didn't know how to begin. When the woman started going through Tina's get-well cards for the second time, Tina took the initiative. "What is it, Mom? Something's making you crazy and it's doing the same thing to me. Have I been evicted? I don't think any of my bills are that overdue."

"Have you watched TV today?" her father asked as her mother shot him a warning look.

"Not really. Is there something bad on the news?"

"Boat World's new ad is on the air." Alice Morton couldn't quite meet Tina's eyes. "That teenager is—well, she's not at all like you."

Tina pointed at her legs. "I should hope not. What's she like?"

"Blond. And tall. You're so small that you always made the boats look bigger than they are," her mother pointed out with loving exaggeration. "But this child practically over-powers the boats."

Tina smiled at what her mother was trying to do. "I doubt that. If there's one thing Larry is, it's a shrewd business-man. He isn't going to let anything detract from his boats, not even his models." Maybe it was being off work for a week that was doing it, but Tina felt detached from the way she earned her paycheck. "Mom, I knew Larry wasn't going to put his business on the back burner simply because I'm out of commission. It won't bother me to see the ad."

"I hope not." Her mother still didn't look convinced. "But I don't think it's showing much loyalty for Mr. Par-dee to replace you without a word of explanation to the public. Honey, you're what the public wants to see."

"Life goes on." Tina looked for a way out of her leth-argy but none materialized. "So. What have you been up to?"

Tina's mother reached into the shopping bag she'd brought and pulled out a filmy nightgown that practically floated as she dropped it onto the bed. "Now that you can get out of bed, you won't have to wear those indecent hos-pital gowns anymore," she explained. "I brought some-thing that should make you feel feminine."

Tina smiled. She appreciated her mother's offer, but the gown really was impractical. Tina intended on spending as much time as possible trying to get her sea legs under her now that Al had promised a walking cast. She couldn't possibly leave her room in that see-through piece of noth-ing. But she wouldn't tell her mother that—buying clothes for Tina was something the woman would probably never stop doing. So she stalled. "I'll put it on a little later."

Her mother was in the middle of a discussion about her current volunteer project at the arts center that would showcase the talents of high-school students, when Joe came in. Alice stopped in midsentence, her eyes never leaving him. Most of the time Tina's parents' visits hadn't coincided with his, which meant they didn't know how often Joe came to see her, but that hadn't stopped her mother from commenting on the obvious differences between "the man who helped you" and "your fiancé," as she referred to Joe and Paul respectively.

Joe acknowledged her parents and then stepped toward her bed with a bag of his own. He pulled out a couple of five-pound dumbbells and placed them in Tina's hands. Their fingers didn't touch but that didn't stop Tina from reacting to his nearness. "Al said you could start working with these," he explained.

"Oh. Are you sure?" She knew this was Joe's domain but she still felt nervous, especially with her parents in the room.

"I'm sure. Don't be afraid, Tina."

The dumbbells felt heavy in her hands. She wasn't sure she wanted to attempt anything with them. "I wish you'd mentioned this to me before."

Joe stood back, waiting for her to begin. "You don't want to walk out of here a ninety-eight-pound weakling, do you?"

"Tina isn't a weight lifter," her mother protested. Her voice had risen an octave. "She's never been very strong."

Joe remained patient. "I understand your apprehension, Mrs. Morton. Believe me, I wouldn't be suggesting this if her doctor hadn't okayed it. But this is precisely the time for her to start building some muscle strength. It'll give her something to do. It'll improve her circulation. And it'll help her self-confidence."

That made sense. Especially the business about having something to do. Just thinking about another day of doing nothing except wait for Joe made Tina a little crazy. "It can't hurt, Mom," Tina said a little tentatively as she started to bend her elbows as she'd seen others do. She felt the strain in her lower arms, but it certainly didn't hurt. "Who knows?" she teased. "I might get into bodybuilding."

Joe gave her a look. "That's not what I had in mind."

"What *did* you have in mind? You aren't afraid I'm going to try to take away your trophies, are you? I might become so strong I'll break the world record."

"Don't talk like that, Tina," her mother warned. "Mr. Rustin, you're making a mistake. Men don't like women to have too many muscles."

Tina flinched. No matter what she did with her life, her mother continued to focus on one thing—how Tina looked. Tina had heard that type of thing for so long that she seldom challenged her mother anymore. "I don't think we have to worry about that," she said a little weakly. She continued to pull the dumbbells toward her body, but without the vigor that she first had.

Joe, too, had little to say. He sat down in his chair and listened to the older woman as she went back to her story about the rewards of charity work.

Tina was restless. Although she was pleased that her mother kept busy, she'd heard a thousand conversations like this one before. She was relieved when her father got to his feet and reminded his wife that they had to drop by the grocery store before heading home.

Tina let out a shaky sigh once her parents were out of the room. She and Joe were alone and she could speak freely. "I think I've seen more of my folks since I got hurt than I have in the past six months," she told Joe. "My mother exhausts me."

"She's concerned about you. She's protective; the accident has made you a child again in her eyes." He had started to reach into the bag he'd brought but now he paused.

"I know," Tina agreed. "But it's more than that. My mother has this thing about my marital state, or maybe I should say, how well I show up in the marriage market. Joe, she grew up believing that all women could be were wives and mothers—with a little volunteer work on the side. She's worked so hard at staying attractive for my father. She thinks all women should put their best foot forward at all times." Tina's eyes glazed as she spoke. Her mother would agree with what she'd just said and yet Tina hated thinking that the older woman's life was limited to that.

"Hence the gown," Joe said with a smile, pointing at the pile of fluff still at the foot of Tina's bed. "Seductive but not very practical." He pulled his hand out of his bag and held a tropical patterned garment in front of Tina. "I figured it was time you got out of institutional clothes, too, but I had a different idea."

Joe's choice had a front zipper, fell to the ankle and was made of a soft cotton that would allow her complete modesty. For a moment Tina couldn't speak. She'd had men buy her clothing before, but she didn't think any of them had ever given it as much thought as Joe had. The front zipper would allow her to get in and out of the gown easily, and it was long enough to hide her legs and yet not so long that she might trip. She could clump up and down the halls to her heart's content and not be accused of wearing bedclothes.

"It's perfect," she whispered. Joe was in his usual uniform of worn jeans and a stretch shirt but he knew what a recovering accident victim needed. She tried to picture him walking into a dress shop and sorting through racks of garments until he found the right thing. "When did you buy it?"

"The day after the accident."

He'd been carrying the gown around for days, waiting for her to be able to dress herself. "Thank you," she said softly.

"I wasn't sure whether you'd need it," Joe explained. For the first time he sat on the side of her bed, slowly lowering his body so as not to jostle her. "I thought your folks or Paul might bring you something."

"Paul didn't bring me anything." Tina dropped her eyes.

"Does that bother you?"

Tina shook her head. "Paul hasn't had much time for me. I think I understand." She touched Joe's cheek. He needed a shave.

"Do you love him?"

Tina wondered how long Joe had been waiting to ask that question. "I don't know. A week ago I would have been able to answer that. But Joe, I don't feel I'm the same person I was before the accident. The ground rules have all changed. I don't know where I fit anymore. I like the journey, I just don't know how it will end."

"A crisis can do that. But don't rush things, Tina. Give yourself time to get in touch with your feelings." He covered her hand with his own and slowly pulled it away from his face. "Your hand's so small," he said reverently, hesitantly. "I don't ever want to see you hurt again."

I won't be as long as you're here. Tina didn't know where the thought came from or why she felt so strongly that it was the truth. "I don't want to be hurt again," she said because something was expected of her. She was used to being on top in social situations, to holding her own against the come-ons she experienced. But she wasn't used to wanting to be the aggressor.

Joe released her hand and gently placed his fingers on either side of her neck. Tina couldn't see anything of the room. He blocked out everything, every thought. He'd saved her life, and she knew that he would never hurt her.

"Al said the stitches will come out soon. He's going to give you a walking cast so you can go home." The weight of Joe's body tilted Tina toward him on the bed.

"Home." The word sounded good but not as good as feeling Joe next to her. "When?"

"Maybe before the end of the week."

"I'll be ready."

"So will I."

Tina didn't have to ask Joe what he meant. His lips found hers and gave her the answer. She wrapped her arms around his neck and brought him down to her. His chest brushed her breasts. His hands were still on her neck, and he caressed the pulse points behind her jaw with his fingertips. Tina felt both possessed and a possessor. The feel of Joe's lips was soft and gentle.

But that wasn't enough. She needed to know what the rest of his body was like. Tina arched her back and flattened her breasts against his rock-hard chest.

For a moment Joe cradled her against him. Then, so quickly that it left her hungry, he eased her away. "I don't think that's wise, Tina."

She tried to reach for him. Don't do this to me. "Why?"

"Because—Paul."

"Joe, something's happening to us." Tina took a deep breath. How did a woman say such things to a man? "Let it happen."

Joe was no longer sitting beside her. He'd risen to his feet with a dancer's grace and was silhouetted against the room's white walls. "It isn't that simple, Tina." He turned toward the door. "Not for me it isn't."

As usual, he left without telling her when he would return.

Joe had been gone an hour and Tina was watching TV with her mind on his leaving when the phone rang. She grabbed for it, hoping to hear his voice. Instead it was her mother.

"Did that man stay long?" she asked. "I know he saved your life, Tina, but I want you to be careful."

"Careful?" Tina tried to shake herself free enough of Joe's image to concentrate on what her mother was saying.

"Yes. Honey, he could hurt you. I want you to be very careful."

After their conversation Tina hung up, wondering why no one else was able to see past Joe's overwhelming exterior. She fell asleep, thinking about the fates that had brought her a man like him.

Chapter Four

He was a damn fool. All right, maybe there wasn't anything terribly wrong with seeing Tina a couple of times—he couldn't just walk out of her life after what they'd shared. But Tina Morton was surrounded by her parents. She had friends who came around every day. She didn't need him.

And he didn't need her. He wasn't good for her.

"Enough," Joe told the image staring back at him from his bathroom mirror. He'd played the Good Samaritan role and it had felt good. But now it was time to move on.

But that wasn't all he'd done. He'd felt close to Tina, and being close to any woman after Shannon wasn't something Joe Rustin should be doing. Distance, he told himself. Keep your damn distance. Tell her goodbye.

It wasn't going to work. Joe had never been good at giving himself a talking-to. For years now, he'd given vent to his emotions by pumping them out of his body. Although he'd been home less than an hour and would have to be back at the gym by eight the next morning, Joe was reaching for his workout bag. He was thinking too much—and not understanding his thoughts—as he got into his truck and drove toward the Muscle Mill. It would take dead lifts, dips and pushdowns, but Joe would drive Tina from his mind—and he wouldn't let her back in again.

Early Tuesday morning, Al called Joe at the gym. "I figured you'd want to know when Tina is being released," the young doctor said by way of introduction. "You can come pick her up tomorrow."

"Tomorrow?" Tina was getting out of the hospital. "Al, I can't. I mean, what about her parents? And what's-his-name?"

"Are you stalling?" Al pressed. "Come on, man. The way you've been hanging around, I figured you'd have my hide if I didn't let you have the honor."

"I can't get away."

"The hell you can't. You own the place. What is it, Joe?"

"Nothing." Joe knew his friend would never buy that.

"Then what are you afraid of?"

"Nothing."

"Don't con me, Joe. We go back too far. I know too much about you."

Joe stared at the weight room just beyond his office, seeing not his grunting clients but the past. "Yeah. You do know too much about me. That's why I'm not coming."

"Then you're a bigger fool than I thought you were. That young lady's exactly what you need, Joe. Don't do this to yourself—or to her, either."

Joe turned away from the now silent phone. The past was supposed to be dead; why the hell couldn't it be like that for him? He would give a year out of his life to be the one to take Tina out of the hospital. He would never try to deny that. But no matter what Al thought, it was better this way.

"I want you out of here, young lady," Al was telling Tina the next morning. "You've been taking up space in this high-price hotel long enough."

"Now?" Tina breathed. "I can leave now?"

"As soon as you can get Joe over here. The paperwork's done. I want to see you back on Thursday to begin some very basic physical therapy, but take it easy today and to-morrow. See if you can get your sea legs back under you."

"Joe?" Tina questioned. "Why not my parents?"

Al grinned. "I can give you a half-dozen trumped-up excuses or the truth. Which would you like it to be?"

Tina was able to return the doctor's smile. "The truth."

"I was afraid of that. Look, you happen to have a very persuasive friend. She was by here last night. Actually, I took Ginger out to dinner. I don't think she was particularly impressed when my beeper went off twice. That lady doesn't mince words, you know."

"I know. But what's the point, Al?"

"The point is, Ginger thinks that asking Joe to take you home is what both of you need."

"Oh? Oh. Have my folks talked to you about my going back to my apartment?" Tina asked. "They have reservations about a place with stairs. They want me to move in with them."

"Do you want to?"

Tina could barely keep horror out of her voice. "Oh, no. I mean, that's very sweet of them but—"

"But you're a big girl and you like having your own place and space. Yes, I've talked to them. That's why I thought it might be easier if Joe was the one to spring you," Al explained. "I told your folks that stairs are going to be good exercise for you, but I'm not sure they agree. You're still their little girl, you know."

Tina sighed. "Do you think our parents ever see us as adults? Are you sure this isn't going to inconvenience Joe? I mean, he's done so much for me already."

"The man's been after me for days asking when you'll get out of here," Al lied. "He'd probably cancel my gym membership if I didn't let him know you were being released."

"I'm not sure how much of an honor packing me out of a hospital will be," Tina said to cover up the small thrill that went with knowing Joe would be with her soon. He hadn't come by yesterday. Somehow she'd managed to keep from calling him. "You're sure he won't mind? He's taken so much time from work already."

"Why don't you let Joe decide that. The way I see it, you either put yourself in Joe's hands or entrust yourself to your parents."

That was all Tina had to hear to make her reach for the phone. She dialed the Muscle Mill number from memory, holding her breath until Joe answered. He sounded wary. With his tone influencing her, Tina found it all but impossible to make her request.

"You don't—I mean, if you're too busy—"

"It's not that. But—what about Paul?"

"What about Paul? Joe, Al suggested I call you." She turned around, but the doctor was closing the door behind him. Tina stammered but forced herself to surge ahead. "I don't know what to say to Paul anymore. I don't even know where he is today."

"What about your parents?"

This was a mistake. She shouldn't have called Joe. And she shouldn't be feeling like a thirteen-year-old making her first call to a boy. "I don't want them to pick me up. I called you because I wanted you to have the honor."

"Tina, I'm just not sure it's a good idea."

"You're not sure what is a good idea?" Tina's hands were sweating.

"Our being together."

"Oh." Tina felt as if she'd been punched in the stomach. And yet he was right. He was much more perceptive than she was. "Joe, I'm sorry. I didn't mean to push you."

"That's not it."

"It's just that—I can understand if you don't want to do this." Could she? "I mean, I've taken up so much of your time lately. It's just that—after the accident—I feel so close to you, Joe."

Five miles away Joe closed his eyes. The accident. A force without substance pulling him to his feet, propelling him into the water where a woman waited to be saved. By him. "I'll be there in fifteen minutes."

Joe showed up carrying a rose that didn't look as if it had come from a flower shop. He placed it in Tina's hands without saying a word. Still, when their eyes met, Tina believed he was here because he wanted to be and not because she'd forced him. While Tina settled herself in the wheelchair he'd rounded up, Joe busied himself with tossing cosmetics into a paper bag. He hadn't touched her; Tina accepted that.

Tina broke the silence. "I feel like a kid on the last day of school," she admitted, holding the fragrant flower to her nose. "My apartment's going to look fantastic after all this white. Where did you get the rose?"

Joe had opened the room's closet door. He answered while adding the nightgown her mother had bought to the paper bag. "Some yard between here and the gym."

"And you just walked up and snitched it?"

"Do you like it?"

Tina loved it, just as she loved having Joe lean over her as he guided her out of the room. There were things they would have to talk about—later. But he was here. They would have some time together. She waved at several nurses and took a long, grateful breath as Joe pushed her past the hospital front doors. "Free," she breathed. She felt reckless. "How would you like to take me break dancing? I want to hear music, watch people having a good time."

"You're heading home. I'm sorry."

He really means it, Tina acknowledged. "Ah, well—" she sighed with mock sorrow "—I haven't had breakfast. Could we at least stop for something?"

Joe nodded. A few minutes later he was placing their order at the drive-up window of a fast-food restaurant. Tina managed not to gasp when his order came to triple what hers was. They ate as he drove. Joe consumed his egg, sausage, cheese and biscuit breakfast with nothing less than reckless abandon. "Not bad," he remarked as he washed it down with the last of three cartons of milk.

Tina whistled. "I guess not. Do you always have that much for breakfast?"

"Most of the time. When I was younger I was always cutting back to weigh in for a contest, but my body's pretty settled now. I don't have to worry about calories."

Tina shook her head, deeply envious of someone who didn't have to watch every mouthful. "It takes a lot of food to feed all that muscle, doesn't it? What do you think?" she teased, flexing her small biceps. "Do you think I should get into bodybuilding?"

"I'm not one to encourage bodybuilding," Joe pointed out as he started down the street that led to Tina's apartment. "That's pretty different from power lifting."

"Okay," Tina relented. "Do you think I should become a power lifter?" She glanced at her small muscle and grimaced. "Do you think there's any hope for me?"

"Maybe. But only if you really want to do it."

"Maybe we'd better wait." Tina laughed. "One step at a time. Thank heavens for a walking cast. It certainly beats crutches."

Tina was embarrassed to need Joe to carry her up to her apartment, but she was the first to admit that the stairs looked formidable. She wrapped her arms around Joe's neck, making jokes about the possible condition of her plants to take her mind off being in Joe's arms. He let her down so she could unlock the door. "I'm home," she called out to the empty apartment. Tina turned on the living-room light and looked around. A spider fern near the patio door was wilted.

"It smells so musty," she observed. "There's something sad about a house with no one living in it."

Joe laid her belongings on a glass-topped coffee table and straightened. "It needs fresh air." He didn't come near her. After he'd opened a couple of windows, he went into the kitchen and returned with a glass of water. "If you think this is lonely, you should be in a schoolroom in the summer." Joe slowly upended the glass into the planter. "You know what I hate? Going into stores and seeing plants people have forgotten to water."

Tina had been thinking about settling into her recliner, but put it off while concentrating on what Joe had just said. "I thought I was the only one who felt like that. Once I went into a public rest room and came out with a dripping paper towel to squeeze over some poor dying plant. I know the clerk thought I was crazy." Strength flowed out of Tina's body. She sank into the nearest chair. "What do you know about being in a school in summer?"

Joe took the couch five feet away. "My mom was a teacher. I used to tail along to help her put things away." He leaned back, eyes half closed. "I'd walk down the empty halls, certain I could hear the echoes of a thousand footsteps."

For a moment Tina forgot that she was supposed to keep up her end of the conversation. Joe had told her about making a name for himself as an all-state football player and wrestler. She knew about the sports scholarship that made it possible for him to go to college. She knew about the months of unrelenting work that went into making the Olympic weight-lifting team. What she didn't know was what Joe had felt inside while all this was going on. "That sounds like the basis for a camp-fire story," she said finally. "The ghost of students past."

Joe was smiling. "I think I was about six when I came running to my mom telling her there were ghosts in the hall and I was afraid of them. Mom said we should never be afraid of ghosts—that they're our link with history."

Tina was fascinated by what the smile was doing to Joe's eyes. Maybe he hadn't wanted to be with her today. Maybe he would soon be leaving. She would take whatever he gave her. "Your mother sounds like a wise woman."

"She was a good teacher. She taught me when I was in the third grade." Joe leaned forward and rested his elbows on his thighs. "Mom was the rock in my life. My father was gone a lot of the time, working construction on bridges and dams, things like that. I look like my father, but—" Joe paused to tap himself on the chest "—I owe what I am inside to my mother."

Tina's eyes blurred. She was happy for him, but he was painting her a picture far different from the one she'd experienced. "I don't think we're really aware of our parents' influence on us until we've grown up. When we're teens we're busy trying to be independent. Then—" she sighed softly "—then we grow up and see that our folks have left their mark on us."

Joe was watching her and his response came slowly. "True. Is there anything you need? I have to leave."

"Oh." So soon? "No. I don't think there's a thing I need."

"Your folks are probably going to show up any minute." Joe got to his feet. He wasn't coming close to her. "They'll get you some groceries, won't they?"

"I don't think they know I've been released. I should have told them."

"They'll figure it out. What if I call you later and see if there's anything you need?"

The only thing I need is to have you stay here. "Thank you," Tina said softly, feeling the loss although he was still in the room. "Thank you, Joe. I'm glad you brought me home." She glanced down at the rose she still held in her hand. "Do you think you could put this in water for me?"

A minute later Joe was sliding the stem of the rose into a thin-necked vase and putting it on the coffee table. His hands were so large that Tina could barely see what he was doing, but she had no fear that he would damage anything. She wasn't sure what she was going to say was wise, but she would weigh the consequences later. "I'm glad I met you. Maybe not under those circumstances, but if I had to have an accident, I'm glad you were there."

"So am I, Tina." Joe had started toward the door, but he retraced his steps. He leaned over her, his presence blocking out the room—the world. His lips on her uplifted, willing ones were gentle and chaste. Tina's reaction was anything but. His mouth was a tease, a catalyst for emotions that flowed through her veins and settled low inside. Tina lifted her hands from her lap, spreading her fingers over the vastness of his upper arms. Joe Rustin could lift close to a half ton off the ground; he could also move a hundred-pound woman in ways that were both new and timeless.

Stay, Joe. Stay with me and we'll find a way to make being together work. "Thank you," Tina whispered when he straightened. She slid her hands down his arms and tried to encompass his wrists, but ended up squeezing his fingers. "For everything."

Joe's chest was rising and falling rapidly. "Thank you for everything, too, Tina. I'll call you tonight."

The house felt incredibly empty after Joe left. Tina wasn't used to being home during the day, but that wasn't what made her turn the TV on loudly. She busied herself by dusting and watering the rest of the plants, but that small exertion drained her.

She was grateful when her parents phoned, even though their call was followed by a visit that was smothering. After her mother helped her with a shower, Tina insisted on dressing in shorts and she caught both of them staring at her thigh bandage. "Al says the bandage will come off when I see him on Thursday," she explained, wondering at her detachment. "He told me to expose it to the air as much as possible."

Alice Morton shivered. "You need to take it slow and easy, honey. Don't do anything that might stretch the—that might hurt you."

"That might stretch the scar," Tina finished for her. She didn't mean to put her mother on the spot; it was just that saying the word *scar* held no meaning for her. "Have you heard from Paul? Does he know I'm out of the hospital?"

Her father looked confused. "I thought he brought you here. That man doesn't know what to make of any of this. He's so—"

"Joe brought you home, didn't he?" her mother interrupted. "Dear, you can't blame Paul for feeling abandoned. I mean, how would you feel if someone else came muscling his way into your life the way this Joe has? Paul should be with you these days, but Joe's always there."

"Joe's always here because he wants to be." That wasn't true. Joe hadn't wanted to be with her this morning. "Paul would have come to the hospital more if he'd wanted to."

"He's busy," Alice continued. "You know how much time his business takes. He cares for you, Tina. He wants to take care of you. I'm sure of that."

Tina didn't share her mother's conviction. She couldn't picture Paul taking care of her, or her wanting that. "Don't make excuses for him, Mom. I'm a big girl. I can handle a little neglect." Paul's neglect, at least.

"Give him time," her mother said, patting Tina on the shoulder in a gesture that reassured only herself. "He'll come around. He just needs time to—"

"Forget Paul." It was Tina's father's turn to interrupt. "Listen to me. I swore I wasn't going to try to run your life. But—I hope you aren't in love with him or anything, because he isn't what you need right now."

"Charles!" Tina's mother gasped. "How can you say that? He's ambitious, wealthy. He can give Tina the security she needs."

"No, Mom." Tina was shaken by the intensity of the love she felt for her father. The man had never quite known what to do with his delicate little daughter and had left much of her rearing to his wife. But today he was reinforcing what Tina knew to be a deep truth. "Paul *isn't* what I need. In fact—" she laughed to lessen the impact of what she was going to say "—I hope I never 'need' a man. I hope I never marry a man simply because he represents security."

"Speaking of security—"

Tina felt exhausted. Obviously her mother wasn't done with her. "What kind of security did you have in mind?"

"I've been thinking." Alice glanced at her husband but hurried on before he could speak. "Do you remember Leo Mentzer, the reporter who did that wonderful piece on the art center? He's such a nice man. Honey, you're news. So many people know who you are. I was thinking—we could get Leo to do an article on the accident and how hard you're working to get back on your feet. Larry would have to get rid of that silly creature who's taken your place." Alice held out her hands, framing her daughter's face as if looking at her through a camera. "Why can't they photograph you from the neck up? I'm sure Leo would be delighted to help out."

"Mom! You haven't talked to him, have you?"

"Not yet. I thought—maybe you would rather make the call."

"I'd rather drop the whole idea." Seeing her mother's crestfallen look, Tina softened her voice. "Mom, I'm not going to try to back Larry into a corner."

"But honey—"

"I'm sorry, Mom. I know you're trying to help, but this is something I have to work out myself."

"I guess . . ." Alice's voice trailed off. "Have you heard from Ginger recently?"

"Ginger? I tried to call her this morning, but they said she was in the law library. Why?"

"Because—" Alice Morton was back to smiling again. "I think she likes your doctor. I saw them together last night. Whatever they were discussing, it didn't look like business."

Her mother's news delighted Tina. She hadn't thought much of the man Ginger had brought out to the lake with her and Paul. Dr. Al, as Tina thought of him, might be the only man who could hold his own with her high-energy friend. She promised her mother that she would call Ginger tonight and pass on any gossip.

However, it was Paul who Tina made herself call as soon as her parents left. For once she was able to catch him in his office. With as few words as possible, she told him that she was home, but he didn't need to let that disturb his day. "I appreciated the attention while I was in the hospital," she said, stretching the truth a little. "I just wanted to let you know I've been let out of hock."

"You don't want me to come see you?"

Tina closed her eyes to make the talking easier. "You said there was something we needed to talk about. But maybe we can do it on the phone."

Paul sighed. "I feel as if I've let you down, Tina. You were hurt, and I wasn't even there to hold your hand. Hell, I didn't even know you were going to be released today."

"I'm a big girl. I don't need anyone holding my hand."

"Who brought you home?"

Paul wasn't a fool. Neither was he afraid of confrontations. "Joe."

"I thought as much. I can be there in a few minutes, Tina. I don't like leaving things the way they are between us."

"That's why I called. But Paul—don't come." Joe's essence was in the house. She didn't want Paul's presence taking that away. "I—I don't know where we're headed."

"Neither do I."

Tina swallowed. She felt sorrow and loneliness, but the emotions weren't deep. "I think— I don't know what I think."

"You don't have to think anything," Paul said softly. "You're doing fine. I'm the one who let you down."

"Don't be so hard on yourself, Paul."

"What I'm trying to be is honest. Tina, I thought I had everything between us in order. I figured, once the golf course was reality, we'd get married and you wouldn't have to work anymore."

Tina turned the thought of being married to Paul around in her mind, but it remained without substance. "I like working."

"Someone like you deserves pampering. I know, you're an independent woman and all that, but I've always wanted you to have an option about working."

Tina tried to work that around in her mind as well, but it made no more sense than marrying Paul. Despite her mother's influence, Tina had always believed that all intelligent human beings—male or female—had a responsibility to carry their own weight. Unless she had the care of small children, she couldn't accept the idea of having someone else support her. "That's sweet. But Paul, I don't want to be dependent on anyone."

"Don't look at it like that. Tina, I've always thought of you as fragile—somehow not like everyone else."

Tina winced at his words. If she were tall like Ginger or strong like Joe . . . "But I *am* like everyone else."

"I know that now."

"Is that it? I'm not the perfect doll anymore. I'm damaged."

"Stop that! Do you really think I'd turn my back on you just because of the accident?"

Tina stopped herself. Attacking Paul didn't make sense. He was trying to be honest with her. "No, I don't think that," she said softly. "But the accident changed a lot of things, didn't it?"

"It proved I have feet of clay. And—I had to accept that you're not as perfect as I thought you were, either. You bleed just like everyone else."

The porcelain doll Paul thought he knew didn't exist. Without regret, Tina said a silent farewell to her. "Nothing's the same anymore, is it? Neither of us are who we thought we were."

"I think I knew what kind of a man I was," Paul said after a long silence. "I just didn't want to admit it. And I don't know what to do with what I've learned about you. Damn! What was the matter with me? I wasn't being fair to you—to either of us."

Tina felt an exhaustion that had nothing to do with her physical condition. "We'd have to get to know each other all over again, wouldn't we?"

"I think so. I'm not sure—Tina, I'm not sure I'm up to that."

"Neither am I."

They said a little more before Tina found an excuse to put an end to the conversation. She settled back in front of the TV, feeling more good than bad. Although their romance had died, she and Paul had emerged with new insight. Maybe, if it was what he still wanted, Paul would one day find a woman who would be content to stay on the pedestal that he would build for her. Tina's relief came from knowing she could stop trying to be someone she wasn't and start looking for who she was.

Tina was sitting on the couch, lost somewhere deep in her thoughts, when the phone rang late in the afternoon. It took until the fifth ring for her to reach the instrument. "Did I wake you up?"

Tina swayed in response to the sound of Joe's voice. "I wish. You know, it's boring here. No nurses to talk to."

"Are you alone?"

"Very. Joe, I talked to Paul."

"And?"

"And nothing. I'd like to tell you about it."

The slow drawing in of his breath took Tina along for the ride. She waited, fearful. Hopeful. "I'll be there in about an hour. Is there anything you need?" he said finally.

Tina explained that her parents had brought enough food to last a month. "Why don't I see what I can whip up for dinner? After all you've done, the least I can do is feed you."

"You don't have to do that."

"I know I don't. I want to. It's the therapy I need right now." Hurry, Joe, Tina thought after hanging up.

She settled on a meat loaf and potatoes, not because she was crazy about the menu, but because it was easy to cook and hearty enough to satisfy Joe's appetite. She felt a little unsure about putting out wineglasses, but today she wanted a celebration dinner for being out of the hospital, not to mention making her peace with Paul.

If they ever got to dinner, Tina admitted to herself as she opened the door to let Joe in. She'd never seen him look so overwhelming before, and her reaction was nothing short of primitive. He was wearing a minuscule excuse for a tank top that exposed his massive shoulders, with the pathetically thin strips of fabric riding close to his neck. His drawstring sweats were cut off, accenting his sculptured thigh muscles. Tina focused on Joe's strongly chiseled jawline, not trusting herself to look lower again. "It's a good thing we're eating here," she said weakly. "I don't think they'd let you in a restaurant dressed like that."

Joe shrugged. The motion threatened to shred the top that bore the name of his gym. "This heat is driving me crazy."

Tina pointed to her own shorts. "You don't have to tell me. I should warn you, the air conditioning in this place leaves a lot to be desired." She stepped back because to stand this close to Joe meant risking what was left of her sanity. "Mom was pretty shook-up when she saw my war wounds, but comfort's more important."

Joe nodded. "Besides, sooner or later your mom's going to have to face facts."

"Such as?"

"Such as that cast," Joe said simply. "You know, she never looks at your legs."

"I know." God! Nothing got past this man. Did that mean he knew what she was experiencing right now? Frantically Tina changed the subject. "How was your day? Anything had to be better than watching soap operas."

"Busy." Joe was standing in the middle of the living room, his arms at his sides as if he didn't quite know what to do with them. "I went to the local college and met with the head football coach. It looks like I'm going to be helping the players get ready for the season."

"That sounds interesting." If she ran her hands over Joe's arms would he relax? Suddenly Tina wanted nothing more than to see him in his gym, to understand that there was a place where this man truly belonged.

"It is. Strength conditioning is important for everyone on the team. It cuts down on injuries."

Tina wanted to digest that bit of information, but Joe's presence was pulling at her. "Are there many women at your gym?" she asked, surprising herself with the question.

"Some," Joe supplied. "But not as many as I'd like to see. Something smells good."

Tina laughed. Laughter was easy now that Joe was here. "I won't guarantee anything. I'm not the world's greatest cook, but give me a microwave and I can stave off starvation." Tina turned as quickly as her cast would allow and led the way into the kitchen. She felt the pull in her injured thigh as she walked, but it was a distant sensation, one that didn't come close to what Joe's presence was doing to her.

Tina pulled open the microwave door and showed him the results of fifteen minutes of work. "I hope you like it."

Joe chuckled. "I eat anything."

Joe was true to his word. By the time they'd finished dinner on the patio overlooking the complex's swimming pool, there wasn't anything left for Tina to put away. She'd allowed herself a rare second glass of wine, enjoying the evening breeze. At Joe's insistence, she was stretched out on a lounge with a pillow under her cast. Joe was seated in a padded redwood seat, a beer engulfed in his hands. They hadn't said much during the meal, but the silence was a comfortable one punctuated by laughter as they watched several toddlers playing in the pool's shallow end.

"They're so free," Tina observed as a little boy discarded his swimming trunks and scrambled off ahead of his mother. "Why were we in such a hurry to grow up?"

"Because we thought growing up would make us independent."

"Freedom without responsibility. That's what I thought I'd get when I grew up." Tina shifted her weight but didn't bother to tug on the hem of her shorts. "I thought growing up meant staying out as late as I wanted, not having to do homework any more, having my mother off my back."

"It didn't turn out that way?"

Tina laughed at herself. "What I found out is that I'm not cut out for late nights. The freedom to do what I want doesn't always work when I have to face myself in the mirror the next morning. Why didn't anyone tell me that earning a living wouldn't be nearly as glamorous as I thought it would be? Nine-to-five is pretty relentless.''

"Don't you like your job?"

Something serious threatened to stir inside Tina, but her mind was on holiday; she wanted it to stay there. She turned the question back on Joe. "Do you like yours?"

"It isn't a job. It's my way of life."

"That's rare." Tina laughed at the wails of the boy who was being tugged back into his bathing suit. "Having your job so closely coincide with your way of life doesn't happen to many people."

Joe leaned forward, bringing his face out of the shadows. "You're in a philosophical mood."

"I am, aren't I? I think it's the time I spent in the hospital." Joe's eyes were too intense and Tina dropped her head to concentrate on what liquid was left in her glass. "I've been thinking about my life. About whether it's going in the direction I want it to."

"At least you have a life, Tina. You almost didn't."

Tina tried to take a breath, but it caught in her throat. Joe had struck at the core of her thoughts. Yes. She had a life—thanks to him. "I'll never be able to thank you enough," she whispered. "You saved my life."

"Don't. I don't know what to say when you do that."

"Don't say anything," Tina started before realizing that wasn't the answer, either. "Just let me rattle on a little, okay? I've been trying to decide if I saw my life pass in front of me that day, but it's still a blank. Al was right. My mind refuses to accept certain things. I don't remember anything of the accident." Absently, Tina scratched at the top of her cast.

Joe was watching. "It wasn't anything you'd want to remember. I'm just glad everything turned out all right."

What Joe had just said was a simple statement, something Tina could easily have passed off. But the unspoken message caught her. Until this moment she hadn't given enough thought to what he had gone through. "You told me something," she started, testing the waters. "You were on shore when the boat hit me. How did you get to me before anyone in the boats?"

Joe shrugged, momentarily distracting her from her thoughts. "I don't know why they didn't go in after you," he said softly. "I just know—"

"That's not what I mean," Tina interrupted. "I'm not looking to blame Paul or Ginger's date. How did you know I was in trouble? Did I scream?"

"If you did, I don't think I could have heard. The motors were making a lot of noise." Joe's eyes slid off her, glazed slightly, and settled on a spot she couldn't follow. "I don't know what happened. I just knew you were in trouble."

Tina let the sound of giggling toddlers wash over her. While she was in the hospital she'd simply accepted Joe's being there. She'd been too wrapped up in getting well to delve into their growing relationship. She didn't want to do that anymore. Had there been an invisible lifeline between her and Joe that summer afternoon? "I wonder why."

Joe leaned forward, bringing his presence closer to her. "Don't think about it, Tina. Everything worked out all right."

"Yes. It did." Maybe, now that Joe was part of her life, things would always work out. "I guess..." She concentrated on the watchful mothers monitoring their children's play. "I've heard that sometimes parents know what's going on with their children even after those children have grown up; that identical twins sense they have a twin even if they're raised apart." That didn't explain what had gone on at the lake, but it was the only explanation Tina had.

"Tina?" Joe said a long minute later. "Are you expecting Paul tonight?"

She hadn't told him. Somehow she'd expected Joe to understand that she didn't believe in complicating her personal life. "I'm not going to be seeing Paul anymore." Tina brought her eyes back to where Joe could read them.

"I'm glad."

It was such a simple statement, exactly what she expected from Joe who, she was learning, said more with the tone of his voice than with words. "So am I," she said quietly.

Joe had gotten out of his chair. He was leaning over her, arms inches away from hers. She thought he was going to kiss her, but he didn't. "I was afraid you were dead. Al said not to tell you that until you were back on your feet."

Because the moment was more intense than she was ready for, Tina settled for a joke. "You call this on my feet?" She tapped the cast without taking her eyes off Joe.

"I felt so damn helpless." Joe straightened and folded his arms across his chest before continuing. "I don't like the feeling."

"If you think you felt helpless, you should have seen things from inside my head." She wasn't intending to be flippant, but she couldn't seem to help herself.

Joe held out his hands and gave Tina something to grip as she pulled herself to her feet. Arm in arm, silent, they moved to the railing so they could watch the toddler who had once again shed his swimming trunks. Joe spoke so low that his voice reached her as a rumble. "When I saw those drunks trying to leave, I almost lost it."

"I'm glad you didn't." Tina leaned her head against Joe's side. She felt warm and safe, and yet the feelings she'd experienced when he showed up at her door were surfacing again. "I wouldn't want you in jail."

Tina sensed Joe's sudden tension. "I couldn't do anything to help you. The only thing I could do was stop the men who almost killed you."

Tina reached up and turned Joe's face toward her. "That's history, Joe. It's turning out all right." She wasn't sure that was true because the cast and bandage were still on and she hadn't tried to go back to work, but her words were what both of them needed to believe tonight. "I'll be back at the lake before my tan fades."

"I hope so. You don't want the lake to spook you." Carefully Joe pulled her against him, breathing in her scent, losing himself in her. He hadn't planned on seeing her again. He'd told himself that a hundred times today and believed it every time he said the words. But then he'd called and brought what he felt for her back to life.

Tina was small, yet she fitted into the places of him that needed to feel her. "I don't want to hurt you," Joe whispered when her arms tightened around his chest.

"You can't hurt me. You could never do that."

Joe closed his eyes and took a deep breath. He wondered if a woman had ever said that to him before. Maybe not, and maybe Shannon had tricked him into forgetting that he could be with a woman and have it turn out right. "There's so little of you," he whispered into her hair.

"And there's so much of you," she said with a smile.

Joe held her close to him with a sigh. While she was in the hospital, he'd felt secure because nurses and doctors were there to take care of her. Now she was on her own and yet he wasn't worried. Maybe she was stronger than he'd thought.

He could smell her, feel her. What would come next? "Is there anything you need?"

"Are you going to leave me?"

"You need your sleep," Joe said, knowing that wasn't it at all.

"I have the rest of my life to sleep, Joe," Tina said from within his warm embrace. "I was wondering—don't we deserve some time together? We've really never been alone."

Joe pushed her away and held her at arm's length, his fingers encircling her upper arms. "Which is precisely why I'd better leave."

Tina tried to meet his eyes but faltered before the gesture was complete. "I feel—" she laughed at herself "—I feel about twelve years old. What are we supposed to say to each other?"

"I don't know, how about good night?" It was the hardest thing Joe had done today, but he released her and walked back through the open patio door. "I'm going to say good night and you're going to get some rest." He could feel her eyes on his back as he walked out her front door.

Chapter Five

Some things just need to be experienced—not analyzed.'' Ginger plopped her long legs on the coffee table and settled into the couch Joe had been sitting in earlier. "I know. I should have told you before. But it seemed silly somehow."

"Silly?" Tina wished she could rest her cast on the table, but she was afraid its weight might crack the glass.

"You know. I mean, here both you and I'd gone to the lake with guys we thought we liked and, thanks to that damn red boat, we're both seeing someone else."

"You really *are* seeing Dr. Al?" Although it was now dark, Tina's apartment was still warm enough that the women had left the patio door open. The only light in the living room came from the shimmering swimming pool below.

Ginger winked and drank from her glass of iced tea. "Is that what you call him? I'm not quite that formal."

"That's what I've heard." Tina laughed. "He certainly moves fast."

"Don't give him the credit. I'm the one who made the first move."

"Why?" Tina asked with a boldness born of their long friendship. "I mean, I thought you and Ron—"

"You thought Ron and I were an item. So did I. But when he tried to defend Paul, we started to argue. After that, we couldn't agree on anything." Ginger shrugged her slender shoulders. "Give me a man with guts any day."

Tina had known Ginger since they'd wound up at the same placement office right out of high school. Even at eighteen, Ginger had believed in speaking her mind. "I'm sorry that happened. The accident changed a lot of things, didn't it?"

"Maybe it was for the best. Sooner or later Ron and I had to learn how different we were," Ginger explained. "I got to thinking—well, we don't know what twists and turns our lives are going to take. Your accident made me start thinking about that. I might have my professional life on course, but I've been going nowhere with my personal life. I just couldn't see sticking with a man who looked at the world so differently. I'm tired of failed relationships."

"Don't be so hard on yourself." Tina tried to find a comfortable position and then gave up. "You've had more boyfriends than I can shake a stick at."

"Boyfriends!" Ginger snorted. "That's like saying I've had more used cars than I can shake a stick at. What I want is a work of art that's going to be with me for the rest of my life."

Tina started to giggle but swallowed the sound before Ginger could hear. "So you decided Ron wasn't a work of art?"

"Something like that. You were still hooked up to all those contraptions when I asked Ron what he thought of our relationship." Ginger's laugh was harsh. "I don't know what I wanted him to say. More than he did, that's for sure.

Tina, I don't want any more boyfriends. I want something permanent.''

So do I. "Did you tell Ron that?"

"Not in so many words, but he got the message. At least I got his answer: I haven't heard from him in over a week."

"I'm sorry."

"So am I." Ginger got up, grabbed a throw pillow from the far end of the couch, put it on the coffee table and laid Tina's foot on top. "I'm going to give 'Dr. Al' a month. If nothing clicks . . ."

Tina sighed. So that was what physical comfort felt like. "That sounds so calculating, Ginger."

"What it sounds like is someone who's tired of playing games." Ginger settled back on the couch. "I can't believe you don't think I've done the right thing. I mean, I don't see Paul around anymore."

"You don't because he isn't."

"And Joe? I think this is the right one, old girl. The man's deep."

Too deep, Tina acknowledged to herself. Much deeper than he was allowing her to dig.

Tina sensed what was happening beyond the Muscle Mill front door before she walked into the room filled with sweating, groaning bodies. Did she want to be here? No matter. She was at Joe's mercy this morning and this was where he'd brought her. As she waited for him to finish talking to the woman manning the reception desk, her ears caught the sound of heavy objects thudding onto pressed-rubber mats. She didn't want anyone to guess that this was her first entrance into an alien world, but it was impossible not to react to the air of intense masculinity reaching her.

Joe sensed what Tina was going through. He'd seen the same wary looks on others the first time they'd entered a place like this. Maybe he wasn't playing fair. Maybe he should have taken her straight to the hospital. Maybe he shouldn't have gone to her apartment at all this morning. But if he didn't take her, she'd have to rely on her parents. And Joe didn't believe Tina's mother had the strength for what was ahead. "It's usually pretty quiet this time of day," Joe explained as he joined her. He was thinking about how delicate, how fragile she'd looked and how he'd known they couldn't linger at her apartment. "Early mornings and evenings are when things pick up."

"I feel like a duck out of water," Tina admitted. "Are you sure those men won't mind my coming in?"

"All kinds of people work out here, Tina. Our oldest member is in his seventies and we have a few just getting into their teens."

"But most of them aren't encased in bandages," Tina explained.

"Which is precisely why you're here," Joe pointed out. "I have to ask you. How do you feel about seeing your leg?"

Tina appreciated the honest question. "I haven't thought about it that much." She ran her hand over the thick padding. "It's like my leg belongs to someone else."

"It won't feel like that much longer. In a little over an hour, you're going to know what it looks like."

Tina felt herself drawing back. "What's your point?"

"My point is, you aren't going to be padded much longer. I want you to start thinking about getting into shape, of making the most of what you have."

Tina thought about pointing out that no one had objected to her shape before, but that might sound conceited. "Let me make that decision."

"I intend to. You have several options." Joe leaned closer, his eyes digging into hers. "One of them is what I have to offer."

"And that's why we're here this morning, isn't it? All right." She took a deep breath. "Show me."

Tina was surprised at how dark the weight room itself was. She wasn't sure what she had expected, but she had been conditioned by the bright workout studios she'd attended. There were a few machines in the middle of the room but none of the gleaming black treadmills, body shapers, tanning booths, or other equipment she was familiar with. Instead Tina saw stack upon stack of weight plates and chrome bars. Some of the weight sets lay on the hard rubber mats that covered the gym floor while others were mounted at chest level on solid vertical posts. Three men were grouped around a hairy giant who'd positioned himself between two of the posts and was in the process of lifting a bar sagging with weights over his head.

"How much is he lifting?" Tina asked while her mind struggled to assimilate everything it was taking in.

"Six hundred pounds. Carl's been here since I opened the gym. He's going to be competing in Dallas next month."

"Oh," Tina said, hoping she'd been able to keep the awe she felt out of her voice. Six hundred pounds. Nothing to it.

"He'll do that for ten reps and then move up twenty pounds for another ten."

"Oh," Tina repeated. She gathered that reps had to do with repeating the exercise a number of times, although why any sane man wanted to put himself through that torture was beyond her. "Does he do that every day?"

"Of course not," Joe said matter-of-factly. "Tomorrow he'll concentrate on the lower body. Head up, Carl. I thought you weren't going to wear those old high-tops anymore. You've got to have better arch support."

While Joe wandered over to give Carl more pointers, Tina held back. A black man wearing sweats and a T-shirt that looked ready for the ragbag was bent at the waist, lifting the dumbbells in his hands out and up. The man was chewing on his lower lip, his eyes closed in concentration. Another man was seated in a machine with handles where Tina expected to find arms. He was pushing against the handles, his face contorted with the effort. A bespectacled man wearing nothing from the waist up stood in front of him. "Piece of cake, Scott," he encouraged. "My grandmother can do better than that!"

Tina turned away in amazement. She noticed a young woman lying on her back on a slant board slowly lifting dumbbells over her head. As far as Tina could tell, the woman was the only other female in the room. She was dressed in a one-piece bodysuit cut high on her thighs to reveal rippled muscle. For the first time in her life, Tina envied a woman's muscles.

"How many members do you have?" Tina asked when Joe rejoined her.

"A couple hundred." Joe was watching the young woman. "I don't count noses as long as the gym stays in the black. Crystal, I thought you were going to do leg extensions."

"Tomorrow, Joe," Crystal shot back. "Did those gloves come in? I swear, I think they're sending them around the Horn in a leaky boat."

Joe explained that he'd called the manufacturer about Crystal's gloves and was expecting delivery before the end of the week. "You aren't warming up enough," he went on. "I heard you had another muscle cramp."

Crystal ducked her head. "Yes, boss. Three lashes with a wet noodle. What happened to you?" she asked Tina. "Lose a fight with a freight train?"

"A boat," Tina corrected, wondering if she had anything in common with a woman who didn't think twice about being locked in a windowless room with fifteen sweating men. Crystal went back to work, grunting and decidedly unladylike as she pumped the dumbbells over her head in a motion that revealed large, firm breasts.

Tina trailed after Joe as he pointed out various machines and explained their use. Tina was intimidated by what she saw, not because this was foreign turf but because the machines seemed to be mocking her, challenging her to conquer them. She'd always admired muscular men and considered the "hunk" calendar Ginger had given her for Valentine's Day a treasure, but until now she'd given little thought to how the hunks got that way. "Has anyone ever hurt themselves here?" she had to ask. "More than a muscle cramp, I mean?"

Joe shook his head. "As long as the members adhere to the gym rules—and I'm very strict about that—there aren't going to be injuries. You heard what I told Crystal about stretching more." Joe pushed Tina ahead of him so she could watch the bearded man named Carl repeat his lifts now that more weights had been added to the bar. "I personally set everyone up on individual programs."

"What kind of program would I need?"

Joe touched her shoulder. "Are you really ready to talk about that?"

Tina wasn't. What she wanted was to go back out into the sunshine, but it was too early to go to the hospital. And Joe wasn't done with her. He wanted her to watch while he went through a workout of his own. "It's what I am, Tina. I'd like you to understand."

She understood much of what he was saying as he went through his warm-ups, but when he started lifting in earnest, Tina could only stand back and watch. Joe didn't seem aware of anyone, not even her, as he straddled a bench with weights supported on vertical rests and inched forward until his arms were slightly behind him. He wrapped his arms around a bar weighted down with several hundred pounds, expanded his chest and lifted the bar off its rest.

The muscles in his neck stood out in relief, his teeth were clamped together, and his deltoid muscles strained against his ancient T-shirt. Joe was staring at something Tina couldn't fathom, his mind focused on nothing except what he was trying to accomplish. Even Carl stopped to watch the gym's owner go through the routine that kept him at a world-class level.

Tina wanted to separate herself from what she was seeing. But she was going with Joe, understanding that physical challenge was the journey and not the goal. It was man against dead weight with the man winning because his will was the greater.

Five minutes later Joe bounced off the bench. He walked over to another weighted bar that stood at thigh level, cinched the thick, heavy leather belt tightly into his middle, and hoisted the weights from his thighs to his waist and back again. The muscles rippling across the tops of his shoulders stood out in bold relief, making him look superhuman.

"This has to go," Joe announced while Carl was adding more weights to the bar he'd just curled ten times. Before Tina could ask what he was talking about, Joe tore off his shirt. He repeated what he'd done before, only this time there was nothing to distract Tina from what the workout was doing to his body.

She'd thought him big before, but that was before she'd seen him with his bare chest expanded, arms and shoulders straining. Even his neck seemed to thicken as he clenched his teeth and lifted 250 pounds ten times before dropping it back onto its rest.

This man had no equal. What was she doing letting him into her apartment, her life?

Tina tried to shake off the thought while Carl told her how Joe had "blown out" his supersuit during a contest last year. Although the terms Carl used were foreign to Tina, she gathered that Joe had so expanded his body during a lift that his heavy-duty suit had exploded. "What happens then?" she asked.

"Then I put on another suit." Joe checked the locks at the end of the bar and again asked his body to do the impossible. This time he completed just six reps before having to slam the weights back into their rest. "Damn!"

"Don't expect us to feel sorry for you, Rustin," Carl countered. "If you hadn't been over at the hospital every minute, you wouldn't be losing ground."

A slow, shy grin touched Joe's lips. He glanced at Tina. "Carl's riding me because he's jealous." Joe ripped off the tight leather belt and sighed in relief. "What do you think? Maybe I should take up needlepoint."

Tina concentrated on the fingers that were totally unsuited for fine work. "You'd hate needlepoint," she said softly. "And I don't see anything wrong with what you just did." But she did. The problem wasn't with the effort Joe had just put out. The problem was with her.

There was no reason to be afraid of Joe Rustin. No reason, Tina repeated. He'd shown her infinite tenderness numerous times, and they'd only just met. But the powerful man pitting his strength against solid weight was different from the one who brought her a rose. This one was at home in a world she hadn't known existed a few weeks ago.

A minute later, as if he had something to prove to himself, Joe repeated the exercise he hadn't been satisfied with. Although he was already sheened with sweat from his exertion, he managed to hoist the heavy weights the required ten times before dropping them to the floor. "Damn! I think I broke something."

"Your brain," Carl observed before going back to his own workout.

Again Joe hitched himself out of his weight belt and turned toward Tina. "That wasn't too smart. Usually if I can't make a weight on the first try I give it up for the day. I'm like a kid trying to impress the girl down the block."

Tina was impressed, all right, but not in the way she knew Joe wanted to hear. She hadn't believed it possible for anyone to be that strong.

She was relieved when Joe was asked to devise a modified routine for a man who'd strained his knee. Tina's first impulse was to retreat to Joe's office, but there were things she didn't have an answer to—things that had to do with powerful men and her own sense of security. The answer, if there was one, lay here in the weight room.

A trio of young men wearing faded sweatshirts bearing the logo of the nearby college had entered the gym and were going through their stretching exercises. Although she felt intimidated by the sheer size of the three, there was an undeniable fascination in being able to watch their healthy young bodies. Football players had always been hooded, padded figures on a TV screen. Now she was being given proof that wearing a uniform meant a great deal more than knowing which direction to run on the playing field.

Despite her frightened defenses, their exuberance reached her. Although their conversation was crude and, she guessed, meant to shock her, she envied them. At twenty-one or twenty-two they had their lives ahead of them. As long as their carefully tempered bodies performed, there wasn't any goal they couldn't dream of attaining.

Joe was power reincarnated. He was also proof of what a man could accomplish if the commitment was great enough. Was self-restraint something Joe never had to concern himself with? Or—and this was what set Tina's nerves on edge—was there ever a time when Joe took what he wanted because no one could stand in his way?

Shaking with the whiplash effect of her question, Tina turned as quickly as her walking cast would allow and marched into Joe's office. On the wall behind his small desk was further proof of what Joe Rustin was capable of. Trophies, some of them so large that they rested on the floor, were engraved with the dates of various contests. Unframed pictures of him in the middle of some superhuman lift were propped on a shelf. There were three plaques proclaiming Joe the best lifter at international meets.

Tina sank ungracefully into a sagging easy chair and waited. She flipped through some dog-eared magazines filled with pictures of men and women posing in tiny scraps of clothing. She didn't try to insulate herself from the sounds coming from the workout room; the scent of human exertion reached her.

What am I doing here? Tina asked herself as she stared at her own delicately shaped fingers. Even the hands of the women in the magazines were muscular. She tried to imagine calluses instead of smooth flesh in her palms, but muscular fingers weren't what Larry Pardee wanted on the woman who promoted his expensive boats.

Although she didn't lift her head from the article she was reading, Tina knew when Joe entered the room. "I didn't see you leave," he was saying. "I should have thought; you've been on your feet too long."

Tina knew it was wrong, but she didn't contradict his reason for her having left. "You were busy." Flustered, Tina waved her magazine at Joe. "I can't believe some of these magazines. Aren't those people embarrassed to pose practically naked in front of a roomful of people?"

Joe shrugged. "Bodybuilders are a different breed. What do you say about getting out of here before someone else wants me?"

Tina had no objection to Joe's suggestion. She felt surrounded—trapped, even—by her environment. Some fresh air would do her good. With Joe's help, she got to her feet and made her way out of the gym. Joe had pulled on a knit pullover and checked the drawstring tie on his sweats as he watched Tina's slow progress to his truck. "Al's a real stickler about physical therapy. He'll get you back on your feet."

Tina settled herself into the passenger side feeling less overwhelmed than she had in the gym and yet not free. Joe hadn't asked whether she wanted him to serve as her driver. She repeated her earlier statement. "You don't have to do this. My folks can take me to the hospital."

Joe started the engine. "I don't think that's a good idea. Don't you want me there?"

"I didn't mean that," she said defensively. "But Carl said you've been taking a lot of time off."

"I'm the boss. I can work as much or as little as I like."

Tina knew that wasn't true. Although her boss was successful, Larry retained his edge only through long hours and personal commitment. "I appreciate you doing this. I know—I already said that. But you might have to wait around. I have no idea how long I'm going to be there."

Despite having resigned herself to hours at the hospital, they were in and out in less than forty-five minutes. In that time Tina was forced to come to grips with what a few seconds of someone's carelessness had done to her. Al met Tina and Joe in a room that looked like a cross between an office and an examining room. He explained that he'd finished morning rounds, but had arranged to see Tina at the hospital so she could talk to the therapist in charge of her case. The therapist was a bull-necked young man with a bedside manner that instantly put Tina at ease. He threw out words like *stamina*, *flexibility* and *balance* in ways that allowed Tina to understand fully what her therapy was supposed to accomplish. Thanks to the short leg cast, and the need to rebuild the inactive muscles in her right leg, Tina would be starting limited stretching exercises and leg raises immediately, along with continuing to work with the light weights Joe had given her. Whirlpool baths were promised as soon as the cast was off.

"I know you'd like to be set completely free," Al said as he started snipping at Tina's thigh bandage. "But that'll have to wait. At least you can get rid of this contraption. I'm curious to see if Wallace is as good a seamstress as he professes to be."

Tina looked. A five-inch knifelike slice ran down the outside of her thigh.

"Not bad," Al was saying. He gently touched the flesh around the scar. "There's hardly any swelling left. You know, if I could make stitches that precise I'd change specialities. What do you think, Joe?''

Tina felt disjointed. She sat quietly while two men peered at her exposed thigh. Al was right. There wasn't much swelling and the stitch marks were almost nonexistent. What had once been perfect flesh no longer existed, and yet Tina felt nothing.

"How does it feel, Tina?" Joe was asking. "Is it very tender?"

Carefully Tina stretched and then contracted her thigh muscle. There was some discomfort but nothing she couldn't handle. "It itches."

"That's the healing process," Al supplied. "I know it's summer and you're dying to work on your tan, but I don't want you to expose this to the sun for a while. The less you fool with your injury, the more your body will thank you for it."

"What about follow-up? Is the plastic surgeon going to have to see her again?" Joe asked while Tina touched her thigh for the first time. So she had a scar; at least she was alive.

"That's up to Tina," Al explained. "Once the healing is complete, she might want to have some surgery done to reduce the scar. Don't worry, Tina. That all comes later."

Tina was still trying to come to grips with what had been forever changed about her when Joe drove her back to her apartment. "I guess I could go back to Bodies Unlimited," she muttered. "Al said low-impact aerobics would be good once the cast comes off."

Joe looked at her for longer than he should have while driving. Nothing about the day had felt right, and yet he wouldn't have tried to change anything. He needed to know more about her reaction to the Muscle Mill, how she felt about his place in it. But more than that, he needed to know more about how she was handling the changes to her body.

That was why he was here. "You aren't interested in my gym?"

She'd said the wrong thing, or at least she'd said something Joe hadn't wanted to hear. Joe was waiting for a logical argument, which Tina didn't have. "I don't feel—I can't lift any of those weights, Joe."

"That's not the point. You don't feel comfortable there, do you?" Joe pulled into the apartment carport.

Tina wanted nothing more than to lean on Joe the way she had while she was in the hospital. But that balance no longer existed. She was on her own turf, expected to make her own decisions. "That's your world, Joe. It isn't mine."

"It can become yours."

Joe was trying to reduce things to their simplest common denominator, but it wasn't that simple. "You're expecting too much of me," Tina countered, once they were in her apartment and she was surrounded by what was comfortable for her. "I haven't tried to sell you a speedboat. Don't try to sell me on lifting weights."

"All right." Joe drew out the words. Tina thought he was going to sit down, but he wandered to the picture window and stared out at the cloudless sky. "Are you afraid?" he asked without turning around.

Tina stared at a back broad enough to block out the sun. "If you're trying to goad me into turning into a jock, that approach won't work." Tina dropped her eyes to her cast. Freedom would be so welcome. Just being able to drive would give her back the independence she craved. "I never was one of those kids who'd jump off a roof just because someone called me chicken."

Joe turned back around. His eyes, which had always telegraphed his empathy for her, were hooded. "I'm not asking you to jump off a roof, Tina."

"What are you asking?" Tina hated her words and yet she couldn't stop them. Before this, their relationship had been delicate and untested, and Tina knew that was about to change.

"I'm asking you to challenge yourself in a way you never have before. You told me you don't like having your boss see you as a sex symbol. But—" Joe frowned. "That's what you believe you are, Tina. Appearances are very important to you."

That wasn't fair! "What's wrong with how I look? We happen to live in a society that puts a great deal of emphasis on physical appearance. Maybe I *have* capitalized on that in my job, but so have a lot of other people. You have."

"And you're proud of being a sex symbol?"

"Stop that! It sounds cheap when you put it that way." Tina leaned forward. "I haven't called you King Kong."

Joe folded his arms across his chest in a way that had never failed to take Tina's breath away. It was the same this time, but she wasn't going to let him know that. "We aren't talking about me," he said softly. "You're a beautiful woman, Tina. But you can be so much more. You don't have to be afraid to realize your full potential."

His gentleness in the midst of an argument threw Tina off balance. "How?" she challenged. "Do you want me to go back to school and become a brain surgeon? The world needs boat salespersons as much as it needs giants of industry."

"I didn't say anything about your brain." Joe took the steps that ate up the distance between them. He unfolded his arms and placed a warm hand on top of her head. "You have a brain. Maybe you aren't using it as much as you could, but that's your decision."

He shouldn't have touched her. He was making it nearly impossible for Tina to concentrate. "Thanks," she said sarcastically. Maintaining the tone was a battle. "What I don't like..." She knew she should have pulled back. Physical distance would lend impact to what she was saying. "What I don't like is being told I can be more than I am. If I'm such a failure, why the hell are you wasting your time with me?"

"I've made you angry." Joe was no longer touching her, but he was still standing too close for Tina to feel comfortable.

"You're damn right you have." Very few people had heard Tina Morton swear—profanity didn't fit with the image she had of herself—but things were different with Joe. He'd scraped below the surface. "I haven't called you a dumb jock."

"Maybe I *am* a dumb jock."

"Are you fishing for a compliment? Sorry, you aren't going to get one from me. You're an intelligent man and you know it. As long as you know that, it doesn't matter what anyone else thinks."

To Tina's consternation, a grin shattered Joe's grim expression. "Bingo!"

"Bingo what?"

"You just said that my knowing what I am is what's important. The same holds true for you."

"And what is that supposed to mean?"

"It means..." Joe leaned forward. His hands on her shoulders were heavy and yet she felt no discomfort. "It means that I don't feel I have to prove anything with my brain. I am what I am. You, however, are looking over your shoulder."

"And what am I looking over my shoulder for?" she asked sarcastically.

"For someone to see that there's a brain in that body. You're afraid, Tina. Afraid that people see only the exterior."

Why was Joe here? All he was doing was slashing away at her self-confidence. "What does this have to do with my working out at your gym?"

"Everything. Maybe nothing."

"That's no kind of answer, Joe." Her anger had spent itself and she had no idea what remained.

"I know. But—maybe that's all we should deal with today." Before she could ready herself for him, Joe claimed her lips. She felt his presence above her, reaching for her, finding her. Despite the time they'd spent together, what they shared was incredibly fragile. They'd come dangerously close to severing that slender thread. He was doing what needed to be done to avoid that danger.

Tina thanked him for that as she gave in to what Joe was offering. She'd had relationships with men that had spluttered and died before anything could come of promising beginnings. Afterward, Tina had felt regret at the loss, but she had been able to go on with her life.

It wouldn't be that way if Joe left her.

Today, she believed, she didn't have to think about losing him. Joe was the sum and substance of her day and a witness to every emotion she'd experienced. He'd seen her imperfections and he felt no hesitancy about them. He accepted that she hadn't yet made her peace with his powerful world. He acknowledged her intellect with as much respect as he acknowledged the frail feminine qualities she'd always been told she should capitalize on. A man like that was incredibly rare.

Tina found Joe's arms and spread her fingers over the rock that formed the base of his forearm. Slowly, drawing out the experience, Tina parted her lips and brought her tongue into play. She was tasting Joe's soft inner lips, and found his tongue waiting to make its own contact. Earlier, his impact on her senses had been like a sledgehammer; this time it was a tender, teasing approach as precious as the exquisite softness of a newborn kitten.

Tina offered no resistance when Joe pulled her to her feet and wrapped her within the refuge created by his strength. His quick breath gave him away. "Is this what you call making up?" she had the courage to ask.

Joe ran his lips slowly down to her jaw. "I think it's called a truce. We haven't decided anything yet. We have a long way to go."

Tina shivered. "I know."

"We have to do something about that." I have to be honest, Joe thought. Someday. Somehow.

"I know." Tina stopped him with her lips. Not today. Today was for satisfying certain needs. Today was for tasting what might become for the two of them. Tina needed Joe holding her and taking away the world. She needed to give him as much of herself as possible without taking the step beyond which there was no turning back.

He was a mountain she'd never climbed. The mountain might prove to be more than she could handle, but today Tina willingly acknowledged the challenge. Joe was testing her in a way she could come to regret, but he was a song reaching her senses on a level that went beyond words. Beyond thought.

A song, the right driving beat, could reduce her to tears. Tina wasn't feeling tears, but she was leaving her body. She was being lifted to another plane where her heart might feel things it had never felt before; where even her fingertips could feel what they'd never felt before.

It should be possible for them to bridge their separate worlds and beliefs and commitments. With him stirring her physically, Tina could believe that all things were possible.

She wasn't content with simply holding on. Her blood was warming, her lungs needed more oxygen. The only way Tina could satisfy those needs was by placing her hand on the flesh exposed by his shirt. There she found the strong pulse that led to his heart.

For the first time Joe touched her breasts. He covered the hardened tips beneath her soft cotton shirt and Tina found support in the arm Joe had placed behind her back. Her hand remained on his pulse, her lips stayed hungry for his.

Joe explored her small, firm breasts with a reverence that made her feel rich beyond all reason. The thin fabric that existed between them only served to stir a deep restlessness, a deep need, and yet Tina willed herself to allow Joe to set the pace. Her eyes closed in reaction to having his palm on the soft mounds.

"I can't feel your heart," Joe whispered.

"It's there," she whispered back. This was the man who lifted hundreds of pounds over his head. But he was capable of such tenderness that she was left weak in its wake.

A long minute later, Joe spoke again. "I don't want to hurt you," he said as she arched her back, bringing herself closer to him.

"You can't hurt me, Joe." Tina wrapped her arms around his neck, molding their bodies together. "I'm not going to break. I'm not afraid."

"I hope you never have to be." He also hoped someday she would understand. Joe held her, fighting down his need, knowing he'd gone beyond turning his back on Tina Morton. And yet, until he could be honest, he would stop with simply holding her.

An hour later Joe's words were still echoing inside Tina, but because Ginger was once again sitting on the couch where Joe had been, Tina was forced to concentrate on other things than why Joe had, once again, left her. "Your mom called me last night," Ginger was saying.

"Why aren't I surprised? What did she have to say?"

"She asked if you were still seeing Joe." Ginger laughed. "That man really has your mother uptight."

"Because he isn't as rich as Paul?" Tina rolled her eyes for Ginger to see. She'd never tried to keep anything from her best friend where her mother was concerned. "I have no idea how much money Joe has. It hasn't come up. His truck is new."

"Money is the least of it." Ginger tugged at the sleeve of her formfitting top. "Or maybe I should say your mother's too much of a diplomat to bring up money."

"What did she bring up?"

"Not much, other than a little matter of size."

Tina sipped her tea. This time Ginger had made it with more lemon than Tina liked, but she was grateful for the pitcherful cooling in her refrigerator. "Mine or Joe's?"

"Both." It was Ginger's turn to roll her eyes in the timeless way of the younger generation discussing the one that came before. "I'm afraid the man's, shall we say, 'muscularity,' has thrown your mother for a loop. I think she's afraid he's going to hold you down and have his way with you."

Tina stopped her reaction before it could show on her face. Actually, Joe's having his way with her, on the heels of the emotions he'd brought to life, was probably the only way she'd get much sleep tonight. "What does she want me to do? Stop seeing the man? He saved my life."

"I'm just relaying the message. Actually—" Ginger grinned "—I think your mom called me so I'd wind up here telling you what I am. You know how it is with mothers. There are certain subjects they don't like to bring up with their daughters. She's using me as the middleman."

"And you're doing a creditable job," Tina acknowledged. "What's the rest of the message?"

"Basically that women who weigh a hundred pounds don't have any business hanging around men who can give Arnold Schwarzenegger a run for his money."

Tina's head bobbed slowly as she absorbed that piece of information. "Even if the man saved my life?"

"Hey." Ginger held up her hand to ward off Tina's question. "I'm not the one you have to convince. Personally, I think Joe's a great improvement over Paul. At least Joe wasn't afraid of a little blood. How is it, anyway?" Ginger indicated the injury covered by the comfortable housedress Tina was now wearing.

"Healing nicely." Tina gripped the hem of her dress. "Are you brave?"

Tina had to give Ginger credit. Although her eyes widened when Tina exposed her scar, her friend wasn't repulsed. "There goes the Miss America contest. How does it feel?"

"Itchy. And kind of weak. Actually," Tina admitted, "my whole body feels pretty weak. That's what I get from lying around. However, thanks to your 'friend'—" Tina winked "—I plan to start going through my paces at the hospital. The physical therapy program will either make or break me."

"I thought Joe might have you pumping iron," Ginger said on her way to the kitchen for more tea. "I get the impression he's pretty sold on that stuff."

"He is," Tina called after her. She waited until Ginger had returned before continuing. "He took me to his gym this morning."

"And?"

"And it scared the hell out of me. I'm just not ready. Unfortunately Joe doesn't want to hear that."

"Trouble in paradise?" Ginger asked.

"I don't know." Tina sank lower in her chair and placed a frosty glass against her suddenly pounding forehead. "Mom's right about one thing. Joe Rustin's not your everyday man."

Chapter Six

I'm not kidding. That child gives new meaning to the phrase 'can't think her way out of a paper bag.' I think Larry's already regretting hiring her. Those idiot salesmen are falling all over themselves trying to be helpful, but the child is dense.''

The comment from Boat World's soon-to-be-retired secretary and only other female employee helped, but it still didn't make things a lot easier. Tina had been out of the hospital one week and she was here to try to convince Larry that she could handle the duties of a saleswoman.

Tina listened to a little more gossip, but her eyes were on Larry's office. She'd borrowed Ginger's car, as it had automatic transmission, and had managed to drive herself—despite her mother's contention that she should wait until she was stronger, or better yet, not press Larry at all. Her fashionably baggy slacks covered her cast, and she looked crisp and professional. She'd taken extra pains with her makeup and given her short curls that carefully tousled look. Actually, Tina admitted, she looked pretty good. She felt terrific.

"I'm sorry you had to wait, Tina," Larry said as he joined her in the showroom. "You know how it is with bankers. Once you get them talking about money, there's no getting them to shut up."

"I know," Tina agreed. Larry was trying to look at her without making it too obvious. In the past she would have let the awkward moment slide, but she'd spent the time, when she wasn't with Joe, wondering how she was going to ask her boss to let her come back to work. The direct approach was the only thing she'd been able to come up with.

"Not too bad?" she asked, holding her arms out and turning slowly. The movement was a little awkward, and Tina felt as if she was putting herself on display. She touched the side of her neck. "The bruises are gone. I should have had before-and-after pictures taken."

"Are you sure it's all right for you to be up and about?"

Oh, yes, the Barbie doll isn't that fragile, Tina thought before she squelched it. "Would you like me to bring a note from my doctor?" she asked in what she hoped was a teasing tone. "He said there was no reason why I couldn't go back to work." Even if she was stretching the point, she'd put the ball in Larry's court.

Larry frowned; Tina could tell he wasn't ready for this. "I don't know...."

Tina waited until one of the other salesmen had moved in and out of earshot. "What don't you know, Larry? You haven't fired me, have you?"

"You know I haven't, Tina. Look, why don't we go in my office and discuss this," Larry said, resting his hand on the small of her back. Larry had placed his hand on her more times than Tina liked to think about. But this time she wasn't thinking about personal invasion.

Tina led the way past gleaming boats capable of bringing out the macho in the most mild-mannered man and opened the door to Larry's office. She sat unceremoniously in the plastic chair to the left of Larry's desk and crossed her legs in a casual gesture designed to let Larry know she hadn't come here hat in hand. "How is my replacement working out?" she asked before Larry had time to sit down.

"Angel? Well, the ad people were pretty taken with her."

Angel. Tina's spirits plunged. She could hardly put on the gloves and go ten rounds against a teenager named Angel. "I'm glad to hear that," she said insincerely. "What about on the floor?"

"On the floor?" Larry seemed reluctant to pursue the question. "The salesmen are going out of their way to show her the ropes."

I bet they are. Tina was dying to ask Larry if Angel knew anything about financing, boating regulations or a given manufacturer's reputation, but it would sound catty if she did. However, there was one hard question she could ask. "Is Angel going to be working here on a permanent basis?"

"I hired Angel so we could keep the advertising campaign going, Tina. You know we were all set to go when you were hurt. I have to tell you, she can handle the modeling business."

But can she think? Tina took a deep breath. "What are you telling me?"

Larry got to his feet. In the past when her boss got too close, Tina looked for a way to keep her distance. But because she had more important things to concentrate on, she didn't flinch when he laid his hand on her knee. "I'm not trying to tell you anything, Tina. You did an excellent job as spokesperson. You had great camera presence. And you weren't nearly as uncomfortable speaking as Angel is."

"I can still do it, Larry."

Larry's eyes settled on the cast outlined beneath her trousers. "Not now, you can't, honey. We can't photograph you from the waist up."

Of course not. Leg shots were expected of Boat World ads. Tina bit back her bitterness. "That's not what I'm talking about," she stressed. "I can't believe Angel has had time to learn everything she needs to in order to be an effective saleswoman. I can do that."

"But what— Are you sure it's wise for you to be on your feet all day?"

Tina explained about the physical therapy that was getting her back to preinjury form. "Larry, I want to work. I'm going crazy sitting around my apartment."

"But you can't model, Tina."

Modeling was a small part of her job. She didn't know why Larry couldn't see that. "I thought Angel was doing that."

"She is. And she's doing her best with the customers. You can't—"

There it was. Tina didn't know why it had taken her so long to understand Larry's reluctance except that maybe she didn't want to face reality. Larry saw her as a come-on both on and off camera. He'd never given her credit for the fact that she had more sales than any of the other salespeople. "I can't what?" she asked, surprised by her capacity to ask for a slap in the face.

"I'm just thinking of you, Tina. You know how much the customers enjoy your perky nature. A woman in a cast has lost a little of her—bubbly—qualities."

Perky? Bubbly? Why didn't Larry come right out and say that a woman in a cast wasn't sexy? "What if I grow a beard and wear a tie? Do you think the customers would be able to stomach me then? I'm sorry." Tina ran a heavy hand over her eyes. "I'm going a little stir-crazy."

"I understand." Again Larry patted her on the knee. "I hope you don't see Angel as taking your job. Actually—" Larry lowered his voice "—I'm having to spend a lot more time with her than I thought I would. She has a lot to learn."

Larry wasn't giving her credit for not needing to be led around by the hand when she first came on the job, but Tina didn't waste energy trying to point that out. "I saw the ad," she compromised. "Angel photographs well."

Larry brightened. "Doesn't she."

"How long will she be doing that?" Tina was surprised by her nerve, but it was too late to back down.

"I can't say, Tina. Between you and me, I've been getting some negative feedback from the ads Angel is in. Something about her not giving the impression that she knows what she's talking about."

"They're used to me," Tina said in what she hoped was an unassuming tone.

"That's probably a lot of it. Angel's trying, but she doesn't have the gift of the gab you do."

Gift of the gab! Tina sounded knowledgeable about boats because she was. She didn't know why it was so hard for Larry to admit that. "Then put me back in front of the camera, Larry."

"I wish I could. But you can't wear a bathing suit yet."

Tina bit down her anger. "The cast will be off in a few weeks."

"And in a few weeks we'll discuss this again."

Tina almost choked on his dismissal, but she knew better than to make an issue of it. Larry was in a condescending mood; she'd be a fool to act anything but grateful.

By the time Tina left Larry's office, she wasn't sure there was anything to be grateful for. Larry had magnanimously agreed to let Tina ease herself into the secretarial position. He'd remained adamant about not wanting her on her feet eight hours a day. Although Tina had seen through to his reluctance to have her in front of the public, she was too tied in knots to force the issue. His reaction to her asking when she might be able to start doing the TV advertising again had rendered her almost speechless with fury.

"We have to consider that scar," he'd said. "I don't know if makeup can cover it up."

"I can't believe the man," Tina spluttered to Ginger when they met for lunch. "What am I, damaged merchandise? There's this cute little bubble-head screwing up more sales than she makes and Larry won't let her go because I'm no longer photogenic. He can't see that I'm an asset to his business because I know my business. Oh no! I'm flawed. For two cents—"

"For two cents you'd find another job. So?" Ginger challenged. "Do it."

Tina groaned. "And throw three years down the drain? I'm not going to give the man the satisfaction."

"Then what *are* you going to do?"

Tina didn't have an easy answer. She'd bide her time until the cast was off and then push home the point that she should be allowed to go back to selling again. Once she'd re-proven herself, she'd ask to be given a chance in front of the camera.

Unfortunately all of that would take time. Tina would rather die than tell Larry, but the truth was, she hadn't recovered enough to weather eight hours on her feet anyway. "I've got to stop feeling like an accident victim," she said as she finished the last of her lunch. "Do you know what I was thinking as I was leaving Larry's office? I wanted to ram my fist through a wall. Instead, I left feeling like a weakling."

"Are you going to join Joe's gym?"

Tina fought sudden panic. She'd tried, really tried, to come to grips with her feelings about the Muscle Mill, but it remained an alien environment. "I didn't say that," she hedged. "Joe—I know he's waiting for an answer. How can I tell him I can't see myself in there? It's just too intimidating. There's a lot of other places I can look into. I'll tell him—something."

Although Tina spent the afternoon inspecting a half-dozen gyms and health spas, none of them struck her as right. At two she would have to fork over a month's pay in order to be properly attired. At another, the emphasis was on aerobics, and with an instructor who looked as if she was in competition for the Olympics, Tina knew she'd be so intimidated that she'd quit within a week. The other three didn't have anything specifically wrong with them. The staff was friendly and helpful, the facilities clean and well lit. But most of the members were too much like what she'd been last year—interested in nothing more than staying fit and socializing. After watching Joe and the members of his gym, Tina knew she needed to be surrounded by people with more commitment.

What she needed was Joe.

"Okay, so I like being with the man. What's wrong with that?" Tina asked when she reported to Ginger via the phone. "He'll keep me from backsliding."

"I thought his place intimidated you."

"It does. And sometimes Joe does, too. But—"

"But you like being around the guy. Look, it's your decision. I'm not going to say anything one way or the other. I just want to remind you that your mother is going to throw up some opposition."

"My mother wants to see me settled with a CPA." Tina laughed. "So far, all I've done is disappoint her on that score. One of these days she's going to give up and let me make my own mistakes."

"Your mother give up? That's wishful thinking and you know it."

"At least with her I know what I'm up against." Tina turned serious. "I just wish I understood Joe as well as I do my mother."

"What's not to understand about him?" Ginger asked. "From my totally unbiased point of reference, any friend of Al has to be all right."

Tina crossed her legs and started rubbing her aching instep. "I take it you and Dr. Al are doing all right."

"So far. But you know me. I have a way of opening my trap when I should keep it shut. Don't change the subject. How are things going with you and Charles Atlas?"

Tina sighed. She didn't want to think about the wall she knew existed around Joe's emotions. "Don't you have any easier questions? We've seen each other every day since I got out of the hospital. But—I'm the one who keeps making the contact. Sometimes I think he doesn't want to have anything to do with me."

"What makes you say that?"

It wasn't anything Tina could put her finger on. It was good, generally, when they were together. Joe kept her from going crazy by taking her for long rides along quiet roads. He played nurse while she attempted grocery shopping and last night they'd gone to an early movie. But they talked about the weather, speculated on how Al and Ginger's romance was going, complained about the lack of funds that kept the city from repairing the street in front of Tina's apartment. They didn't talk about their relationship. And Joe hadn't kissed her again.

But Tina couldn't tell Ginger that.

Joe was in the middle of installing a new leg-curl machine when the woman manning the front desk informed him that Tina Morton was on the phone. "Do you want her to call back?" she asked. "I don't think she's going to want to hear you cussing at that machine."

Joe pushed himself off his knees, grateful for this particular excuse to put down his tools and the frustrating instruction booklet. "I'll take it in my office," he said, not caring what the woman might infer from his desire for privacy.

Despite his need to hear Tina's voice, Joe hesitated. Things hadn't been going right between them, but until—

unless—he told her certain things, he didn't know how to improve their relationship. Was that why she was calling, to let him know it wasn't going to work? That she needed more? If she was, he couldn't blame her. Still, he reached for the phone.

"Am I keeping you from anything?" Tina asked. "I can call back."

"Nothing important." Joe briefly described his problems in trying to follow the directions that came with the long-awaited equipment. He was stalling but he couldn't help himself. "Is there anything you need? Any problems with Ginger's car?"

"Ginger's car is fine. Joe? I went to see my boss today. And I made a decision I need to talk to you about."

Joe didn't want to hear about this over the phone. "I can be out of here in about an hour. Have you had dinner?"

Tina explained that she hadn't had time to think about food. But, she insisted, she wasn't going to impose on Joe anymore. "You know, I've never seen your place. Could we meet there? I'll pick up something on the way."

She wanted to see where he lived. She wanted to see him. Joe gave her directions before returning to his task with an enthusiasm that went far beyond the gym. Why had he tied himself in a knot? Tina wasn't going to give up on him; he was wrong to start every day thinking it might be the end for them.

Less than an hour later, one of his employees was testing the machine and two members were waiting in line. Joe took time for a shower before changing into a pair of his tailor-made slacks and a knit shirt. He slid into his truck and spread his arms, feeling the power of a summer evening.

Tina was already there when he arrived. She'd gotten out of Ginger's car and was wandering around his yard. She turned and waved as he pulled into the driveway but didn't attempt to come back. "The food's on the front seat," she called out. "Could you grab it? I love your house. Someone's done a lot of custom work on it."

Joe joined Tina as she completed her survey of the home he'd added onto until what was once a well-built but unspectacular two-bedroom house now suited his life-style. Although he could afford to have had the wraparound redwood deck built for him, he took pride in having done the work himself. He felt the same way about the addition that housed his weight room and home office.

"The workmanship on the deck is excellent," Tina said as they stepped inside. "Did you really do it all?"

"Guilty as charged." She was close enough now that he could smell the lavender scent she used in her bath. She was carrying something wrapped in tissue, but his attention was on the loose-weave short-sleeved top and white trousers. "Are you an expert on construction?"

Tina hesitated a moment as she took in the slate entryway and beyond that an oversize living room with two paneled walls. "I have to know quality in boats. I appreciate workmanship in all forms. I love the paneling. What is it?"

"Birch. I wanted wood in the living room, but nothing too dark." He couldn't remember ever discussing his home with a woman before.

Tina was still looking at the room and not at him. She hadn't shied away. Neither had she come any closer. "My guess is you spend more time inside than out. I hate to say this, but your lawn could use some work."

Joe struggled to keep up with the conversation. "I'm usually not home until dark. What are we supposed to do with this food?"

"Eat it." Tina laughed up at him, but before he could react, she was leaving him to run her hand over a leather chair. "I knew it would be like this. Masculine. I hope you have a vase." She turned toward him and held out the tissue-wrapped bundle.

Joe dropped their dinner onto the oak top of the low shelving that held his stereo and tape deck. He unwrapped the tissue to find a half-dozen long-stemmed roses flanked by ferns. For a moment no words came to him. "Roses."

"You gave me the idea." Tina's smile was tentative. "After everything you've done for me, I wanted to do something for you. I hope you don't mind."

No one had ever given him roses; it was a beautiful gesture. "What do they call that color?"

Tina's smile gained in strength. She'd made the right decision. If she could be assured of another of his gentle smiles, she would send him roses every day of her life. "Amethyst. I asked. I know, women are supposed to know things like the colors of flowers, but I was absent from Miss Peabody's finishing school the day that was taught. Do you have a vase?"

Joe had to admit that vases were something he'd never concerned himself with. "There must be some kind of glass they'll fit in." Lightly he touched the small of her back, propelling her toward the kitchen. "Why don't you look for something. I can warm up dinner in the microwave."

Joe took quick note of his kitchen, pleased that he'd put the breakfast dishes in the dishwasher, after all. Sunlight streamed in through the window facing his backyard. "You do like things bright, don't you?" Tina asked, running her hand over the butcher-block countertop.

"I guess so. I haven't given it a lot of thought. The only place I have curtains is in the living room. Did you find anything?"

Tina held up a tall iced-tea glass. "How come you only have one of these?"

Joe shrugged. He was expected to supply an answer, but words weren't coming easily. The kitchen had always seemed large enough before, but now that Tina was in it, there was nowhere he could stand where he wouldn't sense her. "I don't know what happened to the rest. I think they broke."

"And I think cooking is not high on your list of priorities. From what I've heard, bachelors don't usually have kitchens this clean."

"I eat out a lot."

Tina's sigh reached him. He risked a look that lasted longer than a glance. Although she was wearing makeup, he thought she looked paler than usual. "You look tired."

"I am," Tina admitted. She hated this weakness, this sense that, once again, she would have to ask Joe for help. But maybe it was all right. He'd never refused her. "I did a lot today."

Before she could protest, Joe wrapped his arms around her waist and lifted her onto the counter. "Why didn't you say something before?" he asked with his hands on her knees. "You didn't have to come here."

The strength seeping from her muscles had nothing to do with her day and everything to do with his touch. Surely he understood that. "I wanted to. Didn't you want me to come?"

"It could have waited," Joe said roughly. With a heavy gesture, he turned toward the microwave. The Styrofoam containers revealed four hamburgers, a mound of fries and a couple of milk shakes. He slid the hamburgers and fries into the microwave and set the timer. Tina watched his movements without blinking. He'd looked out of his element in the hospital. She'd sensed his unease while he was at her apartment. Before tonight she'd thought there was only one place—his gym—where he belonged. But that was before she'd seen him in his home. She was glad she'd come.

"Joe?" Tina's use of his name stripped Joe's mind. "I really don't want to eat sitting up here. Would you help me down?"

Her small giggle made things easier for him. "I guess I could do that. Where would you like to eat?"

"How about your deck?" Tina suggested as she stretched her arms toward him. "There's a marvelous breeze tonight."

Once again Joe slid his arms around her tiny waist and held her carefully against him. This time it was even more difficult to let go. The faint scent of lavender he'd caught earlier seemed even stronger now. It invaded his senses, his memory even. The first time he'd held her, she'd smelled of lake water and a hot Texas afternoon. "Are you going to be all right?" he asked without making a move to release her.

"I am as long as you're here," Tina whispered. She was looking up at him, her hands resting lightly on his arms. He knew she was no more ready to move than he was. "I love your home, Joe."

There wasn't anything he needed to say in response to that. Or if there was, the words escaped him. What was it he'd told himself on his way here? That he was going to keep his distance—let the lessons of the past dictate the present. Fool! He wanted her, and the only way he could stay in control was not to touch her.

But it was already too late for that. A three-hour workout, instead of sapping him, had only made him more aware of his body. Now he was touching her exquisite softness. Her scent invaded his nostrils. He would never have enough of looking at her. Joe did the only thing he could—he kissed her.

Her lips were waiting for his; there wasn't any time to fathom the wonder of that simple gesture. She was sweetness and light and something that had been missing from his life for a long, long time. Joe could lose himself and his past in her, and he knew she could give new meaning to his future.

The timer on the microwave blasted away Joe's thoughts. He was asking more of Tina Morton than he had a right to, risking more than he dared. "That's what I call lousy timing," he heard her say.

He could have ignored their hot meal. Food was the fur-thest thing from his mind. But Joe couldn't wipe away what he'd seen in Tina's face. She'd been too long on her feet to-day. The least he could do was see to it that she put enough fuel in her body to keep it going.

"That's not the best meal, you know," he chided once they were balancing paper plates on redwood lounge chairs with the setting sun turning Tina's hair from black to dusky flame. "No vitamins."

"I know." Tina grinned. "I figured you'd say some-thing, but I've been so good lately that it's disgusting. Don't you ever want to chuck it all and bury yourself in choco-late?"

She was making it easier for him to regain his equilib-rium, but Joe still had to monitor the amount of time he spent looking at her. "Not chocolate," he admitted. "Doughnuts, maybe. But you were going to tell me what you did today."

Tina was finished with her hamburger before she was done with her story. While she told him about the confron-tation with her boss, she'd been looking at what there was of Joe's back lawn, but now she was meeting his eyes again. "That's only half of the story. I'm tired because I've been looking at every gym in the city—coming to a decision." Tina lifted her hand and then let it drop. "Joe, your place is so masculine. It still intimidates me. But I want to give it a try."

"Why?"

"Do you really want to hear this?" she asked, sounding uncharacteristically unsure of herself.

"I wouldn't have asked if I didn't want to." Joe reached for his third hamburger but didn't lift it to his lips. Having her here was like a fragile spring rain. She could, he be-lieved, disappear from his life as quickly as she'd entered it—and he wouldn't try to stop her.

"Because—" her eyes faltered but finally held to his "—because I want to prove to myself that I'm not a ninety-eight-pound weakling. Joe, I've been trading on this damn body of mine almost all my life." She jabbed at her flat stomach. "I'm not very proud of that. I'm ready to make some changes; maybe the Muscle Mill's the way to get started. And I want to be with you."

"Are you sure?"

Tina blinked. When she was done, there was moisture in her eyes. "Oh, I'm sure, all right. I walked myself into the ground today wrestling with that question, but I'm sure." She ran a shaky hand over her forehead. "You've been so good to me, Joe. Put up with so much. I don't want you to think I'm running after you."

"I wouldn't think that," Joe said in a tone light enough that he hoped it would hide his deeper emotions. "It was my suggestion that you come to the gym in the first place. I wouldn't have made the offer if I hadn't meant it."

"You mean that?"

She should be surer of herself than that; someone like Tina Morton shouldn't be uncertain of her impact on any man. Did she have any idea how much she was revealing? Any idea how much he needed to know that? "What do you want me to say?" Joe put down his hamburger. "You're making this more complicated than it has to be, Tina."

Tina was looking up at him with shining eyes. What he saw in them made the decision for him. He was going to take her in his arms and damn the consequences. He was going to, somehow, break free of the past and start to live again. "You'll start me off with an easy program, won't you?"

"Why don't we worry about that later?" Joe held out his hands and helped her to her feet. "Did I thank you for the flowers?"

She was nestled against him, a small warm pocket of life for him to hold on to—maybe forever. "I didn't know if that was the right thing." She was still whispering. "I mean, maybe I should have brought you—I don't know what."

"Roses are perfect. I'm like everyone else, Tina. I need a little beauty in my life." He wasn't sure he was like everyone else, but that didn't matter tonight. Tonight he felt that everything was going right—so right, in fact, that it terrified him. She didn't shy away when he wrapped her against him. Her lips were ready to meet his, her tongue eager to make an intimate exploration.

After a kiss that went on seemingly forever, Joe pushed her away just enough to find a haven for his hand under the hem of her loose-fitting top. He'd forced himself not to stare at her during dinner, but it was impossible not to be aware of her femininity.

Her breast fit perfectly within his hand. He felt her nipple pushing gently against his palm and wondered at the grand design that made women that way. He bent over to kiss the strong pulse at the side of her throat. She was holding his upper arms, giving him her warmth. There was nothing in her response to tell him he might be asking for more than she was capable of giving.

Tina felt herself flowing into Joe and thought about her mother's concerns about him. They just didn't make sense. This powerful man was everything that was gentle and good in her life. She couldn't even remember what she'd drawn away from at his gym. Now the only thing she wanted was his love.

Joe didn't think Tina would protest if he lifted her into his arms and carried her into his bedroom. If he allowed himself to follow his desires, she might spend the night.

Joe put off the moment. He turned so he could bury his face in her curls. Even her hair smelled of lavender. Either that or he was too intoxicated by her to separate fact from fantasy. She was everything that he'd needed in his world and that had evaded him since Shannon had left her mark.

She was what he'd no longer dared to dream of having.

But Tina was no dream. She was pressing herself against him, giving him access to her body, challenging the limits of his self-control.

Tina was the first woman he'd wanted to get emotionally close to in a long time. But—if it was going to work—he didn't dare rush the journey. This time, if there was going to be a "this time," it had to be right.

"Don't," he whispered raggedly when he realized that she'd run her hand inside his shirt and was caressing the smooth skin of his chest.

"Why not?" she asked in confusion.

"Because I want you to too much."

"What's wrong with that? Joe, it's all right. I mean, we can make it all right."

Joe stopped breathing. Inside he died a little. "I don't think so." He forced out the words and moved away from her.

Tina reached for him. She'd known this was going to happen. Despite the precious seconds when nothing existed except what they were learning and giving and experiencing, Tina had known they wouldn't take that last step tonight. Still, she wasn't strong enough to give up. "Don't tell me no, Joe. Don't you know what I'm asking? Please. I've never asked a man to make love to me before."

Joe believed her. But, much as he wanted to give her the answer she deserved, she didn't know what he did about himself. "I want you to be sure."

"I am."

"I want you to know who I am."

"I do, Joe. And I know that I care for you a great deal."

"No." He wouldn't let her touch him. "You don't know me at all."

Chapter Seven

It was Monday, two months after the accident, and Tina was immersed in the business of Boat World. But instead of working, she was staring at a snapshot of Joe taken the year before. In the background was the interior of a school gymnasium. Flanking him were massive men in athletic clothing—their eyes on one thing: Joe.

So were Tina's eyes, as they'd been countless times since she'd found the picture buried in a stack of magazines in Joe's office. Joe was standing on a raised wooden platform. To his right was what Tina now recognized as a chalk stand. On either side were judges ready to flash their green or red lights. Because Joe was now part of her, Tina understood that he hadn't been thinking about the judges when the picture was taken.

Everything that breathed and lived and loved in Joe Rustin was centered on the awesome weight muscled over his head. The superhuman effort had made him unrecognizable, yet she was drawn again and again to the intensity of the photograph. His bare arms bulged; his chest was naked under the straining supersuit. His widespread legs exuded a power she could barely fathom.

It was in his eyes. They were telling her that Joe Rustin had found his personal mountain and conquered it.

No matter what she did, the memory of Joe Rustin followed her everywhere. It amazed her that, despite the distance he'd put between them since that almost perfect night on his deck, she continued to be drawn to him.

Tina started at the sound as Bob Wilson, one of the other salesmen, approached her. She tucked Joe's picture back inside her purse and turned to begin her day. For weeks now, Tina had done little except go to work, show up at the hospital for the prescribed physical therapy and drive over to the Muscle Mill where she would find Joe—where she would watch him in his world and ask herself if she had a place in it. Her cast had come off almost two weeks ago. She should be feeling glorious freedom and yet her life was too unsettled for that emotion.

"How's it going?" Bob asked. He flashed the heady grin he usually reserved for female customers. "I see you're back in a skirt. I bet you're glad to have that contraption off."

"I am," Tina admitted. She wanted to tell someone that it didn't feel as good as she thought it would, but Bob wasn't that person. At thirty-one, Bob was playing the role of the hip, single male. He'd been married at twenty and divorced three years later, and now that he was making a decent living at Boat World he was making up for lost time, as he put it.

"So when's Larry going to let you get back into sales again?" Bob glanced around to make sure they were alone in the brightly lit showroom. "Don't tell me you've fallen in love with paperwork?"

"Hardly. But Larry and I struck a bargain. Actually, he set the ground rules and I nodded agreement. We'd see how this present arrangement worked out. He thought I might prefer this end of the business.''

''Tell him you hate it. Tell him we need you back on the floor. Between you and me, I can hardly wait for Larry to tell Angel she isn't cutting it.''

Although Tina knew exactly what Bob was talking about, she had no intention of playing the catty female. ''I'm shocked,'' she teased. ''I've seen you watching her. Admit it, she's easy on the eyes.''

''And on the brain.'' Bob grinned, pleased with his turn of the phrase. ''I never realized how competent you are until you got benched, Tina. If I've told Angel once how to handle warranties, I bet I've told her a hundred times. Well, maybe I'm exaggerating. Angel has a long way to go before she sells a hundred boats. And she knows zip about motors.''

Tina nodded. It was an unwritten part of the salesman's job to keep the new motors tuned. Boat World had a service department, but the repairmen had their hands full working on used motors. It didn't take much to figure out how to adjust high-powered engines fresh from the factory. At least Tina had never had any doubts about her ability to lift the cover off an engine and attack it with a few basic tools. ''Larry didn't hire her to repair motors,'' Tina said in defense of the giggly, unsure young woman.

''Yeah, I know. He hired her to grin at the camera. Hell, she can't even do that. Ask her to open her mouth and nothing comes out unless someone else has written the script.''

''You're being rough on her.''

''Rough, nothing. It's the truth and we both know it.''

''All right,'' Tina conceded. ''Angel isn't very good at winging it.'' Although it didn't matter whether she was a visible part of Boat World, Tina resented having to write the scripts Angel used during commercials. Tina felt she was being taken advantage of, but she quite frankly didn't know what to do about that. There was no job security at Boat World. Larry called the shots. It was either accept his orders or look for work somewhere else.

Was that what it boiled down to? Right now, Tina was biding her time. It would be job suicide to try to push Larry. In the meantime, Tina did the boring chores he assigned to her and watched Angel flounder. Tina wasn't an aggressive saleswoman; she simply knew what she was talking about. She knew how to assess a customer's financial status and help that customer make an intelligent decision. And, despite the still-healing incision on her thigh, she knew how to step in front of a camera and make the public believe that Boat World was the only place in eastern Texas to buy a craft. But until Larry faced facts, Tina didn't believe there was much she could do short of heading for the unemployment line.

It was funny—almost—Tina thought as she walked outside to take delivery of a trio of sleek racing boats. Her whole life felt on hold these days—waiting for Larry; waiting for Joe.

Waiting for Joe was much more difficult. Since that night at his house, he'd held her at arm's length. If she hadn't sensed that deep down, physical distance wasn't what he wanted, Tina would be trying to convince herself that what had felt so right in the beginning wasn't going to work, after all. But Joe was just as on edge as she was. Someday, somehow, they'd break through the barriers.

Tina forced herself not to look at the picture of Joe again that day, but the image of him stayed in her mind. Yesterday Al had said she didn't need to come to the hospital for therapy anymore. She had the green light to place herself in Joe's hands. No longer would she be standing on the sidelines watching the gym members challenge themselves. She could start facing those weighted challenges herself—start reaching inside herself.

Tina was whistling when she got into her car and punched her left leg down on the clutch. She felt no pain. She was healed—at least healed enough to start proving something to herself and Joe.

Joe was surrounded by football players from the local college when Tina came out of the women's dressing room. She glanced down at her thighs but decided against trying to pull on the lower hem of her shorts. Her fading scar had become a sort of badge. The scar said that Tina Morton had faced adversity in her life and was rising above it. Because she was already on a light workout schedule, Tina began her stretching exercises, easing out the kinks in her back, arms and legs.

Despite everything he should be concentrating on this evening, Joe's mind stumbled. Until now, Tina had worn sweats and he'd been grateful for their gray, unisex bulk. Her outfit today was proof that she no longer felt the need to hide. Maybe it was also a sign that she would no longer accept the rules he'd set for their relationship.

"We're talking intensity," he continued after too long a silence. "You're trying to blast. There's nothing wrong with that, but you've got to think about the quality of what you're doing. Quantity isn't enough."

Joe's words flowed through the room and over Tina. It didn't matter what he said; every word he uttered reached Tina in a way words had never reached her before. She delighted in seeing the players' heads nodding; in understanding that these highly rated athletes accepted Joe as the professional. But Tina saw him as much more than the one man everyone in the room turned to. For reasons that were timeless and yet beyond comprehension, Tina was finding things in Joe Rustin that she'd never found in a man before.

She wanted to be with him. Even when the conversation was about football, she wanted to be with him. It didn't matter that there were other people in the room; Tina was tuned to the slender cord that existed between them.

She picked up a pair of ten-pound weights before lowering herself onto a parallel bench. She stared at the stark ceiling, concentrating. Out to the side—up—down to her chest—out again. Compared to what some of the women bodybuilders could do, Tina's hand-held weights were puny weapons, but she knew enough to go slowly. Someday soon she would start to test herself; now she was content to re-establish what strength she'd had before her accident.

Tina knew when Joe left the athletes and walked over to her. She closed her eyes, not caring that the muscles in her neck were tense and her mouth open to pull in enough oxygen. Joe had seen her at her worst—and had accepted her.

"How does it feel?" he asked after she finished the routine. "Any pain?"

"Nothing I don't expect." Tina opened her eyes and acknowledged the desire to lose herself in him. For a month now, they'd talked of everyday things and she'd gone home to face the nightly battle. Joe had to know that what they had wasn't enough. "Al's given me the go-ahead. I'd like to start doing something more strenuous."

Joe pulled on the top of Tina's sleeveless tank top so that the narrow strap no longer cut into her shoulder. His fingers came away damp with her sweat. "Why?"

Tina wasn't ready for his question. His touching her had made her lose touch with herself. "Why?" she repeated. "I'd think you'd be the last person to ask me that. Why does a mountain climber want to climb Mount Everest? Because it's there." By tensing her stomach muscles, Tina was able to pull herself into a sitting position. "I want a challenge, Joe. I need one. I've never really wanted one before." She brought her legs onto the bench, grabbed her ankles, and stared at her slender fingers. "Work was always something I could do without much effort. Maybe it's the accident, but I don't want to take anything for granted anymore." Tina stopped, waiting for Joe to respond. She could only hope he understood that the word *challenge* carried with it a complex emotion.

Joe pushed her legs to one side of the bench before straddling it. They were sitting inches apart, their body heat meeting. Tina hadn't had her hair cut since he'd met her and he wondered if that no longer had priority. "What do you want to accomplish?"

"I think I want to be stronger than I am. I *know* I do," Tina amended. "I want to feel the best it's possible to feel about myself."

"You don't have any reason not to feel good about yourself."

Joe didn't understand, but then Tina didn't expect him to. She was just now starting to take a serious look at her life, and she hadn't shared enough of her thoughts with him. "Thank you for saying that. But, Joe, I know what I need. How come half the football team is here?"

A pleased grin settled on Joe's face. The athletes were waiting for him, but they would have to wait. Tina was the only one in the room he wanted to be with. "I'm now officially the strength coach."

"Congratulations. I mean it." Joe had told her that working with college athletes intrigued him and he felt he had something to offer the football team. He wasn't sure he'd be given official recognition, because he wasn't a member of the staff, but obviously he'd been able to convince the head coach of his usefulness. "Are they going to work out here?" Tina asked. "You don't have room for the whole team."

"You're telling me. Not only can't I fit them all in here, but I don't have enough equipment." Joe's smile held. "I've seen the weight room on campus. It isn't a bad start, but they need a lot more. I just heard that some rich alumnus is donating the bucks. Today I was given the green light to purchase everything necessary for complete strength-conditioning.''

"Joe," Tina breathed. "That's wonderful. When do you get started?''

"Next week. Right now we're making do by having a third of the team at a time come in here.''

Tina's spirits fell at the thought of what next week would bring. The demands on Joe's time would be even more than they already were. She wasn't sure how much time they would have—how much time he would give her. "I think we need to celebrate," she offered recklessly.

"Celebrate what?''

"You working with college athletes and my freedom.'' Taking courage from the fact that his eyes hadn't left her since he sat down, Tina's mind switched into high gear. Joe had avoided seeing her privately since the night at his home. All right. She wasn't going to push that. But: "Couldn't we go to the lake this weekend?''

"Are you sure?'' Joe sandwiched her right hand between his. Her skin felt soft and delicate, but underneath he found strength. Keeping his distance from her had been one of the most difficult things he'd ever done—and what had it proven? Nothing. She was still inside him. He didn't want things to continue like that between them. Her words were proof that she didn't, either. Absently he ran his thumb over her palm. "That's where you were hurt.''

"That's why I want to go there. Bury the ghosts, so to speak. I—'' Tina risked a glance at his hands and then looked up. "I could fix a picnic lunch and we could spend the afternoon there. Al said it was okay to work on my tan.''

Joe met her eyes. She saw herself reflected in their depths, noted the softening around his mouth. "Maybe it is time,'' he whispered. "I don't want you to go through life afraid of water-skiing.''

"No water-skiing this time," she amended. "Not only don't either of us have a boat, but I just want to relax. Remember, this is going to be a celebration."

"Are you really sure? Don't push yourself, Tina."

Tina straightened. "That's what people have been telling me all my life. I think it's about time I changed things."

She was right. It was time for her to go back to the lake. If he stayed on the course that had sustained him for the past month, Joe would let her go alone. But he couldn't do that any more than he could stop breathing. "Saturday morning," he said before getting to his feet.

Tina went through the rest of her workout without being aware of what she was doing. When she was finished she reluctantly told Joe goodbye, and accepted it when he didn't walk her out to her car. For a few days after the evening at his place, she'd lived in the hope that Joe would show up on her doorstep, but he hadn't, and she hadn't had the courage to ask him why. Now she resigned herself to yet another evening alone. At least this time she had the weekend to look forward to—and the hope that maybe things would change.

By the time Joe came by to pick her up a little before noon on Saturday, Tina had convinced herself that she was going to do something, anything, to break through the wall he had erected between them. Her tactic wasn't original. She'd bought a vibrant yellow maillot made of a silky, ribbed fabric that depended on stretch and not straps to hold it in place. The suit covered all the necessary areas. It also flattened her breasts just enough to increase what showed at the top. She'd deliberately chosen a French cut as proof that she felt no need to hide her thigh. Over that she wore a short nylon lace cover-up in the same bold yellow.

Joe's expression when she opened the door was exactly what she'd expected, yet she drew back. She couldn't afford to make any mistakes with this afternoon. Tina started chattering. "Fruit salad, deli meats in sourdough rolls, and angel food cake. How does that sound?" She thrust a large box into Joe's hand.

Joe took the box but made no move toward the door. His eyes stayed on her face for a moment before dipping lower. "You look good," he whispered.

"Good?" Tina questioned despite the effort it took her to speak. Joe had pulled a well-used cotton shirt over his chest and shoulder muscles. His gym shorts revealed the expanse of his thighs. She'd planned today as a test of Joe's willpower. Now she realized that she was being tested as well. "That isn't much of a compliment," she finished up.

"You look like someone who should never be allowed out of the bedroom."

It took a second for his words to register. One of the things that endeared Joe to her was his ability to carry on a conversation without resorting to locker-room talk. To hear him say what he just had caught her off balance. "Joe. That doesn't sound like you."

"No, it doesn't. I think we'd better leave."

I think we'd better, too, Tina acknowledged. She'd never had fantasies of being anyone's sex kitten, but the thought of never being allowed out of Joe's bedroom stirred her in a way she wasn't about to admit to anyone, least of all Joe. "I'm delighted you were able to get the day off," she chattered as she demonstrated her ability to negotiate her stairs without limping. "You've been so busy I've hardly seen you."

Joe opened the truck door for her before depositing the box in the back. The cab of the truck was narrow enough that their shoulders almost touched. Although the vehicle came equipped with air conditioning, he had the windows down to capture the day's wonderful breeze. "There'll be a lot of people at the lake," he said as he brought the truck to life.

Tina searched her mind for something everyday to say, but once again her mind failed her. She came up with something about the weather, but when silence settled over the truck, she turned on the radio. Tina turned her head toward the window, catching the scent of warm air. Slowly the driving beat of a popular song made its impact on her mood. So what if she didn't know what to say to Joe? They were together; they had a whole day to work past the strange awkwardness that had overcome them and gain back the ground they'd lost.

Tina didn't want to spend a summer afternoon with a friend; she wanted to spend it with the man who made her fantasize about a lifetime spent in his bedroom—who would understand if she told him about her dissatisfaction with work and the way becoming stronger was helping her to deal with that. Maybe, somehow, she'd find herself in his arms before the day was over. And if she didn't, she would at least have his presence, and his understanding. Finally she broke the silence. "I talked to Ginger yesterday. I've been trying to reach her for a week. Things must be pretty serious between her and Dr. Al. She's never home anymore."

Joe laughed. "Al hasn't been around the gym much, either. He's used to being surrounded by nurses bowing to his every command. From what I've seen, that's not Ginger's style."

"Ginger would make a good trucker." Tina laughed. "I wonder what he thinks of a woman who shoots from the hip."

"We'll probably find out." Joe paused as he watched a couple on a tandem bike. "I'm going to ask Al if he'll talk to the team one of these days. Some of them still believe in protein loading. I'd like to get that nonsense out of their heads."

As they left the city, Joe brought her up-to-date on the work he was doing at the college. He'd already rearranged the gym for maximum efficiency and taken delivery on a combination variable and rotational resistance machine. Earlier this week he'd been approached by members of the track team who wanted him to work with them as well.

"It's going to cut into my own workout time," he explained. "With the competition in California coming up in a couple of months, it's really going to stretch me."

An idea so crazy that it was immediately dismissed flitted through Tina's mind. Instead she turned so she could watch Joe's profile. His jaw fascinated her. Her fingers ached with the need to run over that hard line, to give him a message that didn't need words. "You'll manage it. Dr. Al says you're a workaholic; I believe him. What happens at those contests? I mean, who are you competing against?"

"No one, really," Joe explained without looking at her. "Mostly I'm competing with myself."

"I guess we all are in one way or another." Despite the drugging warmth of the sun, Tina's mind was grappling with weighty subjects. "I mean, we all set goals for ourselves. If we meet those particular goals, we go on to other ones."

"And if we don't meet our expectations?"

It was an honest question. Honest and hard. "Then maybe we're a little diminished as a result. I never—" Tina paused long enough to question the wisdom of revealing what was on her mind. "I don't think I gave myself the right kinds of goals early in life. I was satisfied with Bs. It was a good week if I had a date for Saturday night."

Without looking at her, Joe reached over and took her hand. He laid it on his bare thigh. "There's nothing wrong with that. Most teenagers don't ask for much more."

"Teenagers, yes," Tina agreed. She didn't speak until she'd stilled the need to let her fingers take the journey that might end with Joe losing control of the truck. "But I'm not a girl anymore, Joe. I need more out of life than somewhere to go Saturday night."

"Like what?"

Like making love to you. That wasn't fair; it reduced Joe to nothing more than a body and that wasn't what he was to her. "I'm not sure," she said as honestly as she could. "That's why I'm glad you took me to the gym that first time. There's a lot of goal-setting in there, some of which I've accepted for myself. I want to become stronger, see how far I can go. It isn't the same as becoming president of a bank, but it is something to shoot for."

"You've been doing a lot of thinking about this, haven't you?" Joe asked as they entered the Lake O'the Pines parking lot. He carefully glanced at her relaxed features. The past wasn't reaching her—so far. Maybe if he placed himself in the middle, it wouldn't.

"Yes, and it's giving me headaches. Too much thinking's hard on the brain. Today I want to let it bake in the sun."

They were hand in hand when they reached the grassy slope where several picnic tables had been placed in view of the lake. By late afternoon, shade from the nearby trees would reach them, but now sunglasses were necessary. Fewer vacationers were here than at the more open areas, but Tina didn't mind. She wanted as few distractions as possible.

A group of young people had set up a volleyball net a few hundred feet from where they'd decided to settle. It was obvious that the game was little more than an excuse for some hands-on contact between the sexes. "That takes me back a few years," Tina mused as Joe spread out a blanket for them to sit on. She slowly pulled off her loose blouse, delighting in the sensual feel of summer sun on her bare back. "I'm not going to admit how many times I skipped spring classes to do exactly what they're doing."

Joe pulled his shirt over his head. He hadn't had time to drop it to the ground before he was noticed. A couple of the young men stopped in their tracks and one long-haired blond woman gave out a loud wolf whistle.

"I think you're attracting attention." Tina settled herself on the blanket, her legs stretched out in front of her.

Joe dropped to his knees. "I know."

"How do you feel about that?" Tina reached for suntan lotion. "Turning heads, I mean."

"It's okay, I guess. You look beautiful today, Tina."

Tina squeezed some of the lotion onto her hand. "Thank you."

"I mean it," Joe said, taking the lotion from her. "You're the most beautiful woman I've ever known."

Tina was undone. "I feel beautiful when I'm with you," she said with rare, frightening honesty.

"Do you mean that?" Joe slid around until he was facing Tina's back. His broad hand warm and silky on her back sent shafts of pure emotion through her.

Tina could think of nothing save the exquisite tenderness Joe was capable of. Slowly, seductively, he spread lotion up her neck, across her shoulder blades, down to the top of her suit. He didn't have to linger over the task, but despite the danger, Tina wanted him to go on forever. Somehow she managed to speak. "That wasn't easy for me to say. I feel confused when I'm around you. I never know—what's right."

Joe pulled her against him. She settled spinelessly along his strength, letting her head drop back until it rested against his shoulders. For more days and nights than she wanted to think about, she'd accepted the distance he'd placed between them. Now, suddenly, maybe, the chasm was being bridged. "I haven't been fair to you," he whispered. His breath puffed past her ear. "Have I?"

"No. You haven't." Tina was staring up at the cloudless sky. She could smell water and fresh-cut grass and suntan lotion. That, and Joe.

"I'm sorry, Tina. You deserve an explanation, but I hope you'll wait. I have some things I have to work through first."

"What do I do in the meantime?"

"I don't know." Joe groaned. The only way he was going to get through today with his sanity intact was to get to his feet and walk away. It was already too late to do that; it would have killed him to try. "That's the hell of it. I hope you'll remain part of my life."

How could he even think she'd leave him, Tina asked in the small space of time allowed her before he touched the tip of her ear with his tongue. Once he'd done that, she was beyond thinking. "You're making me crazy, Joe," she said because the truth was all she had to give.

"I'm trying to," Joe said, toying with her slender, dangling silver earrings. "It's funny, you know. I've never thought much about earrings before. But they look so right on you. So feminine."

Tina's skin was on fire wherever he touched her. If she was honest, she'd admit that the sensation went far deeper, far lower than that. When had her ear become an erogenous zone? She made a futile, lying attempt to pull away. The effort lasted only a few seconds. "You act like a monk for weeks, and now—" She stopped, knowing that the words weren't necessary.

"I know. I'm sorry." Joe left his exploration of her ear and pressed kisses along her neck. Tina leaned into him, not attempting to still the low moan he'd brought to life. "It hasn't been easy on either of us," he went on. "I wouldn't blame you if you walked out of my life."

"I wouldn't do that, Joe." I can't.

"I didn't know." His sigh was as deeply born as her moan had been. "Hell, I don't have any explanations. Just that— I was afraid to touch you." He nipped the side of her neck and the nearby sounds of play were stripped from Tina's brain.

"You're touching me now."

"I can't help it. I don't know if what we're doing is right or not, Tina. I just know there's nothing I want more than to be holding you like this." Joe lifted his head and wrapped his arms completely around Tina's bare shoulders. He held her tight and safe against him, wondering why he'd thought he wouldn't be able to tell her how he felt. Maybe soon, he could be honest about his past. For the first time since admitting that Tina had become part of him, Joe no longer believed he had to defend himself against her.

They sat like that for a length of time that could have been seconds or minutes or hours. Tina sensed warm sun, a faint pine-scented breeze. The beating of Joe's heart against her back was the only sound she cared to hear. She hadn't really wanted to come to the lake. Despite what she'd told Joe, the memories were bad. But the man who'd saved her life was with her. He was her bulwark against those memories.

When he helped her stretch out on the blanket and covered the backs of her legs with lotion, Tina held herself still. That done, he lay down beside her. Her nerves needed much, much more than what they were experiencing, but she was content to wait. Not much had been said, but it was enough. Joe had given up on keeping his distance, and the future seemed an exciting adventure.

She wasn't sure whether she'd dozed off or not. Probably. The sun on the trail of a restless night sapped her of any awareness beyond the simple pleasure of having Joe next to her. When she became aware of a tender prickling between her shoulder blades, Tina pulled herself into a sitting position and looked down at his sleeping form. Like her, he'd taken off his sunglasses. When she touched him he squinted up at her. "You woke me up," he whispered.

"We're going to get burned." The group of young people who'd been playing volleyball were lounging around several ice chests. "Besides, I'm hungry." Tina put on her glasses and handed Joe his. "I think I'm getting dehydrated."

"That's because you're sweating." Joe ran his hand quickly between her breasts and then held up wet fingers. "See."

"Joe! What if those kids see?"

"What if they do? They aren't going to say anything." He was holding his hand dangerously close to her breasts. "Besides, they're too busy doing the same themselves to notice what we're up to."

"You think so?" Tina asked, forcing astonishment into her voice. What she wanted was to lean forward until he had no choice but to rest his fingers against the spot he'd so briefly touched. But that would be right only if he made the first move. Tina reached for the box holding their lunch and with a flourish handed Joe a huge sandwich. "I accept only compliments," she warned him.

"Then I'll only give you compliments," he said as he removed the wrapping and took a bite.

"That's an improvement over the silence I've been getting." Tina hated herself for what she'd just said. The day was perfect. Why did she have to mar it? "I'm sorry, you don't owe me any explanations."

But he did. And someday soon, Joe would lay everything in front of her. "You're a good cook, Miss Morton. That's the freshest tomato I've tasted this year."

Damn him! He was ignoring her! Suddenly, despite a loathing of what she was doing, weeks of frustration exploded inside Tina. She crossed her legs, leaned forward, and folded her arms across her chest. "Forget what I said," she whispered tightly. "You *do* owe me an explanation."

Joe stopped eating. "For what?"

"Maybe I'm incredibly naive but I thought you wanted to make love to me that night at your house."

"I did," he said softly. "You have to know that."

"I'm not a mind reader, Joe. All I can do is guess. And question." She relented a little. "Why didn't you? You knew how I felt." Tina was grateful for the dark glasses that, hopefully, hid her embarrassment. She wasn't ashamed of her actions, she just wasn't ready to find words for what she was feeling. "You've changed, Joe. You aren't the man I found standing next to me in the emergency room."

Joe shook his head wearily, like a fighter answering the bell. "I haven't changed, Tina."

"The hell you haven't. I felt like we were headed somewhere while I was in the hospital." She dropped her head, not quite brave enough to face him. "Do you know something? I honestly thought I'd be spending the night when I came over that evening. It—was what I wanted." She sighed, took a deep breath and continued. "I thought it was what you wanted, too. I guess I was wrong."

The pain in her voice muscled its way into Joe's heart. He was trapped in a corner by a woman who cared for him—who had no reason not to. "You weren't wrong." He took her hands. "How can you say I didn't want to make love to you? I'm thinking about it right now."

"I—know." She was staring at his hands and not his face.

Joe couldn't yet give her everything of himself that she had a right to, but he could give her something. "This is new for me," he admitted. "I'm not used to talking about my feelings."

Tina smiled a little and lifted her head. She was squeezing his hand. "I understand. I feel the same way. We can talk about everything except what we feel inside. But—if people care about each other, if they trust, they can take chances."

Joe wanted nothing more than to be able to take a chance with Tina. But the scars Shannon had inflicted on him remained. Like an accident victim retraining injured muscles, he had to start slowly. "My body's one thing, Tina." He lifted her hands to his mouth and ran his lips over her knuckles before going on. "My heart's something else. I think—part of that is because of what I do." His eyes glazed. "People notice me so much physically that sometimes I get to thinking I'm nothing more than a shell—muscles and very little else."

Tina stopped him. "You're much more than just someone who can lift a half ton. I know you have a brain—and a heart."

Tina's last words were Joe's undoing. He'd been speaking the truth when he told her that almost no one had tried to see beyond the surface. He was used to that. He was content with that—at least he thought he was until he started speaking. He held her hands against his chest, pulling his thoughts up from his heart. "Maybe—if my father had seen that, then maybe I'd have never become what I am."

Because Tina didn't say anything to break the spell, Joe continued. "Dad was a redneck blue-collar worker. He earned his living with his hands. When he wasn't doing that, he was in a bar drinking with his buddies."

"What are you saying?"

"I'm saying—" Joe took his eyes off Tina long enough to stare at the sky. A single, drifting cloud marred its perfection. "I'm saying I learned there was only one way to get my father to notice that he had a son. He's a man's man. He works hard and plays hard and believes that a real man shows no tenderness, no vulnerability. He has a wife because there are certain things he needs in life. He has children because that's proof of his masculinity. But when those children are born and need someone to hold them—that wasn't something my father knew how to do."

"Oh, Joe." Tina freed her hands so she could cover his cheeks with them. She slid closer to him, bringing her almost naked body in contact with his thigh.

Despite that, Joe went on. "I don't know when I decided I wanted my father to know I was alive. I needed him. I went about getting his attention the only way I knew how." Joe turned his eyes back on the sky. This was hard. "Boxing, fighting, football, hard drinking—that was my father's world. I was too young to join him in the drinking but not too young for the other things.''

"You started fighting?''

"Some,'' he acknowledged. "Then I discovered football. Or maybe football discovered me. I'm not sure which it was. I started playing the game in elementary school. That's when I made a discovery. The boys who made the starting lineup had fathers who boasted about them.''

"Damn,'' Tina breathed. Now it was she who was holding his hands. "I hope today's fathers are wiser.''

"I hope so, too. I made the starting lineup. I was big but soft. Dad didn't do much boasting. I knew my size wasn't going to remain an edge very long. That's when I started trying to find out how I could get stronger. A coach started me on weights, and as they say, the rest is history.''

But it wasn't. Tina held on to Joe's hands with a strength that came from more than her recent workouts. He had said so much and yet it was what he'd left out that told the whole story. "What's your relationship with your father like now?''

"He went to all my high-school football games. When I went away to college he bragged about the athletic scholarships I'd gotten.''

"That's not what I'm asking, Joe,'' Tina pressed. "When you get together, what do you talk about?''

"Women.'' Joe laughed harshly. "He wants to hear about my conquests. Not what the women are like as human beings, just how many there have been.''

"In other words, the two of you really aren't close.''

"No. I don't tell him about wanting to be a father someday. About being homesick when I went away to college. About power lifting being my own personal goal and not just a test of strength.''

He did understand. Tina didn't know whether her love for him was being given root this afternoon or whether the seed had already been planted. It didn't matter. The two of them were bridging gaps they hadn't attempted to cross before. "What kind of a father do you think you'll be?"

"A better one than my father was, I hope." Almost casually, Joe picked up his sandwich. "He said he didn't hold me until I was six months old. He was afraid of hurting me. I want to hold my children as soon as they're born." Joe smiled a little. "I don't care what my children do as long as they set goals for themselves and work toward those goals. I want them to be proud of themselves. And I want to tell them I love them."

Tears blurred Tina's vision. The roots of her love burrowed deeper into the soil of her heart. "You're going to make a good father."

Joe was chewing mechanically and swallowed heavily. "I've never told anyone those things before."

Tina had been right to want Joe Rustin in her life. He was capable of touching her in ways she'd never been touched. "You're a special man, Joe." Boldly she placed her hand high on his thigh and sealed her eyes with his. "I want to show you how special."

Chapter Eight

Tina and Joe were the last to leave the lake that day. Despite the unspoken electricity arcing between them, they managed to spend the daylight hours swimming and sunbathing and dozing. With Joe to take courage from, Tina sat at the edge of the lake and watched ski boats sweep past, towing enthusiastic skiers. They hiked along several of the quiet roads that led to secluded spots under oak and pine trees. They walked out to the tip of the peninsula and spun fantasies about building a glass-enclosed home there. They walked to the dam's spillway and talked to an elderly couple about their catch.

As late-afternoon shadows chased away sunbathers, they finished the food Tina had prepared and Joe helped several families bring their boats out of the water. At one point Tina entertained two preschoolers while the mother maneuvered the family car and Joe and the father jockeyed a heavy older fishing boat onto the submerged trailer. Despite the distraction of the tired youngsters, Tina was aware that the volleyball-playing crowd was watching the big man dressed only in wet shorts and tennis shoes.

Tina sent out a silent, possessive message to a particularly well-endowed blonde wearing too little bathing suit.

Not that Joe really was hers, Tina admitted as she turned the youngest child back over to his mother. A certain primitive chemistry existed between them; but that didn't mean that either could lay a claim on the other.

"Why don't we get out of here before you get tied up for the rest of the evening," Tina suggested when Joe rejoined her. She reached as far as she could across his sunburned back. "Have you ever thought about picking up a little extra money as a dock worker? Maybe there's a union you can get into."

Joe cast her a look of mock horror. "That's work. I'm not about to spend my days shoving heavy weights around."

"Of course you aren't," Tina teased back. "Actually, have you thought about opening a florist's shop? That might be right down your alley."

Joe laughed and stooped to pick up his blanket and then started in the direction of the tree-lined dirt road they'd discovered earlier. "I don't want to leave. What about you?"

Tina took in the nearly deserted parking lot. Silence was quickly replacing the earlier noise and activity. She didn't want to be taken home. She didn't want the day to end—ever. "I don't have to get up early. What about you?"

"There isn't anything I have to do tomorrow." Joe took her hand, holding it at his side as they walked. "The breeze feels good on my back."

Tina looked at his back. Her own prickled. "I think we got too much sun. I hope we don't peel."

"I'm proud of you," Joe started slowly. "I wasn't sure coming here was a good idea."

"I wasn't sure, either," Tina admitted. "But there's still a lot of the accident I can't remember. I think I remember the drive up here and getting the boat into the water, but I'm not even sure about that. Selective amnesia isn't such a bad idea. I guess it's nature's way of protecting us from certain memories.''

''I guess.'' Joe drew out the words. He'd lost interest in the subject. There were other, more important things they needed to talk about. First he had to be sure that the message he was receiving and the one she was giving were the same. ''You really don't want to go home? It's going to be dark in about a half hour.''

''I really don't want to go home. Do you?''

Joe had been carefully choosing their footing along the uneven path, but now he stopped and turned Tina toward him. He'd never liked playing word games. ''I think you know what I'd like.''

Tina shivered. The challenge in Joe's words was subtle and easily avoided if that's what she wanted. She didn't. Husbands and wives had private ways of transmitting their desire for lovemaking to each other. Tina didn't know how couples did that before intimacy became something they were comfortable with, but she wanted to learn. She liked Joe's directness, even if it called for the same from her. ''Yes. I know.''

''I want to be with you,'' Joe went on as they started walking again. ''It's what I've wanted from the beginning.''

''From the first day?'' she had to ask.

Although she had trouble making out his features in the deep shadows of the trees, Tina knew he was smiling. ''Actually, no. That first day—I was more worried about whether you were alive than anything else.''

Tina didn't want to think about how close her life had come to ending. ''That's a relief,'' she said lightly. ''Otherwise I'd have written you off as a little too strange even for me.''

Joe frowned. ''What are you talking about?''

"I have no idea." Tina frowned back. "I think I'm talking just to hear myself."

"Why?"

Tina accepted Joe's lead. They were heading into the woods. "I'm nervous, okay?" she admitted.

"About what?" Joe winced at his question. She had to know where they were going and why. But maybe, like him, she didn't know how to handle the steps they were taking.

"Will you stop with the questions?" Tina's laugh was forced. "I'm nervous because we're alone out here and I'm not sure what's going to happen next."

Joe stopped her. That wasn't what he expected to hear. "Don't you?"

Tina moved easily into Joe's embrace and quickly her nervousness was replaced by desire. How could she want anything but him? "Yes," she admitted. "I think I do."

"Is it what you want?"

"Yes, Joe. It's what I want. Did you—do you have to ask?"

His sigh moved through his body. "I don't want to do anything to you that you don't want."

Tina buried her head against his chest. Joe was warmth and much, much more. He was her present, and maybe her future. "I'm not worried about that," she told him honestly. "We're not talking about something you're going to 'do' to me. I know what other people think when they see you, but they don't know you the way I do." She paused a moment, thinking about how far their relationship had come and how much promise might be ahead for them. "My mother has her reservations. Even Ginger told me to make sure I knew what I was getting myself into. But Joe, they don't know you. Not really."

"And you do?"

Tina understood that Joe wasn't challenging her. He was simply asking for reaffirmation that their making love was right. "I believe I do," she answered. "You told me some things about yourself today that mean a great deal to me. Your relationship with your father obviously isn't something you share with many people. I appreciate that you did. There are some things about you that are still a mystery to me, but that will change. Actually—'' she stood on tiptoe in order to kiss him ''—I kind of like a mystery man.''

"I don't try to be mysterious.'' The seriousness that had been in Joe's voice disappeared. He was feeling good—strong in a way that had nothing to do with physical strength. "Except when I'm trying to psych out other competitors at a meet. And that's not what we're doing.''

Tina was ready for a long, exploring kiss, but after a brief union, Joe turned off the dirt trail and led her into the trees. She waited while he spread out his blanket. They sat on it together, thighs touching, his arm around her shoulder. Tina was wearing her loose cover-up, but that didn't stop his warmth from surrounding her. "Do you think we're alone?'' she asked.

"Probably not. There are a lot of private places like this.''

Tina thought about lovers wanting nothing more than privacy on a summer night. Like those hidden others, she wanted the night to go on forever. Still, she was shivering slightly, unsure of what was ahead for them. She repositioned herself until she was able to reach out and place her hand on the rocklike muscles over his collarbone. Joe shuddered as well.

Growing bolder, Tina cupped her hands around Joe's neck. No wonder the overdeveloped blonde hadn't been able to keep her eyes off him. He isn't yours, she told the blonde's memory. Tonight this man belongs to me.

Fantasy took hold. Tina inched her fingers outward, committing all he was to memory. The vastness of his shoulders mesmerized her. The muscles she found said a great deal about commitment and personal pride and what had become of a boy looking for a way to buy his father's love. By the time she'd explored his limits, her arms and hands were widespread. She rocked forward, bringing her body across his, and tasted him. She found a nipple and reveled in her power when his groan reached her.

Joe's hands had remained on his bent knees while she made her exploration. Tonight could be right; he believed that. And yet because the past still had its claim on him, he willed himself to take the night slowly. Only when he was sure it was what she wanted did he lift his hands and find a home for them within the loose net of her top. His hands felt both cool and hot on her sun-heated flesh. He pushed the net off her shoulders, found her shoulder blades and pulled her close to him. "I was just wondering if they lock up the place."

"Then we'll stay the night."

The night. She was willing to give him that much. Although he shuddered, Joe felt a strength that had never been his before. "You might get cold."

"Not with you next to me." Tina went back to her exploration of Joe's chest. Its salty taste only added to her fascination. She could take his flavor into her, make that small part of him hers. There was more, so much more, but they had all night for the discovery.

Tina straightened long enough to allow Joe to remove her cover-up. When she reached for him again, she found that his body was still, with none of the previous tension. He's sure of himself, she thought, glorying in that knowledge. He's worked through whatever questions he might have brought into the woods with him.

Hands big enough to lift a boat out of the water were spread over her shoulder blades. A chest built from hard work and sacrifice was waiting for her to rest herself against. Tina laid her cheek against that sun-heated chest, surrendering herself to everything he was. She felt a quiet sorrow for the man who'd never taken the time to truly understand what kind of person his son was.

She'd dreamed of being his lover. But it went much further than that. She wanted to take Joe beyond those lonely years and show him that giving his heart to another was what people who trusted did for each other. Joe was already light-years ahead of his father in his ability to reach out. Tina wanted to be the one to tap that potential and soar with it.

Her hands were everywhere on him, drinking him in through her fingertips. She was no longer shy, no longer wondering whether she had a right to him. Her own body was responding with a primitive, driving need that would be satisfied with nothing less than total surrender. Tina had to feel Joe's body consume hers. She was ready to be ignited. She could feel the spark within herself and waited for him to fan the breeze that would turn a flame into an explosion.

"I—don't know how long I can wait," she warned him. "I've been waiting for this for a long time."

"Not as long as I have." His breath was warm and confident against the side of her face. "I won't hurt you. I promise I won't."

"I know you won't." Tina had no fear of his strength. "I won't break, Joe."

No. She wouldn't. But more than that, she was ready to meet him as an equal. His need and her message sealed Joe's fate. He wasn't going to question tonight or get hung up on yesterday. He had a right to everything Tina was offering him. Just as she had a right to all the tenderness and love he had to give.

Tina felt his hands on her arms, then on the top of her bathing suit. He was slowly rolling the suit downward, exposing her breasts to the night. And to him.

Tina sat waiting and eager with the suit clinging to her hips. She willed her hands to remain still. It was his turn to pleasure her now, to teach her wonderful things about her body.

He was a master at it. He knew how to place his hands on the undersides of her breasts and push them upward to receive his open mouth. He knew that the right mix of moist heat and night air would turn hunger into near frenzy. Tina threw back her head in open surrender, losing herself until there was nothing but his hands on her body. She was totally within his control, abandoning herself to the fantasy of being mastered. Somewhere a blond young woman was thinking of a giant of a man with water clinging to legs like oaks. Tina was the one feeling those legs pressed against her thighs.

Tina didn't know when Joe took everything away. One moment there was the ragged memory of a slowly rising moon and the sound of night birds. Now not even that remained. She was hearing the furious beating of her heart, accepting that her body had no existence beyond his touch. Blindly her hands found him; she discovered that even his inner thighs carried no softness.

She leaned forward and brought her mouth to the black hairs that curled over his flat belly. With Joe's hands now on her back, she took those hairs between her teeth, ran her tongue over his skin.

"Don't—do that."

Was he telling her to stop? Didn't he know that was impossible? Now wasn't the time for lengthy foreplay. That could come next time. Now she wanted to bring him to the edge—just as he'd already done for her. "I can't stop," she admitted with the deepest honesty she'd ever expressed to another human being. "You're doing things—"

"Tell me what I'm doing, Tina." Joe's hands dipped lower, pushing the bright yellow suit downward.

Tina jerked away, needing to remove the swimsuit that had become a hindrance. A moment later she'd slipped out of it and cast it away. She came back to Joe. Her hands clamped around his suit. Slowly now, she tried to tell herself. She wanted to undress him, to draw out the moment when he would be exposed to her.

A moment later Joe, too, was naked. He sat back down on the blanket and drew her against him. Nothing could stop them now; nothing could hold Tina back from that most intimate of caresses. He'd taken her breasts again and she ached to take him inside her. She turned to lie down on the blanket.

"No," Joe whispered. "You stay on top."

The position didn't matter. All Tina cared about was that there would be no more waiting. All she could be was honest with her body.

Tina gently pushed Joe onto his back. Then, before there was time to think about what she was doing, she straddled him. He reached up, claimed her breasts again, flattening them against her rib cage. Tina leaned into his hands, her own fingers on his shoulders.

Now Joe became the expert. With his hands and body guiding her, she took him into her and lost herself in the effort. She was somewhere between power and submission, fragments of her mind bouncing off both impressions. A volcano was building within her, slashing its way to the surface. It seemed as though the flames were shooting into the heavens—there was nothing to stand in the volcano's way. Joe was with her, matching her journey with one of his own.

They were one, and they'd never be two again.

When she was once again conscious of her surroundings, Tina was lying with her head on Joe's chest, her body still over his. She felt his fingers on her scalp, his breathing quick and ragged, taking her slighter body with him. Their lovemaking had been over so soon—a moment of ecstasy before the quick, mindless plunge into space.

She kissed his chest and whispered his name as he held her tenderly against his beating heart.

An hour later they made love again. This time, determined to draw out the experience, they played with each other, taking each other's emotional temperatures so there would be no repeat of the first wild explosion. Tina wanted Joe to position himself over her, but he still wouldn't have it. "It's better this way" was all he would say when she asked him.

Tina fell asleep first. For long minutes, Joe lay with her cradled against him. Her body, despite the night air, was hot to the touch. She was so soft, so incredibly soft. A woman's body with a woman's mind.

Joe wouldn't let himself think about how long it had been since he'd held a woman like this. It didn't matter because Tina wasn't just any woman. She was the one his body and mind and heart had been seeking—needing. They'd become lovers, and maybe this time it would be all right.

It was what Joe wanted with all his heart—what he wanted to hinge the rest of his life on. But he'd been injured once before and in the aftermath of the hurt, had given up all self-deception. He'd be grateful for every day, every night he spent with Tina.

But he didn't dare stop being wary.

"I'm sorry you couldn't get me last night," Tina was telling her mother over the phone. Joe had just taken a shower and was waiting for his clothes to come out of her dryer. Tina gave him a lecherous look, but her voice gave away nothing of what she was thinking. "Was it something important?"

"I just haven't heard from you for a few days," her mother went on. "I saw another advertisement with what's-her-name. I thought you were going to get Larry to let you start doing them again."

Tina tried to remember when or if she'd told her mother that. Arguing for the right to see her face on TV wasn't important, but she didn't expect her mother to understand that. "I'm not rushing it," she hedged. Joe looked ridiculous with a towel stretched across his midsection. Ridiculous and very desirable.

"I don't think that's wise. Tina, honey, you only have so many years for that sort of thing. You know how I've always encouraged you to have a career. I don't want you to lose out on this opportunity."

Tina couldn't agree that expounding upon the joys of boat ownership was the career opportunity of a lifetime. What, Tina wanted to ask her mother, was she supposed to do once those so-called vital years were behind her? But she didn't have to ask. Tina already knew the answer. In her mother's scheme of things, before youthful skin had begun to sag, her daughter would have snagged a husband.

"Are you still there?" Alice Morton's question pushed through Tina's thoughts. "Are you alone?"

Her mother had to know sooner or later. "No, I'm not alone, Mom."

"Is—he there?"

"Yes." Tina gestured toward the laundry room, hoping Joe would take the hint and leave her alone for a few minutes. Joe continued to sit. "We went back to the lake yesterday," she explained. "It wasn't nearly as hard as I thought it would be." She winked at Joe who responded by undressing her with his eyes. Distracted, Tina tried to continue. "I don't remember anything of the accident. I'm still not sure how I'd feel about getting back on skis. Of course, between work and working out, that pretty well fills up my life."

"You're still doing that? But I thought the doctor had released you."

"He has. I'm doing this on my own. For myself." The words felt good. "No one has kicked sand in my face in weeks."

"And I don't suppose this Joe Rustin has anything to do with your working out, does he?" Tina's mother asked with a hard candor unlike her. "Has that man let you out of his sight since you met him? Doesn't he understand that people need their breathing space?''

Tina had been on her own long enough that having her mother question her decisions set her hackles on the rise. True, she understood that Joe wasn't someone her mother understood or might ever understand. But Tina's heart had given her certain answers. She needed her mother to accept that. ''It isn't like that at all,'' she tried to explain, wondering why any explanation was necessary. ''Besides, maybe I like the man's company.''

''I know you like his company. That's what I'm concerned about,'' her mother pushed on. ''Honey, the man's huge.''

''I've noticed that.''

''Don't dismiss that, Tina.'' Her mother's voice took on a tone Tina hadn't heard since she was a teenager. ''What if Joe decided to use that strength against you?''

Tina didn't try to answer. Not only didn't she want Joe to hear what she might say, but she sensed that they'd finally reached the core of what was bothering her mother. There wasn't enough time today to put those fears to rest—even if Tina knew how. ''How's Dad?'' she asked instead. ''Has he still sworn off golf?''

''Don't change the subject, Tina. I'm your mother. It's my right to worry. I've never seen anyone that strong; I didn't even know it was possible. Maybe it's my fault. Maybe I should have encouraged you to be more assertive, but you were such a beautiful, delicate child that I couldn't bear the idea of anything hurting you.''

Tina sighed. The subject her mother was on now was hardly a new one.

''We don't know anything about the man. I'm sure he wouldn't tell you if he's been in a lot of fights, things like that,'' Tina's mother pushed on. ''There has to be a reason why he's as strong as he is.''

"There is a reason." It has to do with a distant father and a boy's need for love.

"I can well imagine," Alice went on. "He must have something to prove, some need to be the strongest man around. Tina, I don't like having to say this, you know I don't. But—what if he wanted to have his way with you? There wouldn't be anything you could do to stop him."

There was no way Tina could tell her mother what she thought of that remark. "I think you've been watching too many movies, Mother," she said instead. "Real people are much more civilized than that."

Abruptly Joe got to his feet. He was out of the room before Tina could try to stop him with her eyes. "Mom," she went on distractedly. "I really have to go."

"I'm frightened for you, honey," her mother continued to protest, undaunted. "I don't like to say it because we owe him so much, but the man frightens me. Your father came across an article on him. My Lord, they're saying the man can lift over nine hundred pounds!"

"Which makes him handy for rearranging furniture." This wasn't fair. Her mother was speaking out of love and concern. Still—Joe came first. "Mom, what if I call you back later? I know Joe better than you do. I want to explain some things about him."

"I wonder if you do." Drawn out, the words had impact. "And I wonder if you're blinding yourself to the dangers. Darling—it's just that you're precious to me."

Tina didn't have time to dwell on her mother's words. Something had upset Joe and that's what mattered. She hurried through the kitchen and found him in the small laundry room pulling clothes out of the dryer. "Is everything dry?" she asked, unsure how to start. "I'm sorry. My mother was born with a telephone in her hand. She loves to talk."

Their clothes were in the laundry basket, but Joe hadn't turned around. Every time he started believing that he could live like other people, something like this happened. It wasn't Alice Morton's fault; it wasn't anyone's—except maybe his for being who and what he was. "She's your mother, Tina. You have every right to talk to her."

Tina took a deep breath and let it out. "We were talking about you."

"I kind of figured that." Slowly Joe faced her. He was the most masculine man she'd ever seen.

"She—you know how it is with mothers," Tina said hurriedly. "They hate to see their little girls grow up. The truth is, I'd be hurt if she didn't check up on me. I love that woman. I just—"

"What did she say?" Joe asked abruptly. "What was she warning you about?"

Tina stalled. "We were just talking."

"You said something about civilized people." Joe picked up the laundry basket and brushed past her with it. He didn't speak until he was in her bedroom and had upended the laundry on her bed. "Your mother doesn't think I'm civilized, does she?"

Tina could have tried to brush off Joe's question but she didn't. Honesty between them was essential. She needed to set the example. "She doesn't know what to think of you. You aren't like anyone she's ever met."

"And that's all there is to it?"

Joe was pushing her into a corner and Tina sought the most direct route out. "No. That isn't all there is to it." Tina pushed her fingers through her hair. Then she tightened the belt on her short terry robe. Joe filled her bedroom, giving her emotions too much to deal with. "She's a mother, Joe. She's worried about her little girl getting into a situation maybe she can't handle. She doesn't know you."

Joe didn't want this to be happening. They'd returned to her apartment a little after dawn this morning. After a jointly cooked breakfast, they'd flipped a coin to see who would get the first shower. A few minutes ago he had been wondering what it would be like to make love to her on a bed instead of on the ground. Having the day to spend with Tina was the only thing he was interested in—the only thing he needed. Until Tina's mother had called. "And you're sure you know me?" he asked, testing her—maybe testing himself.

Tina jammed her hands on her hips, bony elbows peeking out from beneath the sleeves of her robe. Her newly tanned legs contrasted beautifully with the white fabric. "I know you a hell of a lot better than my mother does."

But not well enough—because I haven't given you enough. "I should hope so," he said instead. "Please tell me something. Did she say anything that worried you?"

"Like what?" Tina hadn't taken her hands off her hips.

"Like how maybe I might try something."

"Stop it, Joe!" This time when Tina ran her fingers through her hair, it was with hands that had gone white around the knuckles. "My mother's been reading too many police reports or something. Besides, it's not my mother you're talking to. I wouldn't have let you in my bedroom if I thought you were anything less than honorable." Tina paused. "In fact you're so damn honorable it's downright boring."

"Boring?" Joe didn't know whether to be angry or not. "What the hell do you mean by that?"

"I mean—" Tina took a step closer. She lifted a finger and planted it on the tip of his jaw. "Nothing, my dear man. I just wanted to get your attention. I wouldn't be here, or rather you wouldn't be here, if I didn't trust you. Have you got that through your head?"

Lord, she was easy to be with! That was something new in Joe's experience; he needed more time to evaluate what he was learning and what that might mean in terms of the rest of his life. What he *did* know was that when he took her in his arms, he didn't have to ask whether she wanted his strength.

And yet there was the small, never-silenced warning that kept him in check. When he found the tie on her robe and slipped it free, it was with cautiously moving fingers. He wanted to lay her back on her bed, position himself above her and throw his worries to the wind.

But Joe Rustin had been taught by forces more powerful than himself not to do that. His palm was a wind sound on her taut nipples; his legs didn't seek a home between hers until she'd opened herself to him. For a long time he was content to stand in her bedroom holding her, painting her body with his hands. Inside he might be a bomb on the brink of exploding, but he held himself in check. Tina Morton was too precious. He wasn't going to lose her.

Not this time.

Tina was the one who made the first move. "You're making me crazy, Joe," she whispered. She was looking up at him, desire written in her eyes and on her naked body. She was swaying slightly, the muscles gone from the corners of her mouth. "Don't make me ask for it."

With a small sigh, Joe took her in his arms and held her against his heated chest. "You're sure?" he had to ask as he lowered her onto her bed.

"I'm sure, Joe. So sure I don't think I can stand it."

For a moment he looked down at her through eyes that refused to focus. She was stretched out on her neatly made bed, with her legs still and slightly open for him. Her curls were flattened around the sides of her head, lips parted. Even in adolescent fantasies he'd never dreamed of anything this good.

"Well?" She tried to laugh. "Do I pass muster?"

"What? Perfectly," he corrected himself. "You're beautiful, Tina. The most beautiful woman I've ever known."

She lifted her hands toward him. "I don't want to wait any longer."

He wanted to crush her under him, envelop her body and make it his. But when Joe lowered himself next to her, he turned her over and helped her onto him. She muttered a protest, but he knew what had to be.

"This time," she amended as their ability to talk came to an end. "But I want to look up at you, Joe. See nothing but you. Feel nothing else."

Next time echoed through his brain.

Chapter Nine

Tina almost skipped her doctor's appointment. She felt so good that it seemed a waste of both Al's time and hers. Now she was sitting on the examining table while he felt her ankle, telling him just that.

"There must be better things you could be doing with your time," she teased. "Sick people you could be seeing."

"You have a point there," Al agreed. "However, sometimes even us doctors like to see people who aren't going to be putting us in a higher tax bracket anytime soon." He released her ankle and straightened. "I'd say, if anything, that ankle's stronger now than it was before the break. In fact I'd venture a guess that everything about you is stronger."

"Excellent physical therapy." Tina was grateful that Al hadn't asked her to exchange her clothes for one of the clinic's gowns. It was much easier for her to face him as an equal this way. "I sent a thank-you letter to the hospital therapist. I just haven't talked myself into going back there."

"Joe tells me you're pumping a lot of iron these days. That's what I was thinking about when I said you're getting stronger."

"It's a good feeling," Tina admitted. She straightened her back, flexing her muscles in a pose she'd seen the bodybuilders at the gym use. "No more batting my eyelashes to get my way. Now I deliver with a right hook."

"I'll remember that when it comes time to send my bill." Al sat on a backless swivel chair looking as if he had the rest of the day to talk. "That reminds me. Are you going to be able to collect from the joker who hit you?"

Tina didn't particularly like to talk about the legal ups and downs of the suit her lawyer had had to file before the other party's insurance company would accept total responsibility. Just the same, since Al was the one on the receiving end of most of that money, he had a right to know. "It's being settled out of court. My lawyer has the checks now. He just wants to make sure every bill has been accounted for. Talk about a cram lesson in accident insurance," Tina wound up. "I think I could teach a course on the subject now. At least I learned something from the accident." She grinned. "I learned not to let it happen again."

Al folded his arms across his chest. "Then it's all behind you? Have you tried water-skiing again?"

"I haven't tried skiing yet," Tina admitted. "Between work and going to the gym there hasn't been time. And although you haven't asked, work is a bit of a sore subject. I'm starting to think I might have a case for a discrimination suit." Tina frowned. "Forget it. You don't have time to listen to that nonsense. Are you still going to the gym? I haven't seen you there in a while."

"I'm there before any self-respecting person should be. I'm generally out before eight in the morning."

Knowing what she did about Ginger's impact on Al's life, Tina felt secure teasing him. "You don't have time in the evenings? What is it? Night school?"

A grin creased Al's face. "I don't know how it happened. I was perfectly happy playing workaholic. Then this woman came storming into it, and things haven't been the same since."

"Storming is right." Tina leaned forward, concentrating on Al's face. "If there's one thing Ginger has never been, it's subtle. She says what she thinks."

"And the way she wants to say it. That's taking some getting used to."

"Problems?" Tina asked even though she had no right.

"I—don't think so. I need someone who isn't impressed by my title."

Tina started to nod agreement, but Al wasn't finished. "You know, Tina, you're the last person I'd expect to find hanging around the Muscle Mill. You don't fit the stereotype of the lift-and-grunt set."

"Maybe I'm ready to break out of my stereotype," Tina said honestly. "There's something about seeing my life pass in front of my eyes to bring about some changes."

"You didn't really see your life pass in front of you."

"You're right," Tina amended. "Dr. Al? I really can't put why I'm at the Muscle Mill into words. I certainly haven't been able to convince my mother that I haven't lost my mind."

Although he'd gotten to his feet, the doctor didn't seem to be in a hurry to usher her out. "It wouldn't have anything to do with the gym's owner, would it?"

Tina didn't feel like playing games. "Joe's a big part of it."

"I thought as much. The first time I saw the two of you together, I figured something was happening."

Tina had reached for her purse. Now she stopped. "Like what? If I can believe what people told me, I was unconscious."

"Joe wasn't." The athletic young doctor reached for the door. "That man was hovering over you like a worried parent. I think he really believed he was keeping you alive."

Tina didn't know how to handle what she'd been given. "He said I was holding on to him so tightly he couldn't get loose."

"He showed me the marks your nails left in his hand. But he didn't *want* to walk out of that emergency room, Tina. You're good for that man—the best thing that's happened to him in too long."

Although the door was open, Tina wasn't ready to leave. Al was Joe's friend. "Do you really think so?"

"I know so." Al helped her off the high table. "After what he went through, a woman he can trust is exactly what he needs."

Tina could have asked Al for an explanation but she didn't. She sensed a vast chasm between what he'd just told her and what remained unsaid. She didn't want Joe's friend to know that she was unable to bridge that gap without his help. "That's me," she said in a light tone she didn't feel. "Honest, trustworthy and kind. I have more Girl Scout badges than I know what to do with. You don't need to see me again, do you?"

"Fortunately for you, no. If you don't mind getting up at an ungodly hour, I'll probably see you at the gym, though." Al was following her out the door. "Say hello to Joe for me, will you? And Tina, if things turn out right for the two of you, invite me to the wedding."

"Al!" Tina gasped. "You're getting ahead of me."

"I probably am," Al relented. "But at least I shocked you into dropping the Dr. It's just that I'd like to see things go right for Joe. After what happened with Shannon—well, you know what I mean. Those charges he had to face were damn hard, and clearing his name took a lot out of him. There was a long time when I didn't think Joe was ever going to get past that."

"Oh," Tina whispered as a nurse handed Al another patient's file. She shook hands with the tall doctor and walked down the corridor to the front office. Then she got into her car and turned on the ignition. The radio was playing a current hit about sunlit days and some woman in love with a nighttime man.

Tina let the sound wash over her. She didn't know anything about a woman named Shannon. But she was fairly certain that she had a lot to do with whatever Joe was trying to hide.

Even after she'd gone back to work and her boss had dumped a pile of paperwork on her desk, Shannon's name continued to echo through her. Who Shannon was and what the woman had to do with some charges and clearing Joe's name were questions that wouldn't rest unanswered. Tina lived in a world where the people she knew didn't have to concern themselves with lawsuits. That's why she'd been so little help to her attorney. Other people were sued. Other people had to appear in court. Not people she knew.

Not the man she'd made love to—and was falling in love with.

Even when Ginger called to ask her to join her for lunch, Tina was unable to pull herself out of the mire her mind had settled into. It wasn't until Ginger pointed out that they had a lot of catching up to do, that Tina said something vague about not caring where they went and then sat staring at the papers on her desk until Ginger showed up.

"Come on," Ginger encouraged as she tucked Tina's purse under her arm. "Let's blow this place. Things are so good for me these days. Al—" Ginger stopped and stared at her friend. "You look pretty upset, kid. Al didn't say anything bad, did he?"

"Like what?" Tina asked as she obediently followed Ginger out to her car.

"Like—I don't know. I'm not the one who was there. Everything's all right, isn't it?"

"What? Of course. Why shouldn't it be?"

Ginger had started backing out of the parking lot. Now she threw the car into park and stared at Tina. "Wake up, Tina. Do you have any idea where you are or who you're talking to? I had a more stimulating conversation with my cat this morning. I want to tell you about maybe being in love and you haven't even asked."

That caught Tina's attention. "In love? You're sure?"

"As sure as anyone can be about something like this. I thought you'd know what my problem is just by looking at me."

"I'm sorry," Tina apologized. "You *are* grinning a lot. I should have noticed. I just, well, I heard something about Joe. I don't know what to make of it."

"Do you want to talk about it?"

Tina worked up a small smile. "Not on an empty stomach."

Over soup and salad, Tina dumped everything on her friend. If she'd had more time to think about it, she probably wouldn't have said anything, but she and Ginger were close, and it all came tumbling out in a rush that Tina didn't know how to stop once it started. "Joe hasn't said anything to me about this," she moaned. She slowly tore apart a large piece of lettuce but didn't try to eat. "I've told him everything about my problems getting my medical expenses paid for. Not that that's such a big deal, but why doesn't he say anything about this business of clearing his name? I knew something was bothering him. If he would just get it out—"

Ginger shook her head in irritation. "You really are a babe in the woods, aren't you? Look, just last week we started work on an embezzlement case. The man had milked thousands of dollars from his employer over the past five years. His wife didn't know a thing about it. Not a thing. She thought he was simply well paid." Ginger stabbed at an elusive cucumber slice. "Talk about naive. Those two didn't communicate."

"I'm not talking about embezzlement," Tina interrupted. "That's the trouble. I don't know what I'm talking about."

"So ask him."

Tina leaned away from the table, stopping only when her chair complained. Ginger's work for the district attorney's office had taught her to be direct about everything, but this wasn't a legal situation. What stood between Tina and Joe was deeply personal. "Ask him who some woman named Shannon is? Or was? Ginger, I'm not cross-examining the man. If he wanted me to know about this—whatever it is— he would have said something long ago."

"So forget it."

Tina knew Ginger was trying to help by confronting her and she fell right into the ploy. "I can't."

"It seems to me—" Ginger took a cherry tomato in her fingers and held it close to her mouth. "It seems to me that you've worked yourself into a lather, my friend. You can't ask Joe Rustin why he had to clear his name but you can't forget that it happened. If you want my opinion, and even if you don't, you're going to have to come up with some answers or it's going to continue to fester inside. Hiding never solved anything."

"I know," Tina said. "I want to trust Joe. I *do* trust him. I just— Look, am I wrong to feel I have a right to know about something like this?"

"No, you're not wrong," Ginger reassured her. "My bosses won't represent any client who won't be completely honest with them. You shouldn't sleep with a man who won't tell you why he had to go to court."

"Ginger," Tina warned. She wasn't embarrassed because Ginger had guessed what was going on between her and Joe. She just didn't want anyone in the restaurant to overhear.

"Don't Ginger me. I'm serious. Being charged with something, if that's what happened, is serious business. You have a right to know."

Tina believed she did. If she was being truthful with herself, this was exactly why she was having lunch with Ginger. Opposites in the way they approached life, the two women actually served as a balance for each other. Tina was—or used to be—inclined to take the path of least resistance. Ginger was a bulldog—a trait Tina often admired. "But he doesn't want to talk about it," she whispered, staring without recognition at the shredded remains of her lettuce. "It's the past," she went on, trying to convince herself. "Maybe I should just leave it that way."

"Do you want to?"

Tina lifted her head. "No."

"Good." Ginger grinned. "I didn't think you'd want to stick your head in the sand. You could ask Joe what Al was talking about."

"I can't do that." It wasn't that Tina didn't feel she knew Joe well enough to ask him personal questions, it was more a matter of respecting his need for privacy.

"I could ask Al."

That was true. Ginger would take chances with her new romance to help a friend. But that wasn't the way Tina wanted to learn about Joe's past. "I appreciate that, but Al thinks I already know. What's he going to think if he learns that he's the one who let the cat out of the bag? Besides—" Tina gave her friend a level look "—I'm not going to put you on the spot."

"Then it looks as if we're going to have to take matters into our own hands."

By the time the women were done with lunch, the matter had been settled. As Ginger pointed out, it was a good thing Tina had a legal secretary for a friend. If whatever connected Joe and the woman known as Shannon had become a matter for the courts, then a little legwork should uncover the pertinent details. "I still don't feel right about this," Tina was saying when Ginger dropped her off at Boat World. "I wouldn't like it if anyone probed into my personal life."

"This isn't personal. It's a matter of public record. You want to believe the best of Joe, don't you?"

"You know I do."

"Then let's clear up the mystery. If it's nothing, you don't ever have to bring it up. And if it's more serious than we think—" Ginger paused "—at least you'll know."

Tina did her best to dismiss the conversation from her mind during the rest of the day. Because her boss was involved in negotiations to purchase some land and wanted Tina to deal with the real-estate agent, she was busy. By the time she was able to lock up her hopefully temporary office, she wanted nothing more than a heavy workout that had the ability to relieve her body of the stress she was feeling.

Joe wasn't at the gym. However, he'd left her a note saying he was tied up at the college but would call that evening. The bodybuilder who handed her the note teased Tina about being cast in the role of messenger boy, but when Tina refused to rise to the bait, the man asked her to watch and comment on his technique while he did standing barbell curls. Tina cautioned him to keep his head higher and close his stance as he lifted the bar to chest level. She nodded approval when he followed her suggestions. A month ago she wouldn't have had any idea what to look for. But that was before she'd entered Joe's world. She had, she admitted as she went back to her own routine, come a long way.

When the phone rang that evening Tina didn't know whether she wanted to hear Joe's or Ginger's voice. Working out had cleared her mind and renewed her conviction to live in the present. Yes, what Al had said had been a shock, but that hadn't changed how she felt about Joe. He'd been nothing but honorable with her. The man who'd made love to her had been gentle and caring. Her heart wasn't wrong; she knew she could trust Joe—love him.

Why had she said anything? Tina asked herself as she reached for the phone. If it was Ginger, she'd tell her that she no longer cared about Joe's past. She was living in the present with the most exciting man she'd ever known.

Ginger didn't give her the opportunity to tell her anything. "It took a little work to uncover this," Ginger started before Tina could open her mouth. "It happened a little over two years ago. Because the charges were dropped before it came to trial, there wasn't anything in the newspapers."

Trial. The word echoed inside Tina, an experience so foreign to her that she couldn't say the word aloud. "What were the charges?" she asked stiffly when she realized Ginger was waiting. "Why am I doing this? I don't want to hear this."

"I know you don't. However, facts are facts and we both decided you have to face them. Tina, two years ago a woman named Shannon Grayson accused Joe of rape. He was arrested."

Tina reached blindly for the nearest chair and fell heavily into it. A moment ago she'd been aware of sore muscles. Now she felt nothing from the neck down. "Rape." The word sounded like an angry oath.

"I'm afraid so. I'm sorry. This isn't the sort of thing you should be hearing over the phone, but I don't have the time to come over. Do you want to hear the rest?"

Of course she didn't. Two nights ago she'd lain in Joe's arms, her heart singing, her hands unable to get enough of him. That man couldn't have raped anyone.

But what did she know of him before he entered her life? She wasn't the same woman she'd been before the accident. People changed. "I have to," she whimpered. Her living room, except for a soft lamp, was dark. She was staring out at the deck where she and Joe had shared their first meal together.

"That's what I figured you'd say. It isn't pretty, but then I've never seen a rape case that is." Ginger groaned before going on. "For the record, this Shannon person was twenty-four when it happened. I don't know whether you should take that as a good sign or not, but at least she wasn't a juvenile. According to the record, she showed up at the police station one morning and told them that Joe had forced himself on her. He was arrested the same day."

Tina desperately wanted to shut her eyes against the memories lingering on her deck but she couldn't. "What else?"

"Are you all right? You sound terrible. Look, I know this isn't going to make things a whole lot easier for you, but at least she didn't show up at some hospital emergency room. There weren't any bruises. At least the record doesn't indicate there were."

Tina felt as if she'd been sucked into a horror movie without giving permission for it to happen. Last year she would have begged Ginger to say nothing more. This year she had the strength to face anything—even this. "How long was he in jail?" Somehow that was terribly important.

"I don't think it said. Look, why don't you just listen while I tell you what I know. Then if you have any more questions, fire away. According to the record, Shannon said she knew Joe and that they were dating. She didn't deny that. When she went to the police station, the statement she gave them indicated that she'd spent the evening with Joe. He wanted to have sex; she didn't. When she tried to refuse him, he forced himself on her."

"Ginger?"

"I know, kid. I sure as hell wish I didn't have to tell you. However—apparently Shannon submitted to a physical exam, but since she'd showered and everything before going to the police, there wasn't any evidence."

Tina recoiled from the implication of that word. "Why were the charges dropped?" she made herself ask. In the dark her free hand was clamping down on the arm of her chair.

"Because Shannon asked them to be. I'm sorry, but I can't tell you any more than that. To say that this particular record is complete would be a lie. The really frustrating thing is, it doesn't establish guilt or innocence. Maybe Shannon's attorney didn't feel there was a strong enough case for a conviction. Maybe— Hell, who knows what happened. Look, I wish there was more I could tell you. Al really opened a can of worms, didn't he?"

"He didn't know. Thank you, Ginger. I had to know." The word nightmare had taken on a terrible new meaning, but no matter how dark the dream, Tina wasn't going to run away. That wouldn't solve anything. Tina managed to ask a few more questions, but Ginger was unable to supply the answers. Ginger's research had been thorough, but unfortunately there wasn't anything more to tell.

"What are you going to do?" Ginger asked. "Are you going to go on seeing Joe?"

Tina had momentarily forgotten her role in the nightmare. Now Ginger was making her face it. "I don't know." She hated the wounded sound in her voice but didn't know how to replace it with anything else. "I don't know what I'm going to do."

"You can't just walk out of his life."

"I'm not going to do that. That's not what I meant. Ginger, give me a little time."

After Ginger hung up, Tina was left without her friend to act as a buffer. Nothing stood between her and her need to get in touch with her emotions. For several minutes, she sat staring into the dim room, unaware of the city lights that so often drew her out to her patio.

She didn't fault Joe for keeping this from her. What was he supposed to say?—*By the way, I was accused of raping a woman once. No big deal?* If things were turned around, she wasn't sure she'd be able to tell a man she was falling in love with that she'd been a victim of that kind of violence. Maybe she could, once she was certain that their love was mutual.

Tina didn't know what she was thinking. She closed her eyes tightly, trying to picture Joe. Was this man capable of forcing himself on a woman? No was the answer that came quickly to her heart, but the charge had been two years ago. She didn't know Joe then.

Al had said that Joe had cleared his name. The doctor believed Joe innocent. At least that's the way Tina wanted to interpret the words spoken so many hours ago.

Her mother had warned her to be careful. Her mother believed Joe powerful enough to be able to accomplish anything he set out to do.

Damn! Tina pushed herself to her feet and plodded heavily to the sliding-glass door. She tried to rest her numb cheek against the glass, but the heat of the day had left it too warm to offer any relief. She opened the door and stepped outside, drawing in deeply of sweet-smelling night air. There was a dry breeze blowing, memories of the evening spent here with Joe sweeping in to encompass her. Joe, the Joe she knew, was incapable of what Ginger had told her about.

But who—what had he been like two years ago?

Tina had no idea how long she'd been standing spread-legged on the deck when the phone rang. It was Joe.

"That's all right," she said woodenly in response to his apology for being late in calling. "I was—busy."

"I'm going to be tied up here for another hour. I'm sorry," he was saying. "A busted pipe in the men's shower. I'll get there as soon as I can."

Tina's mind's eye filled with the image of a weary, hungry man standing knee-deep in water. He'd be frustrated and irritated, but he needed her or he wouldn't have called. Yesterday Tina would have welcomed him with open arms.

That was yesterday. "Don't, Joe," she heard herself saying. "Go home. Fix yourself something to eat. I'll see you tomorrow."

"I'd like to see you."

"I know." Tina fought off a wave of weakness. Much as she needed to be in his arms tonight, she needed more time alone with her thoughts. "But—look, I'll see you tomorrow. I promise. You have enough on your mind right now."

"Maybe I do," Joe was saying. "Tomorrow?"

"Tomorrow." The word had no meaning. "Good night, Joe." *I love you, Joe.*

Tina slept better than she thought she would for the first three hours, but after a siren woke her, she was unable to return her mind to the quiet place it had been. With nothing to take her from her thoughts, she was forced to replay what little she knew over and over again.

Earlier she'd been able to rationalize why Joe hadn't said anything to her. Now she wasn't sure. Surely he knew that sooner or later she'd hear of this. Didn't he believe it was better to hear the story from him, to listen to and believe his side? If the shoe was on the other foot, she wouldn't be able to remain silent about that chapter in her life.

Or would she?

Tina stared up at the ceiling, hands supporting the back of her head. She'd asked herself a question without an answer. Tina had never been raped. She'd never even known anyone who had been. How could she even guess at her reaction? And if she were the man involved—that was even more of a mystery.

Let it rest, she tried to convince herself. It was two years ago. The charges were dropped.

And yet there had been signs that Joe himself wasn't living completely in the present. There were clues in his earlier hesitancy to bring their relationship to the point of physical intimacy.

Joe was still caught in what had happened two years ago, and because Tina loved him, his past had become hers. Someday, somehow, they would have to confront it.

"Pump it! One more, muscle head! I know you've got it in you."

Tina tried to ignore the shouts of encouragement from Joe's spotters, but she was drawn to the sweating man lying prone under a bar sagging with the weight of almost five hundred pounds. Once, twice, three more times Joe rammed the weight skyward. His eyes were squeezed shut, his face contorted with effort. Tina knew he was existing somewhere deep inside himself, asking for and getting more out of his body than was humanly possible. His spotters stood on either side of the bench, hands ready for a lifesaving grab at the weights, should Joe's strength fail him.

It wouldn't. Deep inside, Tina knew that. Joe was strongly in tune with his body and he knew to the ounce what it was capable of. What was it he had told her? That a man had to have goals. For some men, the goal was fast cars. For others, it was women. For Joe Rustin, it was being stronger than any other man his size.

Despite her tension, Tina envied Joe. Before she met him and walked into his gym, her goals had gone no further than a paycheck, an apartment of her own and a man in her life. Now she was learning something essential about demanding more of herself, of goals set deep within.

Tina returned to her own routine spurred on by the grunts and shouts from the others. The sounds had the same effect on her system as hard-driving music. They were fueling her body and giving new meaning to her existence. Tina felt alive and aware of her capabilities, happy and exhausted and free all at the same time. Work had been hard, because she couldn't get Joe off her mind and because she was going crazy pushing papers and answering phones. Now she was pushing work out of her life.

She'd both dreaded and looked forward to walking into the gym where she knew Joe would be waiting. She also knew he would expect her to say something. But because the plumber had had to come and was just finishing up, Joe hadn't had time to do more than say hello. But that had been fine with Tina. She needed to exhaust both her mind and her body until she was unable to think.

"You're really into it today. For someone who wasn't sure this was for you, you're doing damn good."

Tina was standing bent over at the waist, holding a twenty-pound dumbbell in each hand. She brought her hands together and then lifted them out until they were parallel to her back. Sweat stood out on her headband. The top of her skimpy tank shirt clung wetly to her breasts. She tried to smile at Joe, but her teeth were clenched in concentration. She didn't try to speak until she'd completed her bent laterals and put down the weights.

"How much are the plumbing repairs going to cost? The guys said it really was a mess in there." Tina was aware of Joe's glistening chest and his eyes on her.

"Nothing, if the owner of this building knows what's good for him. It might be a hassle getting him to accept responsibility, but that's what I have a lawyer for. Someday—as soon as I can get out of this lease—I'm going to build my own place." Joe lowered his voice. "I missed you last night."

And I missed you, but it had to be that way. "I'm surprised you had time to think of anything except getting that mess cleaned up," Tina said brightly. "How did it go at the college?"

"What if I tell you over dinner? I'd like to hear how things went with Al. You didn't tell me about that."

"I have a clean bill of health," Tina reassured him, although that wasn't the important thing at all. "Al gave me my walking papers."

Joe grabbed a towel and started wiping at the moisture on Tina's neck and shoulders. "What's that going to mean in terms of work? Are you going to go back to selling now?"

Tina shook her head, weary at the thought of the battle ahead of her. Somehow her job, which had been so much a part of her life, had become no more than a way of filling the hours. "I don't know." She sighed. "Larry's still dragging his feet. Maybe there's something going on between him and Angel. It's crazy, because he's old enough to be her father, but maybe he's ripe for a midlife crisis. Anyway—" Tina sighed again "—I'm going to have a hard time convincing him that Boat World is better off without that teeny-bopper."

"Did he ever try anything with you?"

Tina wasn't ready for that question. She didn't know whether Joe was jealous or concerned, but dealing with male advances was something she'd learned to handle a long time ago. "At first," she said simply. "But it was kind of like he thought I expected it. After I said no a few times, that was the end of that."

"It better be." Joe glanced up at the wall clock. "How about in an hour? We could run out for a hamburger or something."

"I thought you were in training. You need your veggies."

"So I'll have a salad to go with it." Joe gave her a quick, little-boy grin. "And a chocolate shake."

"Make that two of them," Tina amended before going back to work. Before her accident, a dinner consisting of a hamburger and milk shake would have made her cringe in front of the scales the next morning. But since starting working out, she found she could satisfy her appetite and occasional whims without gaining weight. However, if that was going to continue, she'd have to make the most of her workout.

The hour passed quickly and to Tina's relief she found enough water in the women's shower to cool her body down. She slipped into a sleeveless knit top that showed off her firm upper arms and white slacks that skimmed her legs just enough to emphasize her thigh muscles. She exchanged her tennis shoes with arch supports for a few leather straps that passed as sandals. A little eye makeup, a quick brush-through to lift and dry her curls, and Tina was ready to go.

Joe was waiting for her. His hair was still damp, but because her eyes were drawn to the knit shirt straining over his chest, his hair rated no more than a quick glance. Forgetting everything except her stomach and how long it had been since she'd been with Joe, Tina slipped her arm through his and started dragging him toward the door. "I'm starving," she explained as they walked out into the night air that had given her so little comfort last night. "I hope you brought a lot of money."

"Pockets full of the stuff. You're in a good mood."

It was a dangerous question but Tina asked it anyway. "Why shouldn't I be?"

Instead of steering her toward his truck, Joe indicated that they could walk the half-dozen blocks to the thoroughfare known as Fast Food Alley. "You didn't seem to be in a very good mood last night."

He'd noticed. "I know. I'm sorry." They were holding hands, walking with long, swinging strides in keeping with the carefree air that was part of a summer night. "Don't mind me," Tina said softly. She should tell him what she'd learned from Ginger. The time was ripe. And yet being with him was so precious and she knew the wrong words could end everything. "Maybe having to see Al brought the accident back," she lied. "I was on a bit of a downer and then when I heard you'd had a bad day too—"

"I just wish you'd told me." Joe pulled her hand close to his side, brushing her fingers against his thigh. "I was worried about you."

"Joe." Tina stopped. She waited until Joe had turned toward her and then reached up and pulled his head down to her. She stood on tiptoe, pressing her body against his as their lips joined. A passing car honked but Tina paid it no mind. Shannon Grayson was a liar. This man was incapable of violence against a woman—against anyone.

"I take this to mean I don't have to worry about you anymore," Joe said after she released him.

"Not tonight. Tonight everything's perfect."

Nothing happened to change Tina's conviction while they ate and talked. Joe's frustration about the plumbing had disappeared now that the problem had been remedied. He told her about the now completed college weight room and plans that were under way for a workshop with local coaches, doctors and himself. "I just hope it's soon. There's no way I'm going to let anything get in the way of the San Jose meet."

"Are you going to be ready for it?" Tina asked as she snatched one of Joe's French fries.

"I'll be ready, all right. I took first place there last year. I intend to repeat."

Tina stopped chewing. Despite the families sharing the brightly lit interior with them, Joe was once again the only person in her world. "I know you will, Joe. I have no doubt that you'll take first again."

"First, nothing." Joe expanded his chest in playful boastfulness. "I'm going to break the damn record. A 910-pound dead lift."

Over 900 pounds wrenched off the ground. Coming from anyone else the boast would have been just that, a boast. But Joe had the capability to tear the world record apart. "I'd like to see that," Tina breathed.

Joe reached across the table and took both her hands in his massive paw. "With you there I can do it."

Joe wanted her in San Jose with him.

Nothing on earth would keep her away. Not words spoken by Shannon Grayson two years ago. Not an unresolved rape charge. Not even the silent questions she herself hadn't been able to kill.

"I'll be there," Tina whispered.

"Thank you." Joe lifted her left hand to his mouth and ran his lips over the tips of her fingers. Joe wasn't a man to put much stock in intuition. Still, he'd been uneasy since last night, as if something dark and quiet from Tina had stolen into him. Whatever had been on her mind no longer ruled her. He loved what she was giving him tonight. "You're a special woman, Tina. I hope you know that."

"Ah, shucks. I bet you say that to all the girls."

Joe remained serious. What he felt went much deeper than reading and being influenced by her mood. Changes were coming from deep inside him. He'd never wanted or needed a woman around while he was competing. Not before Tina. "No I don't. I didn't think I'd ever meet anyone like you. Sometimes it terrifies me just thinking about that."

Tina paused at his words—a man like Joe Rustin wasn't afraid of anything.

Chapter Ten

It wasn't the first time it had happened, but when Tina slammed down the phone, she knew she was no longer going to keep what she'd just learned to herself. Yet another Boat World customer was calling to complain about the misinformation Angel had given him. Tina rose to her feet and stared at her legs exposed by her slim skirt. Her calves had more definition than they'd had a month ago.

And yet she was still stuck in an office while some bubble-headed teenager messed up more sales than she succeeded with. Tina walked out of her cramped quarters and stalked toward the glass-enclosed room where Larry Pardee ruled. Before her accident, Tina would have missed a month's worth of sleep before challenging the man, but her priorities had changed.

"I have to talk to you," she said as she closed the door behind her. Her purposeful stride had drawn the attention of several salesmen; she didn't doubt that they were watching. She also couldn't care less.

Tina didn't wait for Larry to invite her to sit down. "I just got off the phone with a man named Walt Winters. I have to tell our deliveryman not to bother taking a twenty-five-thousand-dollar cabin cruiser to Mr. Winters' summer place, but I wanted to tell you first."

As Tina expected, Larry paled at the mention of the lost sale. "What's his number? I'll call him. There must be some way we can work this out."

"Don't bother. I already tried." Tina was angry and frustrated, filled with righteous indignation. "Walt Winters, who just happens to be one of our county commissioners, is no longer interested in doing business with Boat World. What I resent—" Tina went on without giving her boss time to speak "—is having to take the heat for a mistake someone else made."

"Who made a mistake?" Larry glanced at the showroom visible through the glass walls. "What's the problem?"

Tina knew she had Larry's attention. Although she had to push aside a momentary hesitation, she felt good about what she was finally going to say. "The problem is that one of our salespersons told Mr. Winters that buying a boat would have almost no effect on his insurance rates. However, when he learned the truth, Mr. Winters came to the not-so-surprising conclusion that someone was trying to make a commission at his expense. His words, if I recall, were that any salesperson representing Boat World should know a hell of a lot more about insurance than she does. And if she does know, he doesn't appreciate being taken for a fool."

"She?" Larry's eyes narrowed.

This was the part Tina thought would be hardest. Surprisingly, the words came easily. "She," Tina repeated. "As in Angel."

Larry leaned forward. It might have been the light, but Tina thought he looked older than he had a minute ago. "It could have been an honest mistake. Each insurance company looks at boat ownership differently.''

''It wasn't a mistake. This was a major company. Larry, I knew those figures a week after I came to work here. Angel's been on staff a lot longer than that.'' Tina didn't bother to say more. If Larry was as astute as she believed him to be, he'd be able to figure out the obvious.

''I see.'' Larry was frowning. ''I appreciate you telling me this, Tina, but I don't appreciate what you're implying.''

So Larry didn't like having one employee blowing the whistle on another. Tina didn't like being cast into that role herself, but facts were facts. ''I'm not implying anything,'' she said calmly. ''This isn't the first time Angel has given customers incorrect information. Sometimes I've been able to rectify matters but not always. I don't—'' Tina sat up straight ''—I don't appreciate being placed in this position. Because you have me doing the paperwork and answering the phone, I'm the one customers yell at when the bottom line isn't what they were led to believe it would be.''

''Why didn't you come to me about this before?''

''I was hoping I wouldn't have to. I understand the position you're in.'' Tina went on although she realized she was giving Larry an out. ''Angel's young. You had to bring her in at a moment's notice. But Larry, you've given her every chance in the book.''

''But it isn't working out.'' Larry's voice didn't make it above a whisper. ''You aren't telling me anything I don't know.''

Tina appreciated her boss's honesty. ''She's young and attractive, Larry. But it isn't helping Boat World to have you treat her like a daughter.'' Tina was pretty sure that a father-daughter relationship didn't cover what was going on between Larry and Angel but that was none of her business. ''You're the one who told me it was up to me whether I sank or swam when I came to work here. A salesperson at Boat World has to carry his or her own weight.''

"And Angel isn't carrying her weight." Larry's frown deepened. He stared silently at Tina for the better part of a minute before speaking. "I wondered who would be the one with the guts to tell me that. I didn't figure it would be you."

"Why not?"

Larry had been sitting behind his desk. Now he got to his feet and came close enough to pat Tina on the knee. "Because you're my sweet, pretty Tina Morton."

Not anymore, Larry. "That isn't really a compliment."

"If you're talking about that scar, forget it." Larry waved his hand distractedly. "You showed it to me, remember? It should heal quite well."

"That isn't what I was talking about. Larry, I'm on the down side of my twenties. I don't want to be anyone's sweet, pretty anything."

Larry lifted his hand off Tina's knee. He was looking at her in a way she'd never seen before. "What do you want to be? You want to get in front of the camera again, don't you? You want to take back your advertising role."

She had it. Without having to hear Larry say it, Tina knew that all she had to do was open her mouth and she'd be at the TV studio for the taping of the next Boat World ad. "You wouldn't even talk about this the last time I brought it up," she reminded him. "What changed your mind?"

"Because—" Larry sighed deeply and sat on the edge of his desk. "I'm going to have to let Angel go."

"When did you decide that?"

"When you sat down here." Larry was shaking his head. "No one's had the guts to tell me about Angel's performance; no one but you, that is. I can't go on pretending things are going to get better with her."

Tina felt the weight of the decision Larry had just made, but hiring and firing was his responsibility, not hers. "You gave her time to prove herself," Tina pointed out.

"A hell of a lot more time than I would have if she was a man. Don't mind me, Tina. I'm telling you things I shouldn't.''

"I have a broad shoulder."

"It's broader than it used to be. I've been meaning to tell you: the business's books and records have never been this accurate. You make an excellent business manager, as well as a secretary."

Tina wrinkled her nose. "It isn't my favorite job."

"But you do it well. Better than I thought you would." Larry was staring at her. "The truth is I figured you'd last a week doing the books. I figured you'd either mess things up or throw up your hands."

"Why?" Tina challenged. "Because I'm a pretty face?"

"I misjudged you, Tina. You've got brains."

"That's the first real compliment you've given me since we met," Tina said as she got to her feet.

"You're also— I'd like you to take back your old job, Tina. You're the best damn salesman I have. The sales records bear that out."

"Saleswoman," Tina corrected automatically. "What about the advertising?"

"That goes without saying." Larry sighed. "Damn. I wish we'd done this a long time ago. You don't know what a load that is off my mind. Your face is the one the public wants to see."

But that wasn't what Tina wanted to do with her face and body anymore. Her job, whatever that was going to be, would have to make her feel as good as working out did. Soon, as soon as she knew what direction she was headed in, she'd tell Larry that.

When she walked into the Muscle Mill later that day, Tina felt stronger than she had in her life. She was whistling, walking with a swagger even. The humid air, massive equipment, groans echoing off the walls had become a potent, welcome drug. She was where she belonged. "Out of my way, buster,'' she warned as she used her hip to shove a six-foot man who was blocking her way. "By the way, your car's taking up two parking spaces."

The man gave her a look of mock astonishment. "See what happens when we let them out of the kitchen?" he said to no one in particular. "Pushy broad."

"Muscle head," Tina shot over her shoulder.

Joe was watching; Tina felt his eyes follow her as she made her way to the free weights. "You're in a fine mood," he said when he joined her.

"I am, aren't I?" Tina wasn't surprised to find that the meeting with Larry had left her even more in tune with herself than before. "It's a long story."

There weren't enough hours in the day anymore. Work had been enough for the past two years, but now that Tina had become part of his life, Joe understood what he'd been doing to himself. He wasn't a machine after all. He was a man—a man with the need for this particular woman. Around Tina, he felt gentle and protective and proud and excited. And more than a little in love. "I'd like to hear it. What are you doing Friday night?"

"Spending it with you?" Tina lifted a pair of rubberized steel dumbbells in her hands.

That was the answer he'd been hoping for. Maybe, when they were alone, he'd find the words to tell her how he felt. "The football team has a scrimmage scheduled. I'd like to watch them."

"So would I," Tina answered easily. To hell with the questions that wouldn't leave her alone. She was feeling too good for anything but sharing emotions and the night with Joe.

Tina dressed for the game with reckless abandon. There was nothing in the fashion magazines that set guidelines for the proper attire for a preseason scrimmage involving two teams minus half of their uniforms. Her outfit consisted of outrageous dangling red earrings, a sleeveless scoop-necked minidress of the same bright red, and red canvas shoes without socks. She'd brushed at her curls until her hair was a billowing cloud, but couldn't believe that she still hadn't taken time for a haircut. When Joe showed up in a faded blue T-shirt and sweats of an indeterminate color, Tina wrapped her arms around his waist and hugged him in delight. "You have all the fashion sense of a railroad tramp."

Joe grabbed for her earrings and missed. "You want me to follow your lead? I'd look like a fire engine coming down the street."

Tina laughed at that. They could be good together; they were good together. "You have a point there. Okay, tell me about this football team of yours. Do they have a chance?"

"That's what we're going to find out. Tina?" Joe's voice roughened. "You look fantastic."

"I look like a small fire engine," she amended. There was something deep in his voice. She could either ask for an explanation or hold to the easygoing relationship that had sustained them recently. Tina took the coward's way out. "Are you ready to leave?"

"No." He held her strong and tight against him, giving her senses no option but to absorb his essence. In another minute—in a second—she'd be opening her heart to him.

"I—think we'd better."

"We'll be back here later."

"I know."

On the way to the game, Tina focused on what had been going on at work because to remain silent for more than a few seconds would bring on too many thoughts about the night to come. There would be a "later." And maybe, if the time was right, she'd tell him that she loved him.

Instead, she told him about confronting Larry and the quick sequence of events that led to Angel not showing up at work the next day. Already Tina had eased back into her former sales position. "I just can't commit myself to the advertising," she admitted, her voice muffled because she was resting her head on Joe's shoulder. "I used to enjoy certain aspects of it, making sure the ad was as good as I could make it. I enjoyed studying the angles the cameraman used, making suggestions for displaying the boats. I don't know," she wound up, "maybe I was getting burned out without knowing it." She looked up at Joe, wanting his reaction. "I don't feel the same about selling, either. It's like I'm playing a game. I need a career change or something."

"You've just been back at it for two days," he reminded her. "Give yourself time."

What Joe said made sense, and yet Tina knew that the woman with the best sales record for Boat World no longer existed. When she was at the Muscle Mill, particularly when Joe was there, she was where she belonged; it was the rest of the time she was worried about.

The scrimmage was being held at the college football field, but because there were no cheerleaders, TV cameras or stands filled with fans, there was a casual feeling to the event. Tina and Joe were able to sit on the fifty-yard line almost at eye level with the field. Before the game, Joe went over to the players' bench and talked to several of them. Tina leaned back in the stadium seat Joe had brought for her and put her feet up on the row ahead of her. Her short outfit rode dangerously high on her legs, drawing glances from more than one football player. She ignored a wolf whistle from a trio of young men sitting a short distance away.

"This is fun," she told Joe when he rejoined her. "We've practically got the whole place to ourselves."

"The game's going to be hard to follow," he warned her. "The coaches are going to be trying out all the players. You'll see a lot more running on and off the field than you get on TV."

Tina thought about telling Joe that watching TV football games wasn't high on her list of priorities, but it wasn't important. What was, was spending a warm summer night with Joe and learning more about what had kept him busy over the past few weeks.

Joe was a good teacher. Not only did he clarify the basic objectives of the game, but he was able to explain what players in different positions were supposed to accomplish. He told her about the need for various pieces of equipment and explained where strength and speed were of the most benefit. Although he left her in order to speak to the coaches several more times, Tina didn't mind. Not that long ago she would have felt abandoned if a date had left her alone in this masculine enclave. Now she was able to use that time to observe the skills of the athletes. She better understood the degree of physical fitness needed. Massive muscles were fine for the linemen; a lean, quick body was necessary to a successful quarterback.

"The center's too tall," she reported when Joe rejoined her. "He can't get down low enough for a good handoff."

Joe gave her a quizzical look. "Do you expect me to tell the coach that?"

"Sure. Tell him that's my considered opinion."

Joe took her hand, brought it to his lips and ran his mouth over her knuckles. "Actually, you're right. They're going to have to do some juggling of personnel there."

Tina didn't answer. She'd been doing fine up until this moment. She was still vaguely aware of grunts and shouts, even the sound of an aluminum can being opened behind them, but Joe's presence was taking her beyond those mundane things. She sagged against him, wanting what she couldn't have.

"Big bastard, isn't he? Must think he's something," were the words that threw Tina back to reality. She tensed, her eyes finding Joe's face.

"Ignore them," she whispered. "They've been drinking."

"All brawn. No brain. All that work just to get a broad to go to bed with him."

Tina tightened her grip on Joe. Beer courage was making the trio behind them say things they had no business saying. She started to turn around but Joe stopped her. "One more word," he whispered.

"And then what?"

"Don't ask."

Tina didn't have long to wait. "Steroids. No question about it. What's the ape trying to prove?"

Joe rose to his feet with a grace that robbed Tina of her breath. Men got into fights in order to defend their honor in the movies, but she'd never known anyone who actually had to do it. But the trio had made a deadly mistake by mentioning steroids. That was one thing Joe was dead set against. "Be careful," she warned him. She knew Joe wasn't listening.

As his long strides ate up the distance separating them and the three men, Tina was struck by a horrifying thought: Joe had been behind bars once in his life; it could happen again, now.

Tina was aware that the players on the bench had swiveled around to watch, but she couldn't take her eyes off Joe. She hated violence. At the same time, she understood Joe's position. The men were goading him. He couldn't ignore them.

She half expected him to start throwing punches. Instead, Joe planted himself in front of the three men, rested his hands on his hips and stared down at them. "If you have something to say, say it to my face." There wasn't anything intimidating in his voice; his physique took care of that.

"You heard me," one of the men responded in a slightly slurred voice. He got to his feet, standing on a higher bench than Joe so he didn't have to look up. "I'm saying you're pumping yourself up with steroids. Hell, I could look like that if I didn't care about digging my own grave."

Joe reached for an unopened beer can and destroyed it with one hand. The foamy contents sprayed out in all directions.

"Hey!" one of the others protested. "What are you doing?"

"I'm making a point," Joe answered him. "The point is, keep your mouth shut. You don't have anything to say."

The third man grumbled something Tina didn't catch. However, she did understand the pointed look the trio shot in her direction. At that, Joe moved so quickly that she didn't know what he was going to do until he'd lifted the speaker into his arms and was holding him above his head.

Turning his back on the other two gaping men, Joe walked over to the stairs and started upward, taking two steps at a time. The man flailed ineffectively at Joe's head, but at least he wasn't so drunk that he risked falling by trying to wriggle out of Joe's grip.

Joe didn't stop until he was at the top of the high, covered stands. Then he turned around so the man had a view of the distant playing field. He said something Tina couldn't hear. Whatever it was caused the man to tightly grip Joe's forearms. For a good thirty seconds neither man moved. Then Joe slowly set the man back on his feet. He turned away and headed toward Tina without saying a word.

Joe was standing beside her when the football players broke out in applause. Their shouts of encouragement and support vibrated inside Tina. She tried to concentrate on Joe, read something of his mood in his eyes, but all she could think of was Joe walking up the stairs with a man held over his head.

What might have happened if he'd lost his temper turned her blood to ice.

"Are you all right?" Joe had sat back down beside her. He wasn't touching her. He didn't know if he dared.

"I don't know. I don't really want to talk about it," Tina said softly.

"I didn't figure you would." Joe was staring out at the field. Damn. This wasn't supposed to have happened. He knew that violence rarely solved anything. He should have stopped with a threat—calm words in contrast to their ignorance. But after what they'd said about Tina— What if she didn't understand? "I didn't have a choice, Tina," he muttered. "I couldn't let them go on talking like that."

"I said I don't want to talk about it."

Silence settled down around them with a life and force all its own. Tina could hardly breathe under its weight and yet she knew she needed some time to think. She wasn't embarrassed by what Joe had done; she applauded the way he'd handled an explosive situation. She hoped she'd be able to tell him that, but now wasn't the time.

Now she was a punch-drunk fighter reeling under the effect of the blows to her emotions. Joe Rustin—the man she'd made love to, the man she'd been ready to turn her heart over to—was a powerful man capable of amazing feats of strength. If his self-control ever snapped—

Was that what was behind the rape charge?

Tina's head pounded. No matter how many times and ways she turned the question around, there was no easy answer. She'd seen enough of life to understand that there were times when even the most self-controlled person could be pushed over the edge. A few months ago she would never have had the courage to tell her boss he was making a serious mistake. That was hardly in the same category as what Joe had done, but she understood that anyone could be forced into a situation where the old rules and guidelines no longer existed.

She'd never seen Joe lose control. But he'd come close today.

"I think we'd better go," Joe was saying. Tina had no idea how long they'd been sitting there.

She rose to her feet on numb legs and submitted to his hand on the small of her back. As they were leaving, she realized there was no sign of the three men who'd been taunting them. Tina wanted to tell Joe she understood that there were times when a man had to defend himself. She knew he couldn't sit passively, pretending nothing was being said.

But if she opened her mouth to speak, she might start saying things from which there was no retreating.

"I'll take you home soon but there's something I have to do first," he said. Tina nodded and followed obediently.

Joe drove to his deserted gym, unlocked it and went inside. Tina trailed after him, but when he went into the weight room and strapped himself into a machine, she stood in the doorway watching silently. He opened with a weight too heavy for someone who hadn't warmed up. But that wasn't enough. He was still a mass of knots inside. Joe added two more plates to the bar and pushed out another set of reps.

He was in love. Was it too much for him to have what other men took for granted? Did he dare ask Tina for an answer? And after what she'd witnessed tonight, did he dare tell her about Shannon? There weren't any answers to his questions; there was only the primitive and essential need to work the questions out of his system in the only way he knew how. When he finally unstrapped himself and got to his feet, his face was bathed in sweat.

He had no claim to Tina. No matter how important she was to him, he couldn't force her to stay.

"Don't ask," he said tightly, as he turned off the lights and led the way back outside.

Joe wondered if Tina understood.

The truck felt like a toy. He'd never been happy with the underpowered machine, but when he was in the market for a truck, he'd allowed himself to be swayed by a friend's enthusiastic talk about gas mileage. Tonight he needed more power beneath him and he wanted a seat large enough to comfortably bear his weight. Tonight he was too big for the world he found himself in. As soon as he could find time, he'd trade this one in for a full-size pickup. He could tell Tina that. Trucks were a safe topic.

Instead, Joe remained silent. Although the quick, hard workout had taken some of the tension out of him, he still carried inside him the image of Tina's horrified expression as he held the man over his head. What shook Joe was that he honestly didn't remember grabbing hold of the man and carrying him to the top of the stands. If they started talking about what happened, he would have to tell her that.

He would have to turn part of himself over to her.

Joe didn't like losing control. Control, given what he was capable of, was essential. He'd always understood that restraint would have to come from within himself, because no one would be able to stop him. He had a gentle side—a side a woman could love. But tonight he'd been challenged; and despite what it had cost him, he'd met the challenge without violence. What turned his fingers into white cords squeezing the steering wheel was knowing that the most important woman in his life had witnessed it.

He didn't want to take Tina back to her apartment. Maybe he could regain the special rapport that existed between them by asking a simple question. "Do you want to go to my house?"

Tina glanced over at him from her side of the cab. "I don't think so, Joe."

Her refusal hurt a hundred times more than anything those three braggarts had said. He could have asked her to reconsider, tell her that anything that happened tonight would be on her terms. But he didn't.

Shannon's memory was in the way. One woman in a lifetime afraid of him was enough.

"You still don't want to talk about it, do you?"

"Maybe after I've had time to think about it." Tina leaned her head against the back of the seat and closed her eyes. She wasn't watching him with the wariness of a trapped creature. It wasn't much. It didn't tell him anything about what she was thinking. But it was something.

Joe didn't move to get out of the truck when he pulled up in front of her apartment. The evening had started with such promise. He'd been looking forward to taking her to the football game and then having the time alone that had eluded them all week. Now he had nothing.

"I'll call you in the morning," he said as she was getting out.

"All right." Tina wasn't looking at him. It took her a long time to close the door.

Joe almost felt relieved when Tina turned away and the night swallowed her. She'd been so close that he could reach out and touch the brick wall that existed between them. He wanted, no matter how hard it might be, to have her tell him how she felt during his loss of control. He needed to tell her that it had been a long time since anyone had challenged him and it might never happen again. But tonight hadn't been right for the telling.

Maybe tomorrow.

Maybe tomorrow he could tell her that he'd fallen in love.

Tina's legs felt as if they'd each gained a hundred pounds and the climb up to her apartment was far harder tonight than it had been in a cast. She heard Joe's truck back out of the parking lot and move slowly down the street. At least he wasn't venting his emotions on his tires.

She had no idea what he was thinking. Her own emotions left little room for anything else. Someday, if anything was going to come of what she and Joe had begun, Shannon's name would have to come up. Maybe she would be the one to ask for the truth.

Probably, she conceded as she let herself in. Joe wasn't going to do it on his own.

She didn't blame him for that. From his distant father, Joe had learned that men were expected to keep certain things inside. That, coupled with the horror of the story it-self, had effectively sealed the lips of the man she loved.

So ask him, she berated herself. Tina walked into her bedroom and pulled the red garment over her head without bothering to turn on the light. The hem caught on her dangling earrings, momentarily distracting her from her thoughts. She couldn't remember how many hours ago she'd put on the earrings, only that the evening's promise had never materialized.

By the time Tina was in her nightshirt, she'd managed to pull herself out of the mental quicksand that had made her numb. Some women would have been delighted to have their boyfriends prove themselves the way Joe had. Certainly the football team had found it much more interesting than the action on the field. Popeye was always coming to the rescue of Olive Oyl.

But Tina wasn't Olive Oyl. She couldn't applaud violence or what had almost become violence. She knew replaying the event in her mind was only making matters worse, but she just couldn't stop herself.

Tina was staring at the inner recesses of her refrigerator when the phone rang. For five seconds she played with the idea of letting it ring. But she knew Joe's voice would be on the other end.

"Are you all right?" he asked.

Don't do this to me, Joe. "I think so," she answered honestly.

"I hope so." Joe didn't sound as if he was doing very well himself. "I changed my mind. I don't think we should wait until tomorrow to talk about this."

"Maybe. Joe, I can't explain how I felt. I owe you more than that, but nothing like that has happened to me before. Those jokers were drunk; they didn't have their brains engaged." She felt as if she was standing off at a distance listening to herself rattle on. "Actually, it was kind of funny."

"It was?" Joe still sounded wary but he also sounded more like himself. Tina silently applauded the courage that made it possible for him to pick up the phone and dial her number.

"You couldn't see that guy's face," Tina explained. "I think he almost lost his dinner. And his friends—his friends were pretty quiet. They quickly learned they bit off more than they'd intended."

"I'm still sorry it happened," Joe repeated. "I was looking forward to the evening."

"So was I," she was able to admit.

"Maybe tomorrow?"

"Tomorrow sounds fine." Tina's mind sprang ahead to a brunch on her patio, sunbathing by the pool, maybe a short drive. Joe had called and let her know he hated this thing that had come between them as much as she did. It was going to be all right. It had to be! "Are *you* all right?"

"I am now. I love you, lady."

Tina believed she understood her role. The words he'd just uttered were a wispy cloud that might develop into something strong and lasting or might be blown away by the next breeze. He wasn't committing himself to anything more than a momentary emotion. He obviously didn't know that she was beyond that point. "I love you too, Joe. Come over when you get up, and bring your appetite."

"I'd like to go truck shopping tomorrow. I'd like you to come along."

Tina told him that that was fine with her. If nothing else, she explained, she knew when a salesman was telling the truth. Truck shopping was a good way to spend the day. But when she hung up, Tina knew that they were fighting to keep their relationship going.

She was also afraid that that was impossible as long as neither of them was brave enough to bring up the past.

Chapter Eleven

The next month flowed by on a smooth if shallow current. Because Joe was in training for the upcoming meet and putting in additional hours at the college, his time was limited. Tina saw him daily at the gym and they were able to snatch a few hours together during the weekends, but as the days stretched on, Tina wondered how much longer they could go on treading water.

Joe felt the same way, but because Tina hadn't brought up the incident at the football game, he tried to convince himself that the present was all they needed. It wasn't hard. Although Joe tried to draw comparisons between Tina and Shannon, Shannon's memory had faded. Never, he believed, had he been tuned in to any woman's thoughts the way he was with Tina. Never had his days and nights revolved around one person so completely.

What Joe was experiencing went deeper than that. He'd never heard this message from his heart before. The message was simple: Loving Tina was right; she was part of him.

Their lovemaking had lost its early frenzy. Tina was delighted with the closeness that came when they had time to slowly draw each other along. Tina loved losing herself in Joe, becoming a little more of him and a little less of herself. She welcomed this slow growth and accepted the pace of their relationship. They were on a journey that could fulfill her as she'd never been before. All they needed was time.

Work was another story. It was something she had to do because there were bills to be paid, nothing more. She felt pressure from both her mother and her boss to commit herself to doing the advertising again. Because it was the height of the boating season, she reluctantly made one commercial, but she didn't come to Larry with suggestions on how they might focus the next one.

"Don't push me, Larry," she told him when he mentioned that he wasn't used to doing the brainstorming himself. "Now that I think about it, I never did get paid for my input."

"Is that what you're holding out for?" Larry asked. "More money?"

Although Tina knew Larry would increase her salary if she asked for it, she didn't jump at the opportunity. "I'm not holding out for anything, Larry," she reassured him. "I'm going to leave that up to you. If you think I'm worth more money, you'll give it to me."

Larry frowned. "You're backing me into a corner, Tina. You know what your sales figures have been since you came back."

Tina couldn't resist. "Yes, as a matter of fact I do know. You kept me in the back room too long."

Larry was still frowning. "I was watching you this morning. Tina, the customer's always right. You shouldn't forget that."

Tina tried to remember what she'd said to a customer this morning. She'd been talking to a man whose youngest child had just left home. The man was looking forward to having more money at his disposal and was eager to invest in the largest, most comfortable fishing boat he could find. But when the man mentioned that he had arthritis, Tina felt compelled to point out that strength was necessary to get the boat he was interested in in and out of the water. In the end, the man opted for a smaller boat he and his wife could handle.

"The customer was getting carried away," Tina pointed out. "I had a responsibility to have him look at all the issues and options."

"And he chose a boat that cost several thousand less."

"He also has one he's going to be happy with for the rest of his life. Larry, I don't like this business of steering the customer to the most expensive boat in the place."

"That's how we stay in the black, Tina." Larry was getting a little red in the face.

Last year Tina would have backed down before the conversation got to this point, but she felt she was right. She was the one who would catch the heat if a customer believed she'd tried to pull a fast one on him. "We also want the customers to recommend us to their friends," she pointed out. "They aren't going to if they think we're con artists."

"What's gotten into you, Tina?" Larry was fairly spluttering now. "I'm the one who sets policy around here. Your job is to sell boats."

Tina hadn't bothered to sit down when Larry called her into his office. It was much easier for her to walk out the door this way. "I'm making more sales than ever before," she pointed out. "I wouldn't think you'd care how I did that as long as the bottom line is in your favor."

"What's with you?" Larry repeated. "You used to be the sweetest thing."

Tina shrugged. She felt wonderful about being able to look Larry in the eye. "I guess I'm not a sweet thing anymore, Larry."

"You're getting to be a pushy broad."

"Thank you. I take that as a compliment."

"Wipe that smirk off your face." Despite his words, Larry was smiling again. "You're good; you don't have to get a swelled head about it."

Tina had a fair idea what that practiced smile was about. Larry was afraid his most valuable employee might just walk out the door. She wasn't ready to do that—yet. "Accept it, Larry. I'm not a yes-man anymore."

"I've noticed that." Larry looked as if he didn't quite know what to do with what Tina had turned into. "It's going to get you in trouble one of these days. No matter what they say about this women's lib business, you don't have all the answers."

"I'm the first to admit that, Larry," Tina said as she reached for the door. "But at least I'm looking for some answers now."

Tina felt good; she continued to feel good about herself for the rest of the day. Talking to Larry had made her even more aware of the changing relationship between herself and the rest of Boat World's staff. In the past, none of the salesmen or service department people had consulted her on any aspects of the business. Although she'd had opinions, she'd kept them to herself. That was no longer true. She was speaking up, and to her delight, the men she was surrounded by were listening.

I *am* turning into a pushy broad, Tina admitted as she shoved aside her workout bag and got into her car. The thought went no further.

Two football players were spotting Joe when Tina walked into the gym. She was surprised to see Al there as well. Because she didn't believe in distracting people during their workouts, she simply waved at him. Al stopped her before she could enter the women's dressing room.

"How's it going?" he asked. "Are you still working for that boat place?"

Surprised that Ginger hadn't kept Al up-to-date, Tina gave Al a brief description of her sense of limbo where work was concerned. "What about you? You haven't changed jobs, have you?"

"Not likely. I'm too old to start over. Tina?" Al looked around before going on in a whisper. "I want to apologize for Ginger."

"Apologize? What for?"

"For sticking her nose where it doesn't belong. It wasn't any of her business to dig into police records."

Any thoughts Tina had had about her workout went out the window. "I'm the one who should be apologizing," she hurried on. "I didn't mean to cause any problems between you and Ginger."

Although before, Al had had the look of an enthusiastic boy, this afternoon he was an old man. "Problems were bound to arise. I don't want to say anything negative about your friend. Lord knows, there are times when she makes me feel pretty terrific. But Ginger's like a bulldog. She says what she wants, when she wants, and damn the consequences."

"I know that, Al," she reassured the doctor. "But anything Ginger did, she did for me."

"Then I'm the one at fault." Al looked so downcast that it was all Tina could do to keep from wrapping her arms around him. "I thought you knew about Joe's past."

"I should have said something, but—" Tina looked around. There was no way out of what had to be said. "I didn't want to admit Joe hadn't been honest with me."

"It hasn't caused a problem between you and Joe? You're still seeing each other?"

Tina answered the easy question. She explained that she and Joe were spending every possible moment together. She didn't tell the doctor that Joe's past remained a taboo subject and that she hated herself for being afraid to bring it up. Al had enough on his mind; if the man was as smitten as Tina believed he was, he had to be miserable about the fight with Ginger. As Al went back to his workout, Tina made a vow to get in touch with Ginger. Despite their differences, Tina sensed the love Ginger and Al felt for each other. She would do anything she could to help keep that love strong.

But first she wanted to let Joe know she was here. "You're going to have to hire a bus to get everyone there," she pointed out when Joe confirmed that the Muscle Mill would be represented by eleven competitors in San Jose. "You really want that team trophy, don't you?"

"It wouldn't break my heart," Joe admitted. "The publicity would be good for the gym."

"It could also backfire on you," she pointed out. "You're bursting at the seams as it is. A little more advertising and you're going to have to build that place you've been talking about."

Joe touched her lightly on the nose. "Are you applying for the job?"

"Maybe." Tina was looking up at him. Even in the middle of a crowded gym, she had him all to herself. "I just about got myself fired today. I might need the work."

Joe looked concerned. "What happened?"

"I shot my mouth off. I told my boss I was right and he was wrong."

"Why didn't he fire you?"

"Because I'm making him too much money. I don't know, Joe." Tina sighed. Trying to come to a decision about her job was exhausting her. "Maybe it's burnout. I'm so tired of talking about boats. They aren't that important."

Joe wound his arm around Tina's waist and pulled her tantalizingly close. "What is important to you?"

You. "Seeing if I can do it," Tina said without thinking.

"Seeing if you can do what?"

"Compete." The word had a life of its own. How long had she been thinking about that?

"In San Jose?" Joe pushed her away so he could look at her. "Tina, you aren't training for power lifting. The program I have you on isn't that intense."

"I know that. I just want to give it a shot. So I make a fool of myself." She shrugged. The gesture might be casual, but that wasn't how she felt. "At least I can say I've done it."

"You're serious, aren't you?" Joe's lips were inches away, making thinking next to impossible.

"Joe, I need some kind of goal. Work just isn't doing it for me anymore."

Joe was slowly shaking his head. "I think I've created a monster. Your boss isn't going to know what to do with you and you know your mother will come unglued."

"Larry doesn't know what to do with me now," Tina admitted. "And my poor mother—she says she doesn't recognize me. But—I need to set some new goals for myself. That's why I want to compete."

"All right." Joe paused. "Let me finish up here and then we'll see where you are." He kissed her deeply, openly, before leaving her.

Tina divided her attention between her workout and talking to Al. She was relieved to find that his usual enthusiasm was returning. Although he didn't mention Ginger again, he wasn't above teasing Tina about what he'd seen earlier. "Fraternizing with the boss, are you? I hope you realize you've given everyone more than enough to talk about."

Tina refused to let Al embarrass her. "If I recall, you've been encouraging this."

"True," Al relented. "It looks as if everything's going well. No problems."

Tina wished that was true. In the best of all worlds, she and Joe would have discovered each other with nothing from the past infringing on the present. But reality was another story. "No more than anyone else," Tina explained.

"Maybe." Al didn't sound convinced. "Tina, I know what those charges did to Joe. You're not going to come away unscathed, either."

Al was right. But this afternoon she didn't want anything to get in the way of her decision to compete. Most of the gym members, including Al, had left by the time Joe was ready to work with her. As he explained, he wanted to determine where she ranked in the three lifts that constituted power-lifting events. For the squat, bench press and dead lift, Joe had her start with weights she could handle and gradually work up until she was near her limit.

"Not bad, for a wimp," Joe observed when Tina declared that she couldn't lift another ounce. "You're not going to set the world on fire, but that's not bad, considering your low body weight."

Tina had to laugh at that. For the first time in her life, being slim was a disadvantage. "What do you think?" she gasped. "First place?"

"If there's no one else in your weight group," Joe pointed out with a dose of reality. "I have to know if you're serious about this, Tina. We've only got three more weeks. I want you peaking at the right time."

"I'm sure." Although she was trembling a little from the exertion, Tina was delighted with her results. She had no idea there was that much strength hidden in her muscles. "Joe! I can squat more than I weigh!"

Joe was grinning with her. "Like I said, not bad for a wimp."

After that there was no stopping Tina. She increased her time in the gym to two hours a day and modified her diet to make sure she took in enough vitamins and minerals. She even told her mother that becoming fit was no longer enough. She needed more.

"You can't be serious," Alice Morton exclaimed when Tina dropped by on her way to work the next morning. "Tina, you're going to hurt yourself. What's Larry going to say?"

Tina didn't bother trying to explain that Larry's opinion meant next to nothing. "I won't get hurt, Mom," she tried to reassure her. "I know what I'm doing. I'd better, after all the time I've been logging at the gym."

"I don't want to hear about it. I don't know what's happening to you these days."

"What's happening," Tina said, taking her mother's hands, "is that I feel better about myself than I ever have. Be proud for me, Mom. Please."

When her mother tried to change the subject, Tina knew she hadn't said enough. "What are you doing this afternoon?" she pressed.

"I was going to lend a hand at the art center. There's going to be a new display. It's—"

"That can wait. Please, Mom?" Tina waited until her mother was looking at her. "I want you to go with me this afternoon. I'd like you to understand what I'm doing."

Although Alice Morton wanted nothing to do with watching her daughter work out in a room full of sweaty men, in the end mother love won out and she reluctantly told Tina she'd accompany her. But she also said she wouldn't like what she saw and she wasn't sure she could keep her opinions to herself.

Tina was satisfied with that. She almost laughed at the feminine and inappropriate outfit her mother was wearing when she came to pick her up, but said nothing. It was important that the two women enter the Muscle Mill with as little tension between them as possible. Tina seated her mother on a stack of rubber mats and started her workout. Because she'd warned Joe earlier what she was doing, mother and daughter were left alone except when Tina needed a spotter. She deliberately chose weights she could handle, wanting to show her mother that she was capable of what she was doing.

"Yes, my muscles get sore," Tina admitted in response to her mother's hesitant question. "But they should with any type of workout."

"But if it hurts, why do you do it?"

"Because— It's hard to put into words. I just know I like myself a lot more when I'm meeting a challenge."

Alice Morton said little during the hour-long workout, but to her credit, she watched everything Tina did and the questions she asked were pointed and intelligent. She winced several times when one or another of the men swore, and when Tina was taking her back home, Alice asked if the rough language bothered Tina.

"I don't think about it anymore. It seems natural. Thank you for coming. Do you understand what I'm doing any better?"

"I'm not sure." Alice rolled down her window. "You need a haircut."

"I didn't ask you about my hair, Mom."

"I know you didn't. Oh, honey—" the words came out in a sigh "—it's just all so strange to me. Your being in a place like that, with a man like Joe Rustin, is the last thing I expected. You have to give me more time."

"I will, Mom," Tina promised. "I just need you to understand that this isn't a whim with me. It's something I want to do, maybe for the rest of my life."

"Oh?" Alice cupped her hand over her hair, a buffer against the breeze. "You aren't my little girl anymore, are you?"

"No, Mom. I'm not."

"I don't know if she really understands," Tina told Ginger the next day. She'd deliberately popped in at the district attorney's office at noon and was now treating Ginger to lunch. "I have to give her credit. At least she didn't run out of the place." Tina watched Ginger pick at her deli sandwich. So Al wasn't the only one who was hurting. "I saw Al the other day."

"Oh."

"He's as miserable as you are."

"Oh," Ginger repeated. She gave up all pretense of being interested in her meal. "What did he say? I've tried to get him to talk about how he feels, but he won't say anything. All I know is—he thinks I have a big mouth."

"You do shoot from the hip."

"I can't help it," Ginger moaned. "You know how it is. I spend my life dealing with cops and lowlifes. I haven't heard drawing-room conversation for so long I wouldn't recognize it. Al's used to nurses who say 'Yes, sir' and walk ten paces behind him."

Tina tried not to laugh, but didn't quite pull it off. "I don't believe that. Al isn't hung up over his title. He just wants— Well, you do sound like a dock worker sometimes."

"I know I do." Ginger shoved her plate aside and leaned on her elbows. "I've been trying to change, I really have. At least I'm cutting down on the profanity. But that isn't the only problem."

"I know." Tina no longer felt like laughing. "Al and I talked—about Joe. I know how Al feels about what you did. I told him that if he was going to blame anyone, it should be me."

"What did Al say to that?"

"That he holds himself responsible. Didn't he tell you that?"

"He hasn't told me anything." Ginger dropped her head. "I haven't been returning his phone messages. The last time we talked— Well, you know me. I said things I shouldn't have. I don't know what to say to him."

Tina impulsively covered Ginger's hand with her own. "No wonder you look like you've lost your best friend. Will you listen to me for once? He's calling, isn't he?" When Ginger nodded, Tina went on. "I'd take that as proof that he hasn't given up on you. He obviously sees something in you that fascinates him. Go for it, kid. Give the two of you a chance."

"But—we fight."

"So, you fight. As long as you're also listening to each other, that's what matters."

"Maybe." Ginger still sounded doubtful, but the life had come back into her eyes. "Speaking of men, what about you and Joe? Have you told him what you know?"

Ginger and she had known each other too long for Tina to lie to her. "I don't know how to bring it up," Tina admitted. "I love being with him. I don't want anything to spoil that."

"It really is good between you?" Ginger pressed. "There isn't anything about him that makes you—nervous?"

"Am I afraid of him? That's what you're asking, isn't it? He's—" She faltered and then began again. "He's almost too considerate. It's like—he's afraid to let go."

"Tina."

"I know," Tina moaned. "There's something not...right about that, isn't there?" She'd kept that inside her for so long. Despite the difficulty in saying the words, Tina was indebted to Ginger for making her say them. "I think I understand," she went on, emotions forming the words. "He's so big, so strong. He doesn't want to hurt me."

"Because maybe he hurt a woman before?"

"Don't!" Tina lifted her hand as if to ward off a blow but then let it drop. Her closest friend had every right to throw that punch. "I don't know."

"You're going to have to ask him that someday."

"I know." Tina recoiled from the image that sprang to life. "Someday."

* * *

On a Friday early in August, Joe and Tina boarded a plane and flew out to California. Tony Dunn, a super heavyweight at 275 pounds, met them at the San Francisco airport. Tina was aware of the eyes that followed them as she walked to the baggage area flanked by two unbelievably large men.

Tony lived in an older house near the heart of San Jose with his wife and infant daughter. As soon as Rita Dunn showed Joe and Tina the room where they'd be staying, the four adults sat down to dinner. Halfway through, the baby woke up and Tony finished dinner with his daughter cradled in his arm.

"You're getting domestic, Tony," Joe teased. "Please don't tell me you change diapers."

"I change diapers," Tony answered easily. A massive man holding in his hand a thirteen-pound infant, he stared down at his daughter. "You ought to try this. Fatherhood is the greatest high there is. It's better than breaking the world record."

As she washed dishes so Rita could tend to the baby, Tina thought about what Tony had said. She'd always wanted children of her own, but had never found the man she wanted to father them. Now she was remembering the softening in Joe's eyes when the little girl curled her fingers around his thumb.

"He's really pumped for this contest," Tony observed when he came into the kitchen to pour iced tea for everyone. "Joe kind of lost his intensity there for a while. It's amazing what a good woman will do for a man."

Tina wasn't sure she could call herself a good woman. She was taking her relationship with Joe one day at a time. Because tomorrow's meet was on her mind, Tina didn't sleep well that night. She tried to remain quiet for Joe's sake, but when she heard his sigh long after they'd gone to bed, she turned toward him and molded her body against his. "Talk to me," she whispered. "Tell me some jokes."

"I don't know any jokes tonight. As many times as I've competed, you'd think I'd be used to this. But I'm not. I'm so pumped." Slowly Joe worked his hand through Tina's hair and began massaging her scalp.

"I wish I could help."

Joe ran his fingers lower until he found the small gold earring Tina was wearing. "You're helping more than you know," he whispered. "This is the first time I've had someone to talk to the night before."

"It is, is it?" Tina teased. "Don't tell me you believe in that old folktale about abstaining before competing."

"I've never been in a position of having to test that particular theory. And unfortunately, I'm not going to be able to tonight, either. It sounds as if the youngest member of the family is getting ready for a night feeding."

Tina and Joe lay in each other's arms listening to Rita as she changed the baby and then started nursing in the living room. Joe's hand was over Tina's breast. "Nursing's a great idea," he whispered. "Milk always the right temperature. Always on hand."

"And the father doesn't have to do a darn thing," Tina pointed out. "Tony's probably snoring."

"I doubt it. His mind's probably doing the same thing mine is." Joe moved his hand in lazy circles over Tina's breast. "I'm glad you're here. You're going to do fine tomorrow."

"I know I am." Tina placed her hand over Joe's. "I have a great coach."

Although she didn't do much sleeping the rest of the night, Tina got up feeling rested. No one ate before leaving for the high school where the meet was being held. The only sound in Tony's car was that of the baby blowing bubbles.

Because of the time she'd logged at the Muscle Mill, Tina thought she would be prepared for what she'd see, but nothing could have prepared her for a gymnasium filled with many of the country's largest men. The wooden stands were taken up with spectators and gym bags and more food than Tina thought anyone could eat. Tina felt engulfed. Her mother had always told her that her diminutive size was what would get her noticed in life. Now she wanted to jump on a box and flex her muscles, somehow prove that she had a right to be here.

Tina was surprised at the number of women in attendance. And she'd expected most of the female power lifters to be rather masculine in appearance, but she was mistaken; the women carried their bodies with cool assurance, yet for the most part they were feminine looking.

Tina found a place at one end of the stands to leave their belongings and then followed the other women into the weigh-in room. Since starting to work out, Tina had gained five pounds. And yet her stomach was flatter than it had ever been. She easily qualified as a lightweight.

The rest of the time until the meet got under way passed in a blur for Tina. Joe insisted that she eat an orange and some carrot slices and drink apple juice. Under Joe's guidance she went through a proper warm-up in the weight room that consisted of light stretching followed by lifts of no more than ninety percent of what she planned on opening with.

"I'm nervous," Tina breathed. She was sitting in her warm-up suit near the rear of the lifting platform. Joe stood behind her, his hands on her shoulders.

"Good. Look, the only thing you're here for is to get your feet wet. Worry about breaking records next time. You don't have a thing to prove to anyone but yourself."

Tina knew she'd never make it without Joe, and yet she was drawing into herself, forgetting everything, even her lover. She stared at the weights she would soon be lifting. She pictured herself squatting with the bar on her shoulders, lying on her back and lifting the weight over her head, pulling the bar off the ground until her knees were locked and back bowed backward.

She could do it. She wasn't going to set the weight-lifting world on its ears but she was going to meet the challenge she'd set for herself. The moments on the platform were for her alone. And—more than just a little—for Joe, too. "Talk to me," she whispered when her name was called. "Please talk to me."

"I love you, Tina. Don't forget that."

Two hours later Tina was finished. In that time she'd stepped onto the platform nine times, three for each event, covered her body with talcum powder, shrugged in and out of her lifting suit, let Joe strap her into the thick power-lifting belt, wrapped her knees with tight bandages and—greatest of all—seen the green light signaling a successful lift nine times.

After the final dead lift, Tina leaned against Joe, hot and sweaty and not caring that her thighs were covered with a fine dusting of white talcum.

"I did it!" She blinked back tears. His words had carried her through. "I had five more pounds in me. I knew it!"

"You're higher than a kite right now. It's going to be a while before you come back down to earth."

Joe was right. Although she was interested in what the other women and lighter-weight men were doing, it wasn't until midafternoon, when the "big boys" began to funnel into the weight room, that she was able to shake herself free of her own second-place finish.

The humidity in the gym had risen by perhaps fifty percent. There were more people in the stands than there'd been in the morning. A local TV station had sent over its camera crew and there were rumors that ESPN was due in shortly to film the top lifters.

When she saw that Joe was staring blankly, she scooted up behind him and started rubbing his neck. She dug in with strong fingers, trying to make an impression on the steel cords beneath his flesh. Joe rolled his head backward but gave no other indication that he was aware of her presence.

To their right was a massive black man and next to him the balding, lantern-jawed man Joe had said was going to give him a run for his money. The black man was lifting in the super heavyweight division, which relieved Tina's mind. She'd spent enough time watching the balding man to believe Joe could hold his own with him.

"I don't know," Joe said with an uncharacteristic lack of confidence. "He's surprised me more than once."

"Stop that," Tina admonished. "You're the best damn lifter here."

"Yeah? Who made you the expert?"

"No one had to make me the expert. I know you."

Joe bent his head backward, trying to look at her. "What do you know about me, Tina?"

Oh, no, you don't—not today. "I know I love you."

The sigh rumbling up from Joe's chest absorbed both of them. "I said the same thing to you earlier."

"I haven't forgotten." Tina ran her lips over Joe's hair, tasting him, taking his essence into her. "I'm glad I'm here." She spread her arms over his shoulders. "I wish we could stay like this forever. I wish we could be like this forever."

"So do I." Again Joe sighed. "Last night, today—I don't want it to end."

"Maybe it doesn't have to." Tina felt tears. Their conversation was simple, but beneath the words ran a deep current. What they were talking about had nothing to do with a power-lifting meet.

"Maybe we can stay here forever?"

"Forever's a long time." Tina wrapped her arms around Joe's neck. He felt strong and good against her breast. "I can't promise you that."

"I know. Thanks for being here. I need you."

Tina didn't look for anything to add. They'd both said things that were better left standing on their own. For a few more minutes she continued to sit behind Joe, rubbing his neck. When he rose to his feet and reached for his heavy bag, she felt lonely. "You'll be rooting for me, won't you?" he asked.

She pointed toward the camera she'd brought with her. "I'll be recording every popped vein. You can do it, Joe." She stole a glance at the balding man who was also getting to his feet. "I know you can."

Joe leaned forward so he could run his mouth across her lips. "You've changed my life in so many ways, Tina."

He was gone. Tina leaned forward, resting her elbows on her thighs as she watched Joe make his way down the stairs and enter the changing room. He didn't turn around to acknowledge her.

Tina pictured him stripping out of his sweats. He would shrug himself into the girdle-tight supersuit but leave the upper part bunched around his waist until he was ready to begin his lifts. He would check the ammonia capsules many lifters used to clear their nasal passages and give themselves a last-minute shot of adrenalin. Then, when the time was right, he would take his place in one of the chairs behind the lifting platform.

The man who reentered the gym wasn't someone she recognized. Joe turned to say something to his spotters; the rest of the time he was locked away with his thoughts.

When it came time for his first squat, Joe took a long time getting to his feet. By the time he'd stepped onto the platform, he'd changed. Gone was the introspective look. In its place was a glare bordering on anger. He slapped his hands heavily on the bar supported at shoulder height, bared his teeth and threw his head back for a whiff of ammonia.

Savagely, Joe rammed his shoulders under the bar and came up hard against the massive weight. Joe was hoping for an 815-pound squat and was opening 25 pounds under that. Tina remembered the camera, but she wasn't thinking about focusing.

She was lifting with Joe. As he became one with the bar and stepped back from the supports, his face turned red. Slowly he flexed his knees, bringing 790 pounds down with him. Behind him, a spotter had his hands on either side of Joe's waist. His eyes were focused on the ceiling, his mouth clenched tightly.

It didn't seem humanly possible to bring 790 pounds up from a position that low to the ground and yet Joe did it with an ease that drew applause from the crowd. Only after the three green lights from the judges flashed did Tina remember to breathe.

Twice more Tina fused her being with Joe while he squatted 805 pounds and finally 815. At the start of his final squat—which represented a personal best for him—Joe's "Yes!" became a superhuman scream.

There was a lengthy wait between the squat and the bench press. Tina thought Joe might spend it with her, but most of the time he stayed with the other competitors. In contrast with the way he mentally prepared himself for the squat, Joe stretched out on the bench without making a sound. Tina marveled at the massiveness of his shoulders and forearms, but the thought of lifting that sagging weight overhead sent sparks of alarm through her. She was grateful for the presence of the two men ready to grab the weights.

Nothing was going to go wrong. Lifting weights was Joe's life.

His back arched away from the bench; his forearms trembled; the veins popped out on his neck—and 680 pounds were thrust into the air.

Joe's second lift of 700 pounds seemed to go even easier, but Tina couldn't pretend she wasn't as pumped as she believed him to be. He was within five pounds of the world record. With his next lift he would be looking to break it.

Tina would have preferred to have nothing said, but as Joe's turn came up again, the announcer pointed out what Joe was going to try to accomplish. Joe seemed oblivious to the attention. Once again he slid under the bar and gripped it with hands so large that Tina couldn't make the connection with the gentle fingers that reached for her in the night.

Joe's legs were on either side of the bench, thighs gripping. He focused on the bar, talking to it, taking his time. In another world Tina might have laughed at his antics, but she'd come to understand words like *mastery* and *power*. Joe had set goals for himself in life; this was one of them.

"Explode, Joe. Explode." Her plea was lost in the encouragement coming from the other lifters.

For a moment, life hung suspended while Joe's elbows remained parallel with his shoulders. Then the slow, strong, upward thrust began. Tina pushed with Joe, feeling the tremendous pressure in her shoulders. Her finger stabbed at the shutter, recording the image of a man pushing his body to its limits.

He'd done it! The bar was slamming back down in its support; three green lights flashed in unison.

"That's the biggest bench press in power-lifting history," the announcer called out. "Way to go, Joe!"

Joe breathed deeply, once, and sat up. He was grinning as he turned toward Tina. She dropped the camera and jumped up on the platform. All she wanted was to feel those massive arms around her, but first she had a job to do. She grabbed the supersuit straps and yanked them down off his shoulders. "You're beautiful," she said from the shelter of his arms. There was more to his scent than sweat. He also smelled of ammonia and chalk. "Joe, you did it!"

"We did it. You handled that last five pounds."

It was almost eight in the evening before the open-class dead lifts began. Tina and Joe had shared sandwiches with Tony and Rita, and Tina had entertained the baby by holding her so she could watch the judges' lights. But now the easygoing banter was winding down again. Joe was in first place, but it was rumored that the balding man had exceeded nine hundred pounds in the gym.

Tina was concerned. A lot had been taken out of Joe already today. He had the added pressure of having attention on him because of his bench. He was pulling away from her, becoming distant again.

Tina was wise enough not to break his concentration. Although she needed reassurance that the man sitting beside her was someone she knew, that would have to come later. Joe was seeking affirmation of what he was as a man, looking inside himself and taking readings.

"They're different at a meet," Rita said after the two men left them. "Competing takes so much preparation. They have so few chances to prove themselves."

"Does Tony talk to you about that?" Tina asked.

Rita shrugged. "You know how it is with men. They don't articulate their emotions the way women do. I've known Joe long enough to know he broods during a meet."

Tina tried to keep her question casual. "How long have you known him?"

"Eight, no, nine years, I guess. He and Tony go back a long way. In fact—" Rita glanced at Tina "—before Tony and I got serious with each other, I dated Joe a few times."

Only a few times? Tina couldn't imagine life without Joe as its center. "I haven't known him very long," she admitted. "I'm still trying to figure out what makes him tick."

Rita snorted. "If you get that figured out, you're one up on the rest of us. Does he— Well, does he talk about himself very much?"

She knows. "I haven't found that to be a problem," Tina lied. Her seat had suddenly become uncomfortable. "I'm going to try to sneak in there for some more pictures."

Joe was already locked into his supersuit. The thick, heavy blue belt cinched around his waist cut into his rib cage. He stood straddle-legged on the platform, an invisible umbilical cord between him and the 850 pounds taunting him on the wooden riser. In his teeth he held an unpopped ammonia capsule. The balding man was going to lift at 855 pounds, but Joe hadn't adjusted his attempts upward. Although the open-class super heavyweights were still to come, Joe was the lifter drawing the most attention. Not only had he created a stir by his bench press, but if he kept up the current pace, he had the best-lifter title.

Joe easily made his first lift. Tina acknowledged the balding man's successful lift without feeling it had taken anything from Joe. Both men wrenched another twenty pounds to knee level and then Joe made his final goal known. He was going for the world record. Tina tried to swallow. Joe had been punishing his body for hours. Did he have enough left in him?

Tina dropped to one knee, camera ready. "Just wait until the nationals," another lifter told her. "He'll go elite. He'll blow them away." Tina stared up at Joe, aware as never before of his place among these mighty men. He wasn't just another lifter—he was a minute away from being *the* lifter.

Sweat broke out between Tina's shoulder blades, and her fingers on the camera trembled.

For a half second, Joe's eyes locked on Tina's. Then he let out a primal scream, stomped his feet on the echoing wooden surface and leaned forward to attack the bar. Up went the incredible burden. Joe's shoulders were thrown back; his back bowed agonizingly. He was standing on widely spread legs, his eyes locked on the overhead rafters. One second passed.

The weight slammed back to earth, the sound boring a hole through Tina's senses. This wasn't a simple, everyday man. In one day, he'd shattered two world records!

And Tina had given her heart to him.

Chapter Twelve

The night before was still playing its vivid picture in Tina's mind during the plane ride back to Texas. Although the balding competitor had made a valiant attempt to duplicate Joe's lift, he'd been unable to lock his knees in place. The two men were still shaking hands when photographers and reporters started in on Joe. He'd submitted to a couple of interviews while meet totals were being tallied. Then came the moment that was magic for Tina. In addition to his first-place trophy, Joe was bringing home the one for best lifter.

And yet, perfect as it was, there was an aspect about the experience that kept Tina's nerves on edge. Joe had gone up to accept his trophies, then he'd jumped on the platform and raised the three-foot-high symbols of his strength in the air and given out a victorious yell. Maybe he wasn't the biggest lifter at the meet, but he was the one who exuded the most power.

He was awesome. Potent. No other words came close to describing what he was.

"I've been thinking—" Joe broke a silence that had existed since the plane took off "—I've donated a lot of time to the college. Maybe I should suggest they hire me. Get on the payroll."

"You have the qualifications," Tina agreed. "I'd think the college would be delighted to have you."

"I won't be able to punch a time clock. They'd have to understand that." Joe leaned back in the seat that seemed ill equipped to carry his weight. "I'll take a few weeks off, and then I'm going to have to start training for the nationals. Hawaii." Joe turned toward Tina. For a moment his smile broke through the tight knot she carried inside her. "You want to go to Hawaii?"

Of course she did. But that meant watching Joe try to exceed what he'd accomplished yesterday. She wasn't ready for the metamorphosis that turned him from someone she loved and trusted into a potent machine. "They said you'd be lifting elite," she sidetracked. "What does that mean?"

"That's the highest class there is."

"Oh." Of course that was where Joe belonged. Tina tensed her muscles to still an unbidden trembling. She was drawn, mindlessly, to Joe's power; she was also terrified by it.

Now Joe was talking about changes he wanted to make at the gym. Because of the purchasing he'd been doing for the college, he'd seen some state-of-the-art machinery he wanted to incorporate into his business. But to accomplish what he had in mind meant moving the gym to larger quarters. "It's a lot to think about," he mused. "I've got so much on my mind these days." He reached out and took Tina's hand without looking at her. "Mostly you."

"Do you think you can get out of your lease?" Tina asked.

Joe answered her question. Before he'd finished, his restless movements began again. Tina understood. She too had been in tune with her own strength yesterday; she hated having to restrain that energy.

At last their plane touched down. Although she could have waited until she got home, Tina wanted to call her parents. "Second place," she told her father enthusiastically. "I was so proud of myself. Is Mom there?" A minute later, Tina was repeating her message. "Next time you have to go with me, Mom. I can hardly wait to get the pictures developed. There's so much I want to tell you."

"Are you sure you haven't hurt yourself?" Alice asked.

"I'm a little sore. But it's okay. I think I'm addicted. I know I can do better next time."

Alice said little in response to that. Although Tina wanted nothing more than to have her mother share her enthusiasm, she knew better than to push the issue. When and if her mother understood, it would have to be at her own pace. "I'll see you tomorrow," she promised before hanging up.

"How did she take it?" Joe asked.

"I don't know. I think she's still in shock." Tina leaned against the closest wall. "I don't know why this is so important to me. I mean, I shouldn't expect my mother to change overnight, to understand why I'm doing this. I just wish— Let's get out of here."

They collected their baggage and went outside to retrieve Joe's truck. When Joe started toward her apartment, Tina drew within herself. The natural, right conclusion to the weekend would be for Joe to spend the night.

And Tina was afraid. She wanted to feel his body next to hers and yet her mind scrambled for ways to postpone the moment. There was too much to Joe to be confined in her bedroom. Instead of sapping him, the contest had left him hungry for an outlet for his energy. He would be expecting her to absorb some of that energy.

"Maybe I won't go to work tomorrow," Tina said, once they were in her apartment. "Maybe I'll go job hunting."

"You make good money," Joe pointed out. He dropped their gym bags in the middle of the living room. "That'll be hard to duplicate." Joe joined her by the patio door but didn't touch her until she'd pulled back the curtain to let in what was left of the day. "You'll make the right decision," he said into her ear. "I have confidence in you."

Tina responded to Joe's unspoken message. She shut herself away from the memory of the man she'd seen lifting over nine hundred pounds off the ground and surrendered to the message her body couldn't ignore. They'd been together for the past three days and yet they hadn't made love. Tina could have stalled—part of her needed that—but she didn't. There were things she had to learn about Joe; only one act would answer those questions.

"I know you do." She reached up to wrap her arms around his neck and stood on her toes to kiss him. "Welcome home, Joe."

"Welcome home, yourself." He wrapped his arms around her waist and held her close, supporting her body so her calves no longer felt the strain of standing on her toes. "I wish we had the rest of our lives to be like this."

The rest of her life with one man was something Tina now realized she'd never seriously considered before. She wasn't going to test the boundaries by asking for more than he'd just given her. No matter what the answers might be, Tina wanted Joe to make love to her. She had to know once and for all what was locked within that magnificent body.

"We have tonight," she said.

"That isn't enough. I want to make love to you until there's nothing left of either of us."

Tina's arms went weak at that, but she didn't think Joe noticed. He lifted her into his arms and took her without asking into the bedroom. A faint rose hue from the setting sun swept away reality. Her room was a place where dreams could be brought to fruition, where the everyday world couldn't intrude. It was where a man and woman could cast off their shells and expose their inner cores.

Joe pulled the knit shirt over his head. Tina's eyes and more were locked on his chest. She'd been right. There was too much of him for containment within her walls.

He was looking at her, his eyes a thousand years old. "Don't you want me?" he asked.

"What?" He was calling attention to the fact that she was standing spread-legged with her arms at her sides. "Yes, I want you." She was breathing through her nostrils and having trouble pulling in enough air. Surely he could see that.

"I wasn't sure." Joe came nearer. "I want you so much, Tina. I've never wanted anyone like this before." His fingers found the buttons on her blouse.

Tina brushed away Joe's hands and finished the job he'd begun. She didn't turn away as she unfastened her bra and unzipped her skirt. Slowly she slid the garment down her hips. Her fingers lingered at the scrap of fabric left clinging to her body, teasing Joe, teasing herself as well.

Even naked, Tina was aware of her power over Joe. The balance of power could shift at any moment; she wanted to remember the hungry look in his eyes.

Joe came toward her and covered her breasts with his hands. "I'm going to make you mine, Tina."

"No one belongs to someone else," she tried. Already she was losing ground.

"In my mind you do." He ran his hands around the outsides of her breasts and then under them, pressing until the points were thrust toward him. "Fantasy has a place in the bedroom, Tina."

He was right, of course. And yet she was alarmed by his choice of words. "I don't give fantasy much thought," she explained almost desperately. Her breasts were firmly within his grip; he was stripping her of her separateness. When he dipped his head to take a nipple between his lips, Tina moaned, knowing that just his touch could take her places she'd never been before.

"Make it good, Joe," she begged him. "Make it good for both of us."

"I will." He gripped her around the waist, lifted her off her feet, stretched her out on the bed. She laughed in nervous anticipation as he yanked at his shoelaces.

He was beside her; he was on his hands and knees looming over her, swallowing her with his size. Tina touched his arms and held on eagerly. They had until tomorrow to explore each other. That was barely enough time for what Tina needed.

Joe was right. The bedroom was the place for fantasy.

Joe was trying to get her to slide on top of him. But Tina wouldn't allow him to do that again. "I want to feel you on top of me," she whispered shamelessly. "I want to be consumed by you."

"Tina—"

"No." She stopped him. "This time it has to be my way."

He was still resisting. "You don't understand."

"I don't understand because you won't tell me." Tina gripped Joe's hips. Her thumbs were kneading his belly, transmitting her need. "I trust you. That's what matters."

"Don't." Joe twisted away but not so far that she lost contact with him. "You don't know what you're doing to me."

The balance of power was back with her again. Joe could master steel, but she could master him. "I'm asking you to trust me, Joe," she whispered, her words coming from her heart. "Please don't hold anything back. I—need all of you."

Joe groaned. Tina sensed the terrible battle going on inside him, but she was too far gone to comprehend what she was asking. There'd always been a part of himself that Joe had kept from her, and she couldn't stand it to be like that any longer. "Sometimes I want you so much that it frightens me," he told her.

Joe's words were lost on her. There was only one thing that mattered, one thing she wanted. Using her body to say the words she was too shy to utter, Tina positioned herself so that Joe could lift himself over her. His elbows and knees bore his weight.

He was everywhere. His breath became hers. She was being swallowed by him. When he entered her, he filled her more than she'd dare to dream.

This time Tina sensed no holding back. The man who'd treated her with such tenderness now assumed her to be an equal partner in their lovemaking. Despite the very real differences in size, he was pushing her against the bed again and again, catapulting her with him. She was being absorbed into him, surrendering her strength to the greater one. There was no stopping now. No mind left to find refuge in. Tina Morton ceased to exist.

At times during the night Tina dozed off, but after a few minutes of peace she would come swimming back. Each time, Joe was ready. He took her without speaking, without asking. No matter where she turned in the bed he was there. Her body was his private playground and his was hers.

At last exhaustion claimed them. They'd been on fire beyond what either of them could bear.

When, at the end of that incredible night, Joe slipped out of bed, Tina was afraid to look at him. If his eyes found hers, he might know exactly how much she'd given him. She turned away and wrapped the blankets tightly around her.

Joe stayed in the shower until he ran out of hot water, but even the cold spray driving against his body couldn't wash away his thoughts. Damn! Last night shouldn't have happened! It felt right—the most perfect thing Joe had ever done in his life—but that didn't make it so. Hadn't he learned anything in two years? Given who and what he was, he had no right abandoning himself to lovemaking with a woman, especially with the only woman who'd truly ever mattered.

She was too precious, too easily gone. Had she really wanted him last night, or had she, instead, let him have his way? Damn! If only he dared ask for the truth.

But he didn't. And until he did, there was only one thing Joe could do this morning.

"I have to go, darling." Joe sat on the side of the bed, overwhelmed by the tender emotions that, like heated waves, washed over him. He didn't think he would ever stop loving her—but maybe they weren't good for each other. He wrapped both her and the blankets in his arms and pulled her close to his freshly showered body. "I'll call you later," he forced himself to say.

Tina lay limp in his arms, acknowledging that her day would be defined by that phone call. "I love you, Joe," she whispered.

"Don't say that, Tina. Not this morning." He gripped her tightly. Why, out of all the things she could have said, had she chosen those words? "You don't know what you're getting into."

"What's wrong? You've never acted like this before, Joe." She had to be honest. "You're frightening me."

Joe released her almost violently and surged to his feet. "I didn't mean to lose control last night. I swore it would never happen."

They were getting too close to the forbidden. Still, Tina couldn't run away. "It wasn't just you. We both lost control."

Joe shook his head. "I don't think we should see each other again today," Joe said abruptly, before leaving the room.

It took the sound of the door closing behind him to make Tina face her own day and the holes he'd bored through it. Still, Joe was right. They needed distance. Somehow she had to pull herself back together. Find what was left of herself.

Tina chased away a few of the cobwebs under the shower, regained a little strength with breakfast, and finally found something to focus on by driving to Boat World.

She stood outside the recently expanded glass-walled building with its inventory of boats, thinking about the months and years of herself she'd invested in the business. When she'd been a young woman looking for a way to earn a living, Larry Pardee had seemed like the perfect boss.

At the beginning it hadn't mattered that her looks had gotten her the job. Hadn't her mother groomed her for that kind of role? But now, the old order no longer held. The thought of spending the rest of her working life deferring to Larry's ego made her ill. A sweet smile and silent resentment would drive her crazy. The job didn't matter, and she intended to tell Larry just that.

"You've been looking for a business manager for the better part of a year now," Tina was telling her boss ten minutes later. "I wrote enough letters and did enough research while I was laid up to know you want to open a new place in Fort Worth. You're going to be putting all your energies into that venture. Someone's going to have to keep Boat World going." Tina took a breath to help calm herself but discovered she didn't need it. Not enough hinged on what Larry's answer would be. "I can be that person."

"You?" Larry looked as if Tina had just informed him that she'd taken up skydiving. "I need someone who can play hardball."

"I can play hardball. I'm a tough old broad, remember?"

Tina froze as Larry patted her on the knee. "One thing you'll never be is a tough old broad. Tina, you're a beautiful young woman. The customers love that."

Tina didn't want to be just a beautiful young woman anymore. "It doesn't take brains to be what you say I am," she protested. "If that's all I was, I wouldn't have the sales record I do. I know I can manage the business here."

"Tina, no one's going to take you seriously." Larry leaned back in his chair, hands folded behind his head. "The competition's fierce. They'll tear you apart."

"No, they won't." Tina didn't know why she was arguing. She and Larry were worlds apart. "I've never tried to cut anyone's throat. I'm honest. I know what I'm talking about. That's what it takes to succeed in this business."

"What's gotten into you?" Larry sounded as if he was running out of arguments. "Why would you want that kind of pressure?"

"Pressure gives me some goals to shoot at. Larry—" She swallowed down a quiet desperation. "I don't want to spend the rest of my life extolling the joys of boat ownership."

"You do it better than anyone else here." Larry smiled indulgently. "You're a people person. The customers sense that."

Wind up the little robot and watch her perform, Tina thought. Slowly, feeling the strength she no longer needed to keep under wraps, Tina got to her feet. "I want the manager's job. I can do it—we both know that."

"Maybe," Larry conceded. "But you have to look at it from my point of view. What is the competition going to think if I leave Boat World in the hands of a woman who couldn't punch her way out of a paper bag?''

Tina was amazed at Larry's ego. "Give me that paper bag. I'll prove you wrong," Tina said, although that wasn't the point at all. "You're afraid of what this would do for your image, aren't you? It doesn't matter that you know I can do the job," Tina said, starting for the door.

"Wait a minute." Larry stopped her. "You aren't thinking about slapping me with a discrimination suit, are you?"

"I'd win and we both know it. But, no. I'm not going to do that. Do you know why?" she challenged. "Because I don't care enough."

It took the better part of an hour for the reaction to set in. Tina had done everything but saw herself off a limb. The next step was hers. Either she would come crawling back to Larry or go looking for another job.

But that decision would have to wait until later. Now Tina was sitting on her still-unmade bed. She closed her eyes and slowly rocked back and forth. She'd refused to accept thoughts of Joe since walking out of the house, but he was waiting for her here. Joe had absorbed her last night. He hadn't forced her—they'd made love because Tina's needs had matched his; yet she didn't recognize the woman she'd been last night.

Just as she didn't recognize the man Joe had turned into this morning.

Tina flopped back on the bed feeling the tangled covers under her. She should call Ginger. No, she couldn't—Ginger would ask about Joe and wouldn't rest until she'd heard everything.

Tina pulled herself upright. The walls were closing in around her. She knew it was recommended that a lifter not work out for several days after a meet, but nothing else could handle her energy.

Besides—Joe would be at the gym. She could tell him about the meeting with her boss. That could be her excuse for seeing him when he'd asked her not to.

Tina had repacked her workout bag with a clean outfit and was looking for her keys when the doorbell rang. The teenage girl holding out two dozen colorful balloons grinned. "This is the most balloons I've ever delivered at one place."

After thanking the girl, Tina jockeyed the balloons inside. She tied the strings to a table leg before opening the small envelope the girl had given her along with the balloons. "Congratulations for accomplishing something that's totally yours. For forging new trails." The message was in her mother's handwriting.

Mom! Tina sank into a chair and let her tears fall. She did understand. Alice Morton was acknowledging her daughter as a person separate from herself.

Five minutes later Tina left the house. Her workout bag banged against her shoulders as she took the stairs two at a time. She felt like singing and like crying some more, too. Joe and how she would earn a living were still unknowns, but today she was filled with joy. She had accomplished something wonderful and her mother loved her for it.

Tina had tried to call her mother, but had to be content with leaving a message on her answering machine. "Thanks," she'd said. "Your note meant more to me than any trophy. The wonderful thing is, I think you know that. I love you, Mom."

Joe wasn't at the gym, but Al was. She asked the doctor when Joe was expected back.

"Not until late, I'm afraid. He said something about being tied up at the college today. Said I was in charge." Al wiped his hot forehead. "You're not supposed to be here, young lady. Let your muscles rest."

"You're not my doctor anymore," Tina reminded him. "I wanted to tell Ginger how I did. Do you know when she might be home?"

"As a matter of fact, I do." Al winked. "You'll never get a trophy for subtlety. Just so you don't have to ask, Ginger has moved her things into my place."

"She has?"

"It makes sense. I have a much larger house. Besides, I had the roof reshingled last year. It isn't going to leak."

"I don't care about your blamed leaky roof," Tina broke in. Had she really been so wrapped up in Joe and getting ready to compete that she'd lost touch with her friend? Ginger and she had talked several times since Tina took her out to lunch, but Ginger had been taking one day at a time, not saying much about whether she and Al were managing to blend their different personalities. "You two are, you know, okay?"

"We're okay," Al reassured her. "Ginger still swears and I still mince my words, but we're working on a compromise. You know how it is. All we can do is live one day at a time. And life is too short to spend it sweating the small stuff."

Was that what she was doing, "sweating the small stuff"? Maybe she needed to put her reaction to Joe's strength behind her, ask him to explain his behavior this morning, and go on with life. Maybe it was that simple. "I'm not going to apologize for being part of any arguments the two of you may have had," Tina emphasized. "At least it looks as if I had a hand in clearing the air."

"You did. If there's one thing I've learned since meeting Ginger, it's that there's no one right or wrong. What am I telling you for?" Al laughed. "You and Joe make a hell of an unlikely pair and yet you've obviously worked out your differences."

No, we haven't, Tina admitted after Al returned to his workout. It didn't seem as if they'd worked out anything. Although Tina didn't try to duplicate her performance in San Jose, her workout lasted the better part of three hours and left her physically exhausted, but still in high gear emotionally. When Al received an emergency call she agreed to man the office. A woman came in to sign up her teenage son; before Tina was done with them, the woman had paid for a six-month membership for herself as well.

The after-work crowd kept Tina stimulated. She teased and boasted and entered one of the never-ending arguments about power lifting versus bodybuilding. Al dropped by again with a lukewarm hamburger as a bribe to get her to stay on until Joe returned. "My roommate's been trying to track me down. Something about an experiment that takes my expertise."

"I'll get you for this," Tina warned. She took a tentative bite of her dinner. "I don't know why Joe asked you to cover for him. He should know how undependable doctors are."

"I don't think Joe had his mind on business today," Al informed her before taking off.

By nine Tina had the gym to herself. She'd tried to reach Joe at the college but no one knew how to get a message to him. She wondered if, like her, he was trying to keep himself so busy there'd be no time to think.

She was getting ready to close up when she heard a pickup pull into the parking lot. Heavy footsteps on cement told her what she needed to know; Joe was here.

"Tina?" Joe wasn't ready for this. The day, despite everything he'd accomplished, had been hollow. And now the person who'd made it that way was standing there, forcing him to confront his emotions. "Where's Al?" he asked tentatively.

Tina stood waiting in the middle of the weight room. She was holding on to an overhead lateral pull-down machine, her arms stretched high in the air. Joe filled the doorway, outlined in the darkened room by the light behind him. "Tina?" he repeated.

"Al had an emergency call." He was magnificent. She understood why she'd lost herself in him last night.

"How long have you been here?" He still hadn't moved away from the doorway.

"Most of the day. I've been waiting for you—we need to talk." Words were coming out of her mouth, but Tina wasn't aware of having planted the seeds.

Joe finally stepped into the room. He straddled his new power bench and leaned against the weighted parallel bar. "About last night?"

Yes. About last night. "I don't think I have a job anymore." Tina couldn't look at him because wanting him was taking her too far from what needed to be said.

"Were you— You weren't fired, were you?"

"I quit." Tina rolled the word around in her mind. "Yeah, I quit. I told Larry I could manage the store. He disagreed."

"What are you going to do now?"

Tina's groan was genuine, but still the reality of being unemployed had yet to sink in. "Find another job. Tomorrow." Tina released the lat grips and came within inches of Joe. She could barely see him in the dark, silent room but that didn't matter. Her body knew what he was like. "Al and Ginger are living together. They'd had a fight—about you and me. But they were able to work through it."

"I'm glad."

It was obvious to Tina he wasn't going to bring up the past. Maybe Joe believed it was a closed chapter, just as he'd closed himself off from last night. Maybe he was shocked by what they'd done. Maybe he regretted telling her he loved her. Maybe—a lot of things. She should respect his need for privacy and yet she couldn't.

Shannon and her accusations were walls Tina had to vault if she and Joe were to have any chance at a future. This awkwardness between them wasn't an aftermath of a night of wild lovemaking, although that, too, was part of it. Last night Joe had given her everything a woman could ask for, and in the morning he'd walked out on her. Joe was a complex man. She wasn't going to leave here tonight without learning how complex.

Tina reached out, resting her small hands on the mountains of Joe's shoulders. She wasn't afraid of him; she could never imagine being afraid of him. He had to know that. "I know about Shannon, Joe."

Silence. Wordlessness that had a life of its own. Tina felt tension radiate out from Joe and enter her body. "Say something," she challenged.

"How?"

"How did I find out? Al said something—he assumed I knew. Then I had Ginger do some digging for me. That's what Al and Ginger fought about."

"I'm— It's history, Tina." Joe tried to stand but Tina planted herself in front of him.

"I don't believe that! It remains part of what you are today." Tina closed her eyes and deepened her grip on his shoulders so she could go on talking. "I hate having you say that, Joe. I don't know what to do."

She knew. And yet—she was here. Promise and hope sparked to life inside Joe, pushing at the weight he'd been carrying for two years. Tina was tearing herself apart with her need for honesty. He had to break out of his prison, if they were to have a future. What did he mean, if? "How long have you known?"

"What does that matter?"

"Why didn't you say anything before?"

Tina's laugh echoed harshly throughout the room. "Why didn't you?"

She was right. This was his burden, not hers. "Because I wanted to let it die. It doesn't have anything to do with us."

Joe was so terribly wrong. "Why? Because I'm not important enough for the truth? Tell me something. Were you ever going to tell me or were you—" Tina stopped. The most dangerous move of her life was ahead of her. She had no choice but to take that step. "Did you think you'd never have to tell me you'd raped a woman?"

Joe was on his feet. He loomed over her, his form a massive silhouette. "I didn't rape Shannon."

Tina refused to breathe. If she did, it would come out as a sigh that Joe might interpret as relief when that wasn't it at all. "Then why didn't you say anything?"

"I didn't know you knew."

This wasn't getting them anywhere. "Think about it, Joe. At first you treated me as if I was a piece of fine china. You held yourself in check and didn't think I'd find anything strange about that? Last night, when you were everything I ever wanted, I felt you hated yourself afterward. Joe! I don't understand."

Joe sank back onto the bench. He was both exhausted and stronger than he'd ever felt in his life. He could, finally, with this woman, say the things that had been eating him up inside—and maybe break free. "The charges were dropped," he began tonelessly. "Shannon recanted her testimony. But—" Joe stopped. Even when he'd had to turn himself over to a lawyer, he hadn't been able to say this. But Tina wasn't an outsider. He loved her; she deserved total honesty. "There was some truth in what she'd said."

Tina placed a gentle hand on his arm.

He went on. "When she went to the police, they asked why she didn't have any marks on her. I guess they wanted some sign that there'd been a struggle. She said she didn't fight because she was afraid."

"You aren't telling me enough," Tina pleaded. "I don't understand what you're saying."

"I know." Joe didn't blink. He didn't breathe. "I haven't told anyone this."

"I'm here."

Joe planted his hands on his thighs and took the breath she'd given him. "Shannon and I were dating, but there was another man in her life. Someone named Mike. I tried to understand why she was seeing both of us, but it wasn't easy." He took another breath. "She'd call me when Mike was out of town. When I was too busy or away at a meet, she'd go to Mike. Once—I asked her to go to a contest with me. At the last minute she called to say she couldn't make it. I learned that Mike had made her a better offer."

"Why didn't you drop her?"

"I thought I loved her," Joe said while Tina fought the blows that came with his words. "Tina, I was just getting the gym off the ground. I didn't have much time for dating. I think I tried to make Shannon into the one stable thing in my life. But she didn't want the role."

"What happened?" Tina prompted, despite the effort this was costing her. "You had a fight?"

"No." Joe let the word out slowly. He was still looking at her, his eyes everything honesty needed to be. "I told her I wanted a commitment. Me or Mike. Not both of us. We argued and then she started crying. She said she was miserable without me. We—made up."

Tina fought against and lost to the image of what the making up must have been. "At least I thought we'd made up," Joe went on before she'd had too long to think. "I was at work when the police arrested me."

"Why?" she managed. "I mean, why were you arrested?"

"I know the answer to that, now. I didn't for a long time." To Tina's surprise, Joe laughed. "Shannon was playing both ends against the middle. She wanted to see which of us would give her the better offer. Mike won."

"What does this have to do with—" Tina didn't know how to go on.

"What does this have to do with my being arrested? Ask Mike. No. There's more to it than that." Joe sighed, making Tina wonder if the hardest part was yet ahead of them. "After the charges were dropped, I asked Shannon to see me one more time. I told her I deserved an explanation."

"What did she say?" Confronting her boss was nothing compared to what she was experiencing now and yet Tina felt no desire to back away. They were nearing the end of a long dark tunnel.

"Mike had asked her why she'd slept with me that last time. I don't know why she told him about us; I didn't ask her that." Joe shook his head. "If I can believe her, she told him she had no choice, that she gave in because she thought I was going to force myself on her. Maybe she thought it would work out better with him if he believed that."

"You're not capable of doing that, Joe." Joe hadn't touched her since coming into the gym, and that frightened Tina.

"Aren't I? I don't know." Under her hands Joe flexed his muscles. He was right. The prison he'd existed within for two years wasn't as solid as he'd believed. He was breaking out. Maybe Tina would be there once the last wall had crumbled and maybe she wouldn't, but the question that had driven him from her room this morning had to be answered. "Answer me something, Tina. If I wanted to have my way with you right now, could you stop me?"

That wasn't the point. "How much did Mike have to do with what happened to you?" Tina asked instead, and Joe let her change the subject.

"A lot, I guess. After she told him about—about our last night together, he told her to call the police and tell them that she'd been coerced into having sex with me. That's what Shannon told me the last time we talked. I believed her. *Intimidated* was the word the cops used." Joe fell silent.

"Did anyone listen to your side?"

"I didn't have to try. The charges were dropped." Joe's voice ran cold. "Shannon decided she didn't want to have to go through a trial after all. I was released."

But the scars remained. They filled the air. They'd molded Joe into something he hadn't been before the police had come after him. "She lied, Joe," Tina whispered. She'd been standing too long. She collapsed on the bench before her legs went out on her.

"Did she?" Bitterness was alive in Joe's voice. "She was crying when she came to me afterward. She—said she was afraid of my strength. She hadn't said no because she didn't know what I'd do."

Tina was trembling with the need to put an end to the agony in Joe's voice, but she had to hear him out. "I've been so careful since then," he went on. "I don't want to intimidate women. Tina, I don't ever want to hurt you."

"You can't hurt me." If she collapsed against him, would he give her support? She couldn't do that. Tonight Tina had to be as strong as he was. If they were ever going to meet on equal terms, this was the time. "I'm not afraid of you, Joe."

"Shannon was."

"That's what she said. Joe, after what she did to you, how can you believe anything she said?"

"Tina." Joe took her hands. His were cold, hers burning. "Shannon dropped the charges because she didn't want to go through a trial. That didn't mean she didn't believe what she said. I was angry the last night we were together. Even when we were—together—I hadn't really forgiven her.

I wanted to make her prove how she felt about me. There was coercion involved."

So that was what had remained behind to haunt Joe for the past two years. Feeling both chilled and close to the end, Tina asked her question. "Did you force yourself on her?"

"I don't know." The pressure from Joe's hands increased. "It's so hard to remember now. There's one thing I do know: I'm never going to let it happen again."

Suddenly Tina was angrier than she'd ever been in her life. "So you intend to hold back and never give a woman all of yourself again!" she spat out. "What the hell kind of a life is that?"

Joe was shaking his head. "I didn't want to hurt her. I don't want to hurt you."

"You're a liar."

"What?" Joe started to his feet; again Tina stopped him.

"I said—" Tina was standing apart from her anger, making it work for her "—you're a liar. And the sad thing is, you're lying to yourself. Last night was more than I ever dreamed lovemaking could be, but you won't admit that. Joe, I lost myself in you. It was the only thing I wanted. You were high on your victory and I believed I was part of that mood."

"You were."

"For once, you let go. You were honest in bed." Tina was speaking too rapidly to be embarrassed by what she was saying. "You gave me more than I knew it was possible for a man to give. You didn't hurt me, Joe—and I wasn't afraid."

Joe was staring at her silently with eyes that bored their way into her soul.

She could spend hours trying to convince him that nothing meant as much as being in his arms, but his scars ran deep. He was the one who was being curbed by his strength.

There was only one way she could free him and in the act break down the final walls between them.

Slowly Tina got to her feet. She was still straddling the bench, her hips and thighs purposely within his reach. She waited until his eyes followed her before gripping the hem of her faded sweatshirt. They had all night, and she intended to make the lesson last until morning.

Tina bunched the sweatshirt in her hands. She began lifting it upward, revealing her ribs, her breasts, her shoulders. The loose neckline slipped easily over her head. "I'm not afraid of you, Joe," she whispered. "I love you. I need you to believe me. I couldn't love you if there was any fear involved."

"Tina—"

"Touch me, Joe." She threw back her head. Her breasts jutted outward, waiting for his hands to give them a home. "Tell me."

His palms pressed against her hardened nipples. Her moan merged with his words. "I love you, Tina."

"That isn't enough."

"I know." Joe was on his feet, pulling her against him, drinking in what she was offering. There were no more walls, only promise. "I want us to be together for the rest of our lives."

"Are you sure?"

In the process of laying out his past, Joe had become free. He finally understood what it meant to be a man in love. There would be times when what he felt for Tina would wash over him like a raging flood and times when he would need to reach for her for reassurance.

Today he was sure. Tina loved him. She'd offered herself to him, heart and body. All he had to do was take the offering, hold those precious offerings next to him. "Yes, I'm sure," he told her. "We're right for each other. I've never felt this way before."

"You haven't?"

He loved away the last of her questions.

Chapter Thirteen

We can't stay here forever," Joe whispered. "People are going to start showing up."

Tina didn't care. Although she'd been in Joe's arms for hours, it wasn't nearly long enough. "Lock the door and put up a sign saying the gym's closed for the day."

"I can't do that, you wanton woman. Honey, neither of us has had any sleep. I've heard of living on love, but I've never known anyone who's actually done it."

"We have." Tina pressed home her point. She slid her free hand over Joe's naked chest, still not believing the incredible night they'd spent on a mat on the floor of the Muscle Mill. "Don't leave me," she protested as he insisted on getting to his feet.

Joe released an exaggerated breath. "I have to, woman. You've done me in."

"I doubt that." Joe had been insatiable; but then so had she. "You really are going to open that door, aren't you?"

Joe glanced up at the overhead clock. "There's a half-dozen men who show up at six in the morning, regular as clockwork. You wouldn't want them to see you lying there, now would you?" He looked down at her naked body. "I'd suggest you take a shower."

"Beast," Tina hissed. Nonetheless she got to her feet and padded unself-consciously into the minuscule women's shower area. She turned on the water and leaned against the shower wall letting stinging needles hit her now numb body.

They hadn't talked that much, but that didn't bother Tina. After the promises offered and accepted, they had the rest of their lives for talking. Their bodies had given out the stronger message.

Tina caught the muffled sound of masculine voices, but still she couldn't bring herself to get out of the shower. Despite having had almost no sleep, she felt reborn. Her body, which she'd always viewed dispassionately, was telling her things she'd never suspected. She was capable of ecstasy. Joe had given her that, along with his love.

Nothing could ever come between them again.

It took the sound of another woman in the room with her to snap Tina out of her lethargy. As she slipped back into her ragged sweatshirt and wrinkled jogging shorts, she came to an interesting realization. She was starved.

"My treat," she bribed Joe when she found him in the weight room. "We could run over to fast-food heaven for something—anything."

Joe shook water from his wet hair on Tina. He'd even shaved in the time they'd been apart. "How can I refuse? Besides, we have a full day ahead of us. A lot of decisions to make."

Although Tina wanted to know what Joe had in mind, he kept her in suspense until they were having second cups of coffee, unaware of curious eyes and a few open stares. "You never did ask me what I was doing all day yesterday," he prompted.

"I assumed you were at the college. That's what Al said."

"Until after dark?"

"It wasn't any of my business. Then."

Joe took her hand and held it lightly. "Yes, it was." He'd been in a loving, lighthearted mood, wondering at the miracles that had given him this woman. Now he turned sober. "I kept telling myself I had to give you breathing room but that wasn't it at all. I wanted to tell you about Shannon but because I didn't know how, I tried to reconcile myself to the fact that you might not be part of my life anymore."

"Oh, Joe."

"Yesterday was miserable for both of us, wasn't it?"

Tina covered Joe's hand with her free one. "That was yesterday. We don't have to think about it."

"No." His smile was coming back. "We don't, do we? There's something I want to show you, but weren't you going to call your mother?"

"Later. I think she'll understand. I want the two of you to get to know each other."

"I'd like that. After all, if she's going to have me as a son-in-law, we need to spend some time together. But not today." Joe winked mysteriously and got to his feet. He waited until Tina joined him before leading the way back outside. "I hope you have your track shoes on. We have a lot to accomplish."

"I really should go home and change," Tina protested. "I look like something the cat dragged in."

"You look fantastic." Joe had his arm wrapped around her waist as they walked back toward the gym. "Besides, if I took you back to your apartment we wouldn't leave."

Tina knew Joe was right. "So where are we going?"

"That's my secret. I'll let you know when it's time."

"That's not fair. It drives me crazy when people won't give me a straight answer." Tina jabbed Joe in the ribs and then escaped him while she climbed into his truck. "You like doing that, don't you?"

Joe reached for her and brushed past the swell of her breast. "I like everything about you."

It was a moment before Tina thought to respond. "That isn't an answer," she pointed out.

"I thought it was. Last night was incredible, sunshine. I'm still not sure I didn't dream it."

"Sunshine." The first name he'd given her. "I had the same dream," she told him honestly. "How many times did we—"

"How many times did we make love? I lost count. How do you feel?"

She could answer him honestly now and know he wouldn't misinterpret her. "Sore. Tired. Ready for more."

"You're insatiable, woman. What am I going to do with you?" He backed out of the parking lot.

"Love me," Tina said boldly.

Instead of pulling onto the street, Joe stopped. "I do love you, Tina. You must know that."

Of course she did. Last night had been all the proof she would ever need that spending the rest of her life with this man was right. "I do. But that doesn't mean I don't want to hear you say it over and over again."

Joe pretended to frown. "Women are strange creatures. Never satisfied."

As a horn honked, Tina tore herself from the distraction next to her. "People are starting to stare at us."

Joe shrugged but started the truck in motion again. He was maddeningly quiet as he drove out of the downtown area where the Muscle Mill was located. He headed toward the section of Longview currently exhibiting the most growth. Small shopping centers, housing developments and several industrial parks were all within a couple of miles of each other. "This is it," Joe announced after he'd pulled off the side of the road in front of a plot of land punctuated by a For Sale sign with a paper Sold sticker slapped over it.

"This is what?" Tina knew Joe was leading up to something and she was ready to play her part. "You brought me out here so I could see an acre of weeds?"

Joe opened his door and got out. Tina joined him. "Can't you see it?" he questioned as they stepped onto the lot. "A brightly colored building with a large glass front, central air conditioning and the biggest damn weight room in this part of the state."

"Joe." Tina understood. Still it took several seconds for her to find her voice. "You're going to build here."

"Yep." Joe wrapped his arm around her, pulling her close, letting her hear his heart beating. Had it been less than twenty-four hours since he'd been here? In that time his whole life had come into focus. "That's where I was a lot of yesterday. First I saw the real-estate agent. Then I went over a million details with my banker. I start signing the papers next week."

"You're going to build a new gym here?" Tina repeated. She felt both exhilarated and sad because she hadn't been part of his day. "I wish I'd known."

"I wanted you to," Joe told her. He turned her toward him, tipped her face upward and kissed her long and gently before continuing. "That was the bad part. Not knowing whether I'd be doing this alone or if you'd be with me. But I had to do something yesterday. Something had to be right."

Tina couldn't be angry at him. The wall between them had been as much her doing as his. "I understand," she said, remembering what she'd done with her own day. "Have you drawn up blueprints yet?"

Joe explained that he hadn't, although he had a good idea of how he wanted the interior to look. Arm in arm, they stepped off the spot where the gym itself would be, and the area reserved for parking. "That still leaves you some room," Tina pointed out when they were through. "You shouldn't leave it in weeds."

"Landscaping?" Joe frowned. "A flower garden wouldn't look right."

"I didn't say anything about a flower garden." Tina shook her head at the quick masculine reaction to the word landscaping. Although her ideas were only half formed, she showed him where a lawn would work and pointed out that fast-growing trees would supply needed shade. "Neutral landscaping," she reinforced. "Something both men and women would enjoy."

Joe sat down quickly, bringing Tina with him. He held her hand close to his mouth, breathing on it. He spoke slowly. "A long time ago you said I needed to do something to draw more women to the gym. I guess landscaping's a start."

"It's only a start." Joe was trying to tell her something. Although she didn't understand what that something was, she tried to help. "It's inside the gym that really counts."

"I know." His breath traced a path of vapor over her knuckles. "Do you think enough women would come to a place like mine? I don't want tanning booths or that kind of thing."

"I came," she pointed out—although they both knew her reasons were tied to Joe and not his business. "Joe, there's enough fitness centers. You aren't trying to duplicate them." She closed her eyes, looking deep inside herself for the rest of what she wanted to say. "You're the reason I started going to the Muscle Mill. But I got something out of it that had nothing to do with you. I'm stronger than I thought it was possible for me to be. That has given me confidence I didn't know I had. I'm not the only woman who needs to feel that way." Tina buried her head against Joe's side. If he understood as well as she believed he did, she wouldn't need to say any more.

"It won't be *my* gym."

Tina forced herself to concentrate. "What do you mean? Is it the money?"

"Of course not. What I mean is, I don't want it to be *my* gym. I want you as my partner."

So that was why they were here. Tina turned toward him and wrapped her arms around his neck. Last night one of them had said something about marriage and the other had accepted. Now Joe was asking her to be even more. With slightly parted lips she found his mouth, sealing a bargain she knew would last as long as they lived. Her eyes closed but she wasn't thinking of her name painted next to his on the outside of a building. Instead she saw a big man and small woman holding hands. Forever holding hands. "I accept."

"I didn't dare think about that yesterday," Joe said when she at last allowed him to speak. "I didn't know where we were headed, if anywhere."

"All you had to do was ask."

"What would your answer have been before last night?" Joe was holding her so close that she felt rather than saw him shake his head. "I sat here yesterday, thinking. I've been dreaming about expanding the gym for a long time— making it attractive to women as well as men. But knowing the dream was turning into reality didn't mean as much as I thought it would. I was here alone."

"Don't." Tina hated thinking of him hurting. That bothered her more than her own pain had. "Please, don't."

Tenderly he stroked her head before running his hand down the side of her neck. It seemed to her that he was trying to read her pulse. "I made myself a little crazy out here yesterday. I also came to an important decision."

"You were going to ask me to be your partner?" she asked.

"No. Not then. We weren't ready for that." He turned her head so she was looking up into his eyes. The first time he'd touched her, Joe thought he was holding a doll in his arms. But the woman who had emerged for him was far more perfect, and complex, than any doll could ever be. "I decided I was going to tell you about Shannon. I knew that it could all go up in smoke if I told you, but we were in deep trouble because of what was standing between us."

"You were going to tell me?"

"I was. But you beat me to the punch. Larry Pardee doesn't know what he's letting slip away. You're a gutsy lady."

Tina could laugh. Today everything was perfect. "I told Larry I was a tough old broad."

"All right." Joe joined her laugh. "You're a tough old broad," he said, as he played with the neckline of her sweatshirt. "That's the kind of woman I need for a business partner."

"Just a business partner?"

"No." Joe got to his feet and helped her stand. "A lot more than that. When do you want to get married?"

Tina swayed but caught herself. "Today. No. We can't do that. I want my parents to be part of this."

"How long will that take?"

"Not long." Tina stood on tiptoe and reinforced her answer in the only way possible. Joe's lips were sweet and alive on hers. "Not long at all."

It was close to midnight before they crawled under the covers at Joe's house. The day had been filled with sketching possibilities for the gym, trips to three fitness centers to make sure they wouldn't be duplicating anything available elsewhere, standing outside a jewelry store looking at wedding rings, breaking their news to Ginger, Al, and Tina's parents.

Although Tina now had her body molded against Joe's, lovemaking would have to wait until morning. She was so tired that her limbs were trembling. Joe's response to her presence was slowed by his own exhaustion. Yet he held her close, still talking. "Your mother's a remarkable woman," he whispered. "She's come a long way since the day I met her."

"She has, hasn't she? The journey isn't over, Joe. It isn't going to be easy for her to accept the changes I'm making. It'll take..." Tina's voice trailed off. She felt herself slipping and struggled to stay awake. "I'm not the girl she thought she raised."

"I hope I'm not intimidating her."

"You can't intimidate anyone." Tina spoke from her heart. "I found the real you. The same will happen with Mom."

"You don't mind a quiet wedding?" Joe reached out with his tongue, touching her ear and the small pearl earring he'd bought her a few hours before. "If you want—"

"I don't want a big wedding," Tina reassured him. "There won't be time for much of anything once we break ground. However—" she paused just long enough to make sure she had his undivided attention "—I do have definite plans for a honeymoon."

"Such as?"

"Hawaii. The nationals, remember?"

"You want to combine competition with a honeymoon? I'm not going to have much time for—"

Tina covered his mouth with hers, cutting off his words. "I know what we won't have much time for. Besides, we'll be an old married couple by then so it won't be a traditional honeymoon.'' She inched her knee between his legs. ''A wedding. Building the new gym. Training for the nationals. Do you think you have the strength?''

''All I need is a few hours' sleep.'' Joe pretended to snore to bring home his point. ''Then I'll show you how strong I am.''

''Is this a challenge?'' Tina muttered. She wanted to concentrate on what Joe was offering her, but sleep had her in its grip.

''Hardly. I already know the answer to my question. But you can give me a demonstration in the morning.''

''There's nothing I'd like better. I love you, Joe,'' she mumbled. ''Let me show you how much.''

''I'll be here, sunshine,'' he mumbled back. ''I'll always be here for you.''

* * * * *

Silhouette Romance™
Legendary Lovers Trilogy

BY DEBBIE MACOMBER....

ONCE UPON A TIME, in a land not so far away, there lived a girl, Debbie Macomber, who grew up dreaming of castles, white knights and princes on fiery steeds. Her family was an ordinary one with a mother and father and one wicked brother, who sold copies of her diary to all the boys in her junior high class.

One day, when Debbie was only nineteen, a handsome electrician drove by in a shiny black convertible. Now Debbie knew a prince when she saw one, and before long they lived in a two-bedroom cottage surrounded by a white picket fence.

As often happens when a damsel fair meets her prince charming, children followed, and soon the two-bedroom cottage became a four-bedroom castle. The kingdom flourished and prospered, and between soccer games and car pools, ballet classes and clarinet lessons, Debbie thought about love and enchantment and the magic of romance.

One day Debbie said, "What this country needs is a good fairy tale." She remembered how well her diary had sold and she dreamed again of castles, white knights and princes on fiery steeds. And so the stories of Cinderella, Beauty and the Beast, and Snow White were reborn....

Look for Debbie Macomber's *Legendary Lovers* trilogy from Silhouette Romance: *Cindy and the Prince* (January, 1988); *Some Kind of Wonderful* (March, 1988); *Almost Paradise* (May, 1988). Don't miss them! SRT-1

Silhouette Intimate Moments

Rx: One Dose of

DODD MEMORIAL HOSPITAL

In sickness and in health the employees of Dodd Memorial Hospital stick together, sharing triumphs and defeats, and sometimes their hearts as well. Revisit these special people next month in the newest book in Lucy Hamilton's Dodd Memorial Hospital Trilogy, *After Midnight*—IM #237, the time when romance begins.

Thea Stevens knew there was no room for a man in her life—she had a young daughter to care for and a demanding new job as the hospital's media coordinator. But then Luke Adams walked through the door, and everything changed. She had never met a man like him before—handsome enough to be the movie star he was, yet thoughtful, considerate and absolutely determined to get the one thing he wanted—Thea.

Finish the trilogy in July with *Heartbeats*—IM #245.

Silhouette Special Edition

WHITE LIES*
by
Linda Howard

Bestselling author Linda Howard is back with a story that is exciting, enticing and—most of all—compellingly romantic.

Heroine Jay Granger's life was turned upside down when she was called to her ex-husband's side. Now, injured and unconscious, he needed her more than he ever had during their brief marriage. Finally he awoke, and Jay found him stronger and more fascinating than before. Was she asking too much, or could they have a chance to recapture the past and learn the value of love the second time around?

Find out the answer next month, only in SILHOUETTE SPECIAL EDITION.

*Previously advertised as MIRRORS.

COMING IN MAY

SSE452

Silhouette Special Edition

NORA ROBERTS'S 50TH SILHOUETTE NOVEL

In May, SILHOUETTE SPECIAL EDITION celebrates Nora Roberts's "golden anniversary"— her 50th Silhouette novel!

The Last Honest Woman launches a three-book "family portrait" of entrancing triplet sisters. You'll fall in love with all THE O'HURLEYS!

>   *The Last Honest Woman*—May
>   Hardworking mother Abigail O'Hurley
>   Rockwell finally meets a man she can
>   trust...but she's forced to deceive him to
>   protect her sons.
>
>   *Dance to the Piper*—July
>   Broadway hoofer Maddy O'Hurley easily
>   lands a plum role, but it takes some fancy
>   footwork to win the man of her dreams.
>
>   *Skin Deep*—September
>   Hollywood goddess Chantel O'Hurley re-
>   mains deliberately icy...until she melts in the
>   arms of the man she'd love to hate.

Look for THE O'HURLEYS! And join the excite-
ment of Silhouette Special Edition!